SWEET, SEDUCTIVE SAVAGE

I must be dreaming, Johanna told herself as he carried her to the bed and lay down beside her.

Hawkeye's head lifted, his dark eyes glittering down at her, hot with ancient sensuality.

"Please let me go," she whispered, but knew she didn't mean it. She was caught in a spell, too helpless to resist him.

"Tell me you don't want my touch," he said harshly. "Tell me you want me to stop."

She knew it was madness to continue. She meant nothing to him. She was only a convenience. Her sense of decency should make her demand to be released. She should be rejecting the sensuous, lingering hands that were stirring feelings that had lain dormant, buried deep inside her body. Feelings she'd never had for anyone else before. . . .

D0596553

ROMANCE FROM FERN MICHAELS

DEAR EMILY   (0-8217-4952-8, $5.99)

WISH LIST   (0-8217-5228-6, $6.99)

AND IN HARDCOVER:

VEGAS RICH   (1-57566-057-1, $25.00)

Available wherever paperbacks are sold, or order direct from the Publisher. Send cover price plus 50¢ per copy for mailing and handling Penguin USA, P.O. Box 999, c/o Dept. 17109, Bergenfield, NJ 07621. Residents of New York and Tennessee must include sales tax. DO NOT SEND CASH.

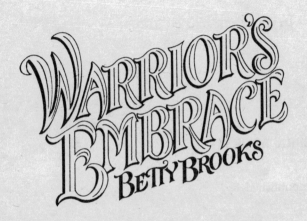

WARRIOR'S EMBRACE

BETTY BROOKS

ZEBRA BOOKS
KENSINGTON PUBLISHING CORP.

ZEBRA BOOKS

are published by

Kensington Publishing Corp.
850 Third Avenue
New York. NY 10022

Copyright © 1989 by Betty Brooks

All rights reserved. No part of this book may be
reproduced in any form or by any means without the
prior written consent of the Publisher, excepting brief
quotes used in reviews.

First printing: November 1989

Printed in the United States of America

10 9 8 7 6 5 4 3 2

Dedicated to Eva

If the choice for another daughter had been mine, you would still have been chosen.

Chapter One

New Orleans,
March 1838

The full moon glimmered softly over the grounds of the Durant Institute. It shed a pale light that filtered into a locked room, illuminating the delicate features of the girl leaning against the door. Her face was pale, her hair dark as midnight, tumbling past her shoulders to rest on the white cotton shift that was her only garment, giving her an appearance that was almost angelic.

But Johanna McFarley's thoughts were far from angelic as she cursed both Michael Durant and the thick wooden door that muffled the voices in the hallway.

"Durant!" She beat on the door with her fist. "Open this door!" She kicked the door with her foot, succeeding only in bruising her toes against the hard wood. "Durant! Damn you! Let me out of here!" Her feelings warred between rage and fear, and she was so overwrought she hadn't even realized she was cursing as no lady of quality would.

"Damn ye!" The voice came from down the corridor, muffled by the heavy wooden door, but even so, it was as familiar to Johanna as her own. ". . . no right to keep . . ."

Relief flowed through her, unknotting her muscles and making her sag against the door. He had returned and found her missing. And he had come for her, just as she had known he would.

"Da!" she screamed, beating her small fists against the door. "Da! I'm in here!"

"Johanna!" his voice answered, closer now, and elation swept through her. "Where are ye, child?"

She pounded harder at the door. "Da!" she screamed again. "I'm in here, Da! He locked me in!"

A shot rang out, echoing through the corridor outside the thick door. Johanna's face blanched and her green eyes widened with fear as a confining mantle of claustrophobia settled over her. She had difficulty breathing as she stopped beating on the door and listened, instead, to the silence.

God! What had happened?

"Da?" Her voice was barely above a whisper.

Muffled cursing reached her ears, then Michael Durant's voice called, "Cooper, get in here. Help me with . . ." The rest of the words were indistinguishable as Durant moved away from the door.

Johanna stood frozen with anxiety as heavy footsteps sounded outside her door, then, a moment later, she heard the sound of something being dragged away down the hallway.

"Da!" she said softly, her face pale and stricken. Her heart refused to believe what her mind told her had happened. "I'm in here," she whispered. "Da? Are you still there?"

No answer.

"Durant!" she screamed, beating her fists against the door. "What have you done? Where is my father?"

She hammered on the wood with her bare hands until each blow sent a cruel bolt of pain down her arms, through her shoulders, and up the back of her neck. She drew deep, gasping breaths as she pounded and pounded until her flesh bruised. Even then, she kept on pounding, screaming for her father, totally unaware of the tears streaming unheeded down her cheeks as she cursed the wood that so easily resisted her fierce attack. Finally, exhaustion took its toll and she crumpled to the floor.

Hours later, the sun tinted the horizon with a rosy blush of color. Robins flitted though the old oak tree located outside Johanna's window, heralding a new day with their song.

The sound of a key being turned in a lock brought her weary head up. Then the door opened on well-oiled hinges and an attractive girl with coffee-colored skin stepped inside, carrying a tray with Johanna's morning tea. The maid barely glanced at the crumpled figure on the floor as she set her burden down on the table. Moving to the window, she pulled the curtains aside and let the morning sunlight stream into the room. Only then did she turn to face the grief-stricken girl.

"You gonna catch your death of cold on that floor, Missy," the maid said, frowning heavily.

"What happened to Da?" Johanna asked.

"Don't go askin' me," the maid replied, reaching down to help Johanna to her feet. "Massa Durant, he skin me alive if I open my mouth. You just set a while and drink your tea. It makes a body feel some better after a bad night."

"Tea won't fix what ails me, Cissy," Johanna told the other girl. "I have to know what they did to my father."

"Massa Durant is the one to ask. Ain't nobody else gonna tell you nothin'." Cissy poured some water in a washbowl and wet a cloth. "I'm gonna wash your face now," she said. "You done cried so much, your face is swole up somethin' awful."

Johanna pushed impatiently at the girl's hands and took the wet washcloth from her. Her eyes felt gritty, as though they were filled with sand, and she pressed the wet cloth to them for a moment, angry at herself for giving in to tears. They were a weakness she could ill afford.

Lowering the washcloth, Johanna met the maid's eyes, feeling surprise to see sympathy there. Hope fluttered to life, surging wildly through her breast. "Cissy," she said, hearing the desperation in her voice. "Please help me get out of here. I must find out what Michael Durant has done to Father."

Her words caused an instant reaction. Fear flared in the maid's eyes and they flew to the door, as though she expected the devil himself to walk in. Twisting her hands, she backed away from Johanna. "Don't ask me," she whispered shakily. "I got 'nough troubles already. I don't want no more."

Johanna grabbed the girl's hand and squeezed it tightly. "Please, Cissy," she said. "You can't enjoy being a slave."

The maid shook her head back and forth. "You know I don't, Missy. But it ain't my choice. I was born a slave. And I always gonna be a slave."

"No!" Johanna said fiercely. "It doesn't have to be that way. Help me get away from here and I'll take you with me."

The maid's dark eyes were sorrowful. "Ain't nowhere to go," she mumbled. "Nowhere that Massa Durant can't find me. He got papers showin' he own me. If I run away, they just bring me back, and Massa have me flogged."

Johanna knew the maid was frightened out of her wits, but she refused to give up. Cissy was her only hope of leaving this place. And she had to leave. She must find her father.

"I know a place where you'd be safe," Johanna said.

"You do?" the maid whispered. "Where?"

"North," Johanna replied. "You could be free there, Cissy. Just think what that would mean. There is no slavery in the North. You would be paid for the work you do."

A flame lit in the maid's eyes, then just as

quickly died. "Down in the shacks, folks talk about a place like that. Some say they is such a thing, some say they ain't. Me, I just listen to 'em talk." Her eyes became soft. "A long time ago, I had me a fella. And he said to me, come on, Cissy. Come go with me to de North." She sighed deeply and her shoulders slumped. "We made plans, me and that fella." She walked to the window and stared through the steel bars. When her voice came again, it held a world of pain. "The night we was goin', the massa sent for me." Her head dipped low in shame. "Massa kept me all night and my fella go. Ain't never seen 'im since."

Johanna's heart went out to the girl. "Did he get away?" she asked.

"Some say he did. Some say he was caught and hanged." She sighed and shrugged her shoulders. "Me, I don't know. Mebbe he's in that place where folks like me can go free." She looked at Johanna. "You reckon so?" she inquired hopefully.

"I'm almost certain he made it," Johanna replied, knowing it was what the maid wanted to hear. After all, she consoled herself, it could very well be true. All the states north of Maryland had abolished slavery and the abolitionists were scattered throughout the South. "I know someone whose sole purpose in life is to help people of color find their way to freedom, Cissy. If we can reach him, he'll help us leave the city."

The maid's eyes were dark and hopeful. "Are you tellin' it true, Missy? You know somebody that would help the likes of me?"

Johanna nodded her head. "Yes, I do. And if you'll help me, I'll make certain you won't ever have to return here."

Fear crossed the maid's face. "I'm mighty scared, Missy. They gonna kill me for sure if I get caught."

"That won't happen if we're careful," Johanna said, knowing she must convince the maid to help her. Cissy was her only hope. Even if she managed to unlock the door, there was still the guard at the gate outside. "Think about it, Cissy," she coaxed. "Wouldn't anything be better than what you have here?" Johanna knew she was taking unfair advantage, because Cissy's lot as a maid during the day and whore for Durant and his men at night must be a hard one to bear.

"It's gonna take some doin'," the maid said softly. "But I know how to get aroun' the guard at the gate. That man's got a pow'ful likin' for the moonshine."

Triumph flowed through Johanna. Cissy was going to do it! She was going to get out of here. She would find her father . . . Her breath caught. She had forgotten about the shot . . . the heavy dragging sound. She looked at the maid for a long moment. "Please, Cissy, tell me what happened to my father."

"He's dead, Missy," the maid said sorrowfully. "They ain't nothin' you can do for him now. It's too late."

Even though Johanna had suspected as much, to hear it put into words pierced her anew. Tears welled into her eyes and slowly fell down her cheeks; she turned her head away from the maid. She had prayed she was wrong in the conclusions she had drawn. But she was not. Now she was completely alone.

Johanna didn't hear the maid leave the room, too overcome by grief for her father. Although she was the youngest of seven daughters, three had died at birth and the other three, Bridget, Mary, and Kathleen, had decided to stay in Ireland when Johanna and her father had fled their homeland. They knew nothing of her plight, but even if they did, they could not help her. Ireland was too far away.

Overwhelmed with grief, Johanna flung herself across the bed and cried until she could cry no more. Then she began to make her plans.

That night, Cissy came to her room carrying a bag. She had been severely beaten, her mouth was swollen and one eye was completely closed.

"What happened?" Johanna gasped.

Cissy's voice was emotionless when she spoke. "That man, Cooper, he likes to beat women before he beds 'em." Moving to the wardrobe, she crammed some clothes into it, then, taking a dark cape from the wardrobe, she brought it to Johanna. "Put this on," she said, fastening the cape around the girl. "We're gettin' outta this place. Nobody's gonna beat me no more. I'm gonna go North and be a free woman."

As they left the room and descended the stairs, a movement in the shadows brought Johanna's head around. She found herself staring into the dark eyes of Joshua, the old negro butler.

Cissy turned when she heard Johanna's fearful gasp. Her eyes fell on the butler and held for a long moment. Then, taking Johanna's hand she tugged at it. "Hurry, Missy," she said. "Old Josh ain't gonna stop us."

Hoping she was right, Johanna followed the other woman from the Institute.

The night mist was heavy, and it swirled around her in a clammy embrace as they crossed the grounds toward the open gate. A shout warned Johanna of discovery just before shots rang out and Cissy crumpled to the ground. Johanna's heart beat fast as she knelt beside the girl whose eyes were already glazing over.

"Ain't nobody . . . gonna hurt me no more," Cissy whispered. Her eyes closed and she shuddered, then was still.

Johanna felt for a pulse, but there was none. She realized instantly that it was too late. Cissy was beyond anyone's help. The bullet had pierced her heart. She was right. Nobody would ever hurt her again.

"Don't just stand there!" Durant's voice penetrated Johanna's consciousness. "Fools! Stop her!"

Johanna made a dash for the open gates, expecting to feel a bullet at any moment. She could hear Durant calling instructions to his men and the pounding of heavy boots as she fled toward the forest. She ran beneath dense branches that were heavily draped with Spanish moss, running for her very life.

She knew the forest better than Durant, had

enjoyed its beauty with her father often and she had no trouble eluding her pursuers as she headed for a small cave, hidden deep in the woods. The entrance was hidden by a bush and she pushed it aside and entered the darkened interior. Only then did she allow herself time to think, to regret having asked Cissy's help. Because of her, the maid had lost her life.

Drawing up her legs, she rested her head on her knees. She stayed in the cave throughout the day, often hearing the sounds of searchers, scouring the woods for her. But no one found her hiding place, and when night fell again, she made her way deep in the bayou until she found what she was searching for.

The house was built on thick stilts that served to protect it from seasonal floods. Although the hour was early, the house was completely dark.

She stared at it in dismay. She wasn't aware of another presence until she felt the press of cold steel against her neck.

"State you bus'ness here," a cold voice said from behind her.

"Patrick?" her quivering voice asked.

"Johanna," Patrick O'Shaunessy said. "What you doin' out here alone, lass?"

"Michael Durant was holding me prisoner at his Institute," she said. "He knows about me, Patrick. And he killed my father."

"I already knew about yore pap, lass," the old man said. "They buried him today. Rumors had it yore pap was set on by footpads."

Hatred flared in her eyes. "Footpads!" she spat.

16

"Michael Durant did it. And if it's the last thing I do, I'll see him pay."

"No, lass," Patrick said. "Thinkin' like that'll get you killed. It won't help yore pap none. He's dead and buried. You gotta think 'bout yoreself now. If that man knows about you, then he'll stop at nothing. You gotta get outta the city. It's what yore pap would say. You know it is."

"I know," she said, lifting her eyes to him. "That's why I came here. Could you get me out through the underground railroad?" she asked.

He sighed heavily. "It's all exposed, lass. That way's closed for now. The people I worked with was caught and hanged. They couldn't even help themselves. But don't despair. We'll find another way."

Johanna knew how dangerous was the job of smuggling the darkies out to be shipped up North. If anyone was caught doing it, they would be killed on the spot. But the underground railroad would continue. Many people of color had already escaped, and there were enough abolitionists around that another group would surface. All they had to do was wait. But Johanna had no time to wait. Durant wouldn't stop searching until he found her.

"You come inside and, after we eat, we'll figger somethin' out," the old man said. "We'll get you out some way."

But it wasn't to happen. Patrick and Johanna had only finished eating when they heard horses approaching. Pushing the bed aside, Patrick lifted a floorboard to expose a hidden compartment. He reached in, removed a pistol and handed it to her.

"Take this, lass," he muttered. "An' you go out an' hide. If them riders don't leave right away, you get as far away from here as you can."

She left quickly and waited in the woods. She couldn't hear what was being said, but from the sounds of the voices, she knew they were questioning the old man.

Realizing she would endanger Patrick if she stayed, she slipped silently through the forest, making her way toward the city. Her mind worked frantically, as she searched for a way out of her situation. As she reached the outskirts of the city, her feet seemed to turn of their own accord to the graveyard. It took only a matter of moments to locate the freshly turned grave. Tears fell from her eyes as she knelt beside it.

"We shouldn't have come here, Da," she whispered. "This is a savage land, and it's filled with savage people." The last was shuddered out in a sob.

They had been told this was the land of opportunity, a place where they could find riches beyond belief, but instead of the opportunity they'd been promised, Johanna and her father had found grief; instead of freedom, her father had found death.

"It's all my fault," she whispered. "Had it not been for me, you'd be safe in Ireland."

Overhead, storm clouds gathered, but Johanna paid them no attention. A storm posed little threat after what she had endured the past three weeks. An overturned carriage—a simple accident—had led to her imprisonment and ultimately, to her father's death.

Somewhere in the night a howl sounded, long and mournful, and Johanna started. Huddling into the shadows, she searched the darkness and waited, her breath knotted in her throat. But nothing more came. It had been merely the howl of a dog, a stray in the midst of the city.

The knowledge that Durant and his men were scouring the countryside for her transformed every rustle she heard in the shrouding darkness into a threat. She felt as though a thousand eyes were upon her, imagined the heated breath of her pursuers on her neck. And a voice within whispered. *Run . . . run.*

Johanna knew it had been dangerous to come to the graveyard, but she hadn't been able to leave the city without at least saying goodbye to her father.

Forcing back her tears, she cast one final glance at her father's grave and hurried toward the cemetery gate. She had almost reached it when the sound of wheels clicking over the cobblestone street reached her. A carriage was coming.

Durant! Could it be him?

Fear crawled up from deep within her, and she froze against the wrought iron fence.

The rattle of the carriage wheels grew louder.

Turning to flee, Johanna's eyes fell upon her father's grave. Cold rage swept over her. She reached into her reticule and stepped back into the shadows, her fingers sliding over the cold steel of the gun Patrick had given her . . . Gripping the weapon tightly, she pulled it from her bag.

If Durant was in that carriage, she would see him dead. Here, in this cemetery where her father lay buried. She would kill his slayer.

Straining her eyes through the darkness, she waited. The carriage neared the cemetery and slowed.

Johanna's heart beat with a slow, steady rhythm. She remained hidden in the shadows, motionless, except for the hand holding the weapon.

Thud . . . thud . . . thud . . . Her heartbeat was the only sound she heard as she watched the carriage stop.

Raising the gun, she used both hands to aim it at the carriage door. Then she waited . . . waited for Michael Durant to appear.

A shriek came from the carriage, followed by a loud masculine laugh, and then a paper-wrapped bottle sailed through the air to crash against the iron rail of the cemetery fence.

"Get me another bottle," declared a husky female voice from inside the carriage. "Hurry, Henri."

The carriage moved on.

Johanna released a ragged breath and dropped her hand, the gun dangling from her fingers. She was actually disappointed the carriage had not contained her enemy. Though violence was foreign to her nature, she had been prepared to kill Durant.

She looked back at her father's grave. Then, whispering another goodbye, she fled the cemetery and made her way down the streets of the *Vieux Carre,* the French Quarter of New Orleans.

The silence of the night stretched endlessly around her as she made her way past iron gates, barred doors and archways that both revealed and hid the private world of the wealthy.

Questions tormented her. Where could she hide from Durant? And what would happen to her if she were found?

But then, she already knew the answer to that. If she were found she would become a prisoner again — locked away — to be brought out and used for profit. And she couldn't — wouldn't — allow that to happen. Not after her father had given his life to set her free.

Propelled by urgency, she gathered up her skirts in one hand and broke into a run. Her gait was uneven; she hadn't completely regained her strength yet. And after a short distance, she stumbled on the roadway and sprawled forward. Her reticule flew out of her hands as she skidded on the cobblestones.

Ignoring the pain in her hands, she crawled after the bag that contained her weapon. Without it, she was defenseless. Her hands closed over it and she gave a sigh of relief. Sitting back on her heels, she breathed in the musty smell of stone and dirt, waiting until her heartbeat slowed down. While she rested, she became aware of her exhausted body. Her legs ached, her muscles were tensed, and the abrasions on her hands stung.

But she couldn't stop now, knew she had no choice except to go on. She had to escape from her enemy.

Struggling to her feet, she brushed the pebbles and dirt from her hands and clothing and moved on, forcing herself to go at a slower pace.

Suddenly, she became aware of her surroundings. She hadn't realized when she'd left the French Quarter behind, but she had. And now she was at the wharf, with the smell of the salt air teasing her nostrils.

She knew this part of the city well. It was almost as familiar to her as her father's house on Chartres Street. For this had been her father's second home, the sea his first love. Because of that, she knew ships as well as she knew carriages.

Perhaps here was her answer.

Johanna was exhausted, knew she had pushed herself to the limit. It was an effort now to put one foot in front of the other. And before her an old weather-beaten merchant ship rocked gently in the Gulf waters.

She didn't know where the ship was bound. Furthermore, she didn't care. As long as it took her away from New Orleans — away from the man who was determined to own her.

Clutching her cape tighter around her neck with one hand and the rope of the gangplank with the other, Johanna crossed the swinging platform. Then she tiptoed across the deck to make her way down a long flight of stairs. Finally, she found concealment between two barrels. A weary sigh escaped her lips as she settled down and drifted off to sleep.

Chapter Two

Where are they all going? Johanna wondered, making her way through the churning crush of people in the new port city of Galveston. She had no way of knowing they were emigrants, each drawn by the huge grants of free land Texas offered.

Perspiration dotted her face and she brushed aside a damp lock of hair. She had thought New Orleans was humid, but it didn't compare to this city. The mid-morning sun blazed hotly above and she had long since shrugged off her cape, but still the sultry heat drained her, pulled at what little strength she had left.

She had remained hidden throughout the journey across the Gulf of Mexico, hidden and hungry. She had slept little on the journey, fearing discovery at any moment, but luck had been with her, and she had managed to escape detection. Now weariness weighted her. Her footsteps dragged, and desperation gnawed at her.

She was a stranger in a strange town, and she had no money for a room. She dared not even rest long on the benches that dotted the cobbled streets, for already she had drawn more attention than she wanted from the rough-looking workers who made up a good part of the crowd.

A feeling of hopelessness assailed her, and she wondered where she could go with no money.

Her only answer was to find work. Although she had never before held a position, she could see no difficulty in securing one. After all, she was well-educated. And Galveston was said to be a civilized town. There must be quality people here who needed teachers for their children.

Determination flared in her green eyes and purpose steeled her backbone as she started briskly down the street. But by late afternoon, very little steel remained in her, and her determination had given way to desperation.

It seemed situations abounded in Galveston, but they were all for men. She had not found one single listing at the newspaper office for a woman, nor had she come across any clerical positions in any of the shops in which she inquired.

Utterly depressed, Johanna wilted on the nearest bench. Her fingers idly caressed the brooch fastened to her dress. Suddenly they stilled. The brooch was very valuable. It had belonged to her mother's family and had been passed down from the seventh daughter to the seventh daughter for generations. There was no way she could part with it.

Her stomach rumbled.

At the same moment she was assailed by weakness. It had been more than two days since she had eaten. How much longer could she go without food?

Her stomach rumbled again.

Tears misted her eyes as she slowly unpinned the brooch. It was all she had of value. She had no choice except to sell it.

The decision made, sheer resolution lifted her from the bench and urged her footsteps toward a nearby general store.

Her fingers clutched the brooch tightly, pressing the precious metal against her flesh. Feeling a sharp pain, she bent her head to peer closer and saw a drop of blood welling from her finger where the pin had pierced the flesh.

Johanna's lips twisted wryly. Durant had pierced that same finger, over and over again. He had seemed to think he could determine her make-up from her blood. He didn't seem to realize—

Without warning, she bumped into a yielding wall of solid flesh.

Durant! He had found her!

Choking off a scream, she pushed hard against the muscled wall of flesh, unaware that she would have fallen except for the hands that curved around her waist.

"Let me go!" she panted. Her flailing feet connected with a shin and her captor swore softly.

"Stop struggling!" a harsh voice commanded.

"I'm not going to hurt you."

The words didn't penetrate her consciousness. Only the sound of the *unfamiliar* voice. Only the sudden knowledge that *it wasn't Durant's voice*.

Lifting her head, she found herself looking into the blackest eyes she had ever seen, unfathomable eyes that seemed to search out her innermost secrets, and yet revealed nothing of the man behind them.

His hat was pulled low over his face, and she was vaguely aware that he was dressed in beaded buckskin. But her attention was focused on his sharply cut features. Even shaded by his hat, she could see he was unlike any man she had ever met.

"I'm sorry," she muttered in embarrassment. "I thought you were someone else."

He was heavily armed, wearing a double holster fastened to a wide belt around his waist. The right hand pistol was worn butt back while the left one was butt forward. And behind the left hand Colt, resting in its sheath, was a big-bladed bowie knife. Johanna had never seen such an arrangement before and she wondered if he was a gunfighter.

Her cheeks flushed crimson as she became aware that she was staring.

Something flickered in his dark eyes as they lingered on her flushed cheeks. "My fault," he grated harshly.

"No," she said. She was unable to tear her eyes away from him. "I w-wasn't watching where I was going."

When his gaze returned to hers, she lowered her eyes demurely and stepped away from him. Her heart was acting in a most unusual fashion, beating a rapid tattoo on her ribcage and, for some reason, she found his presence almost overwhelming.

Uttering another muttered apology, Johanna stepped around him and hurried on her way.

She glanced back over her shoulder as she pushed open the door to the general store. The buckskin-clad man was still where she had left him. Although he had been joined by two other men, he was still watching her.

Johanna stepped inside the store.

The room was stuffy and smelled of stale tobacco and leather. Tables were piled high with bolts of material, ribbons, and scented soaps. Jugs of sorghum stood next to barrels of nails, rice, beans, flour. Every inch of wall space that she could see was taken up with harnesses, traps, pots, skillets, and rifles, and other items too numerous to name. Johanna's gaze swept over the multitude of merchandise and finally came to rest on a display case filled with jewelry.

The middle-aged man she had already spoken to about a position was leaning against the counter reading a newspaper. He looked up. "Something you forgot?" he asked in a slightly irritated voice.

Her hand clutched her brooch. She swallowed, and her throat almost closed over her words as she asked. "Do you buy jewelry?"

"Sprechen zie deutsche?" asked a voice at the same time.

Johanna and the merchant both turned to see an elegantly dressed, gray-haired woman beside them. The woman smiled an apology. *"Ents-chuldigen zie, bitte."*

"Ma'am?" the portly merchant asked, obviously confused.

"Machts nichts," Johanna assured the woman.

"Oh," the German woman said in her language. "I am pleased we can speak together." She held out a gloved hand to Johanna. "My name is Frieda Hoffman," she said.

Johanna's hand was gripped in a brisk handshake as she murmured her own name.

"Johanna," Frieda Hoffman repeated. "Such a lovely name." Her smile multiplied the lines radiating from her faded blue eyes. "It is German, you know." Johanna nodded. "But I think you are not. Well, no matter. Perhaps you will be kind enough to help me anyway."

"If I can," Johanna replied.

"I have just arrived from my homeland with my husband and son," Frau Hoffman explained. "We travel by wagon train to Fredericksburg where we have friends." She smiled proudly at Johanna. "It is to be our new home."

Johanna returned her smile. She knew what it was to be a stranger in a strange land. Such had been her case only a few years ago. "How can I help you?" she asked.

"I come to buy supplies for the trip but I have great difficulty. I have found no one who speaks my language. I cannot make the merchants understand. I fear they will take advantage of my ignorance."

Assuring the woman she would be glad to help,

28

Johanna took the list of supplies and turned to the merchant. "Frau Hoffman has asked me to help select her merchandise."

"Has she now?" he said. "Before you start, you'd best ask her how she's aimin' to pay for it. I ain't takin' no Texas currency."

"Why not?" Johanna asked curiously.

" 'Cause I ain't no fool," he said. "Texas currency is down to forty cents on the dollar. More trouble than it's worth."

Johanna frowned at him, but she relayed his message to Frau Hoffman. After learning the woman intended to pay him with gold, the man's attitude changed. He became most obliging, even going so far as to help Johanna select the items listed.

The merchant, recognizing the woman's ignorance of American products, would have taken the opportunity to rid himself of inferior merchandise at inflated prices had Johanna not been present.

When she picked up twelve bars of soap from the table and handed them to him, he scribbled down the price and quickly hid it from view.

Suspicious of his actions, Johanna asked to see the pad of paper with the figures on it.

"Makes more sense to wait until we're done," he growled.

"If I don't see the figures you've put down, we could be finished already."

His lips thinned. "Nothin' worse'n a woman who thinks she knows more'n a man," he said resentfully.

Johanna ignored him, her eyes intent on the

29

figures he had put on the pad. Her eyes flashed angrily as they ran down the list. Then, she lifted her eyes to his. "You've overcharged Frau Hoffman on the soap, the flour, and the coffee," she said. "Please take the items from the box. We'll get those down the street. And anything else you see fit to overcharge on," she added.

"No need to do that," he said hastily. "It must have escaped my notice."

"I'd appreciate it if you'd give the figures your utmost attention," she said dryly.

Frau Hoffman stood quietly during the exchange, seemingly ignorant of their words. But it was not so, for when the purchases were completed, she took Johanna's hand and placed a twenty-dollar gold piece in it. "Please take this."

Johanna stared at the piece of gold lying on her palm. She had expected nothing from the woman. And yet, here was enough money to pay for a room, to buy a much-needed meal. She wouldn't have to sell her brooch. But would it be wrong to take the money? She had done nothing to deserve so much. Her green eyes were filled with indecision when she lifted them to meet Frau Hoffman's.

Seeming to recognize her indecision, Frau Hoffman reached out and gently closed Johanna's hand around the gold piece. "Please don't refuse," she said. "The merchant would have cheated me had it not been for you."

"But—"

"No," Frau Hoffman interrupted. "I will be insulted if you refuse it. As would Poppa. We

Hoffmans do not like to be in debt. And I am in yours until I have repaid you."

Johanna didn't know what to say, couldn't have said it anyway, for her throat had closed around a sizable lump. Just at her darkest moment, God had sent Frau Hoffman to her. Moisture filled her eyes and she blinked it away.

Frau Hoffman opened her reticule and pulled out a timepiece. She made a sound of annoyance, then threw a look at the crates of groceries she had purchased. "It is time to meet Wilhelm and Gunter at the hotel. Will you tell the merchant we will return for the supplies, Johanna?"

Nodding, Johanna relayed the message to the merchant. "Please see that every item Frau Hoffman paid for remains together," she added.

A surly nod was the only answer she received. Johanna gave an inward sigh. She knew if her brooch had to be sold, it wouldn't be to this particular merchant.

"Would you dine with us at the hotel?" Frau Hoffman asked. "I would like for you to meet my family."

Johanna found herself accepting the woman's invitation. She would eat with Frau Hoffman and her family. She might even pretend for a while that the family was her own. Surely such pretense would do no harm.

Silently, she followed the woman from the store.

Although Hawkeye was deep in conversation with Cremp and Jude, he was aware when the two women left the store and walked down the street toward the hotel.

"I still say it ain't enough money," Jude was belligerently insisting. "Them rifles is the only ones of their kind. Shipped all the way from someplace called Prussia. I hear tell they's some kind of cartridge rifle and they use a steel needle to make 'em fire. They oughtta be worth a hell of a lot more'n five thousand dollars."

"Keep your voice down," Cremp snapped. "You want ever'ybody in town to know what's happenin' here?"

"Five thousand is the price," Hawkeye said. "That's a hundred dollars for each one. Take it or leave it." His eyes were hard. He didn't like doing business with these vermin. But he knew he could not steal the guns and transport them himself. The rifles were closely guarded. But Cremp was one of the guards. He would have no trouble.

Jude's expression was dark but he kept his mouth shut.

"We'll expect the payment to be in gold," Cremp growled. "No Texas currency."

"You'll get it," Hawkeye said.

Cremp exchanged a surreptitious glance with Jude. "When?" he asked.

"How long will it take you to get the rifles?"

"A week oughtta do it." Cremp's eyes narrowed, traveled searchingly over Hawkeye's buckskin-clad form. "You got the gold with you?" he asked.

Hawkeye's face remained impassive. "That would be foolish of me," he said.

"No gold. No rifles," Cremp growled.

"When I get the rifles," Hawkeye said. "You'll get the gold. Bring them to Washington-on-the-Brazos."

"Now wait a minute—" Jude said.

"Shut up," Cremp told him. His eyes held Hawkeye's. "How do we know you'll bring the gold?"

"How do I know you'll bring the rifles?" countered Hawkeye.

Cremp thought about that for a minute. "We got expenses," he said slowly. "We gotta hire drivers for the wagons. We need half the gold up front."

Hawkeye's eyes narrowed, became cold. "What's to stop you from taking the gold and leaving?"

Cremp attempted a smile. "Now we wouldn't do that. You have my word on it."

For what it's worth, Hawkeye told himself. "I'll give you five hundred now," he told Cremp. "It will be enough to hire drivers."

"That ain't enough to—"

"Take it or leave it," Hawkeye said shortly. "It's all I've got with me."

"All right," Cremp agreed. "But it ain't gonna be easy finding drivers for that kinda money."

Hawkeye gave the two men the gold and, after arranging a meeting place in Washington-on-the-Brazos, took his leave of them.

Johanna followed Frau Hoffman into the spacious lobby of the hotel. A bespectacled clerk at the registration desk looked up inquiringly from the newspaper he had been perusing. "Help you?" he inquired.

"No, thank you," Johanna replied. "We're meeting someone."

"You can wait over there," he said, waving at the gold brocade-covered couches along the wall.

They had barely seated themselves when two men entered the hotel. Immediately Frau Hoffman stood up and waved a handkerchief at them. "Over here, Poppa," she said in German.

"Ahhh, there you are, Momma," the older of the two said. "I see you have found a beautiful companion."

Johanna flushed silently at the compliment. Frau Hoffman introduced her husband, Wilhelm, who stood several inches shorter than his son, Gunter, a blond young man who looked to be in his mid to late twenties. "Johanna helped with my purchases," Frau Hoffman said. "The merchant would have cheated me without her. I have asked her to dine with us."

"That is good." Wilhelm Hoffman's gray eyes studied Johanna. "Thank you for your help," he said. "Gunter speaks your language well, but Momma and I have yet to learn. As we will," he added, "for this is our new homeland, and we cannot expect our son to follow us around everywhere we go. We must learn to speak for ourselves."

He turned to his wife. "Our meal will have to wait, Momma. We must return to the wagon train."

"But, Poppa," the woman protested. "We must

34

not. I have asked Johanna to join us."

"Perhaps the young lady could accompany us to the wagon train," Gunter suggested. "I could bring her back to the hotel after dinner."

Johanna felt embarrassed. She should have refused the invitation. Now these kind people were being put out. "Please don't bother about me —" she began.

"Why must we return?" Frau Hoffman interrupted. "We agreed to dine at the hotel."

"I know, Momma," he said. "But the scout for the wagon train is here. He says everyone must return early for a meeting with the wagon master." His eyes returned to Johanna. "You must come with us. If you refuse I will forever be in Momma's bad graces."

Johanna shifted uncomfortably. "It's very kind of you to ask me," she said. "But I wouldn't think of putting you to so much trouble."

Wilhelm took her arm in a firm grip. "It is useless to protest," he said. "I will not take no for an answer." He herded her toward the door. Moments later she found herself sitting beside Gunter in the back of the wagon, headed out of town.

Johanna was made welcome by the other travelers. She sat with the Hoffman family during the meeting, listening to their plans. There was much laughing and joking between the families as they discussed the journey ahead. When the meeting was over, Gunter helped his father bed down the livestock while Frau Hoffman and Johanna prepared the meal.

"Where is your family, child?" Frau Hoffman

35

inquired as she floured the steaks, placing them in a skillet sizzling with hot lard.

"My parents are dead," Johanna said huskily. "I have three married sisters, but they live in Ireland." Would she ever see her sisters again? she wondered. It was doubtful. She couldn't return to her homeland, and her sisters couldn't afford the journey to America with their families. Perhaps it was Johanna's destiny to be alone.

"Where do you live, Johanna?" Frau Hoffman asked.

"Nowhere yet," Johanna said, thinking of the twenty-dollar gold piece she had placed in her stocking for safekeeping. "I've only just arrived in town."

Frau Hoffman nodded. "And you look for work," she said. She studied the girl for a moment, then seemed to make up her mind about something. "You must not return to that town, Johanna. It is no place for an innocent girl such as yourself. You will come with us."

"I couldn't," Johanna protested.

"Whisht, now," the woman said. "Of course you can. You will find a job somewhere else. You are obviously educated. Perhaps you could find a situation teaching school."

Johanna felt tempted to go, but, fearing Frau Hoffman had only made the offer out of sympathy for her plight, she felt she must refuse. She had no intention of becoming a burden to the family.

Frieda, sensing her indecision, said, "It would help us, Johanna. You could teach us to speak

English."

Despite her efforts at control, Johanna's eyes filled with tears. She had been lucky to find such kindly people. "If you will let me work for my passage, I will come," she said.

"Then it is agreed," Frau Hoffman said. "And it is a good bargain we have made."

Yes. It was a good bargain, Johanna thought. She felt as though the weight of the world had lifted off her shoulders. She would travel with the Hoffmans. Somewhere along the way she would find a suitable position. And the farther she went into the heart of Texas, the less chance there was of Michael Durant ever finding her.

If he was still searching.

Chapter Three

Hawkeye guided Diablo around the grove of cedars, his eyes alert for any sign of the wagon train. When he reached the screen of willow trees edging the banks of the Brazos River, he reined in for a moment, his senses attuned to his surroundings.

The water in the Brazos moved slowly for this time of year, making hardly a ripple as it meandered along. Somewhere along its banks a frog croaked and in the distance a whippoorwill called to its mate. The breeze blowing across the river held a hint of dampness, and Hawkeye was aware of the pungent scent of the willows mixed with the odor of sweating horseflesh.

He had been traveling for two days now, stopping only a short time last night to grab a few winks of sleep. Had he been unable to stop, it would not have bothered him, for Hawkeye was used to traveling fast with very little rest and his body was accustomed to it.

Waiting patiently, he listened to the sounds around him: the soft rippling chuckle of the river flowing downstream, an owl hooting in the distance. He waited until the sound was repeated. Then, deciding there was no one about, he dismounted and allowed Diablo to drink his fill.

After quenching his own thirst, he mounted Diablo again, and man and beast continued their journey.

Hawkeye had traveled only a few miles when he found the tracks of unshod horses. The riders were keeping away from the river, heading farther into the hills, perhaps in search of a place to hide until they were ready to ambush an unwary traveler . . . or a wagon train.

As he moved toward the hills, the sweep of his gaze took in the whole countryside. Dismissing the beauty of the landscape—the bluebonnets, Indian paintbrushes, sneezewood, and prairie grass—he searched out all areas of possible ambush.

He saw nothing, had still seen nothing when he reached the foothills. His hands gripped the reins lightly as Diablo picked a cautious path up the hill, over the ferns and lichened granite. When he reached a point which gave him a clear view of the terrain, he sat his horse and waited.

Finally, his patience was rewarded. A rider emerged from the trees, moving at a fast walk. He looked neither to the right or left, just rode straight toward Hawkeye. Even from this distance, his seat in the saddle, the way he held his body, told Hawkeye who the rider was. He was Sky Walker, a Comanche warrior, and blood brother to Hawkeye.

Although Sky Walker's face was expressionless, Hawkeye sensed all was not well.

"You stray far from our hunting grounds," Hawkeye said, as the other man pulled up beside him.

"I'm scouting for Running Deer," Sky Walker explained. "He was told of a wagon train traveling across our lands. We will attack when the wagons stop for the night. Running Deer said we must teach the white-eyes they cannot invade our hunting grounds."

Alarm flickered through Hawkeye. "We've got to stop him," he said. "The wagon train will have to be allowed across our lands." Recognizing Sky Walker's puzzlement, he explained. "While I was in Galveston, I heard about a shipment of percussion rifles similar to my pistols. They are far superior to anything these Texans already possess. I've made a bargain to buy them from the men who guard them. They plan to come this way. If Running Deer attacks the wagon train, the men will hear of it. They'll be afraid to bring the rifles."

Sky Walker was familiar with Hawkeye's weapons, had long been envious of them. The pistols, designed by a man called Colt, were too new as yet to be available for purchase. Hawkeye had met the salesman demonstrating the weapon and had been lucky enough to purchase two for himself. Rifles built in such a manner would give them a distinct advantage over their enemies.

"We may be too late to stop the attack," Sky Walker said.

"Where is the wagon train?"

When Sky Walker told him, Hawkeye knew they dared not delay. The wagon train could even now be under attack.

"We must hurry," he said. "If the wagons are still moving, we may be in time. If we lose the rifles, we stand no chance of keeping the settler from pushing us farther west. The Texas Militia is a formidable enemy. With weapons such as those, they would surely defeat us."

The two men urged their mounts forward, sending dust clouds aloft beneath the horses' hooves. Hawkeye could only hope that he reached Running Deer in time to stop the attack.

The wagon train moved slowly along its way, the travelers unaware of the lone horseman who waited motionless in the dense woods a quarter of a mile ahead.

A breeze touched the man's long hair, ruffling it softly against his naked chest. A lance, flowing rawhide tassels and squirrel's tails, thrust skyward from his right hand, and across his back was a quiver full of arrows fletched with owl feathers and tipped with stone warheads that fit the short bow slung across his left shoulder. Buckskin leggings covered the rider's legs and moccasins encased his feet.

The pony remained still, for he was a well-trained war stallion and his rider need only apply a small pressure with his knees to instruct the horse.

Although the warrior was not from a central-Texas tribe, coming rather from the Staked Plains, he had been here before. Two seasons ago he had ridden down with others of his band to take revenge against a settler who had cheated them. During that raid they had taken cattle and horses, and something even more valuable to them. They had taken a female child to raise to womanhood among his own people. Some day she would bring new babies to his dwindling tribe. If they were lucky, they would take more children today. As was their practice, the females would be used as breeders, and the males would be sold to other tribes which might be willing to buy them, provided the children were tough enough to survive the pace the war party set as they made their return journey to their village.

The warrior continued to watch as the wagon train drew closer. Soon it would be time to attack. He turned and rode toward the place where his brother Comanches waited.

Johanna trudged wearily beside the covered wagon, her face flushed with heat, dust boiling up around her, settling over her clothing and in her hair. The trail had been long, winding endlessly through the cedar and towering oak trees that covered the wild Texas land. When they had first left Galveston, she had marveled at the wildflowers growing in such abundance beside the trails. The beauty of her surroundings could almost rival the fields of her beloved Ireland. If only her father could have been here.

His loss pierced her anew. Six years before, when she and her father had first come to America, he'd had such high hopes for them. Now, because of Durant, he was dead. Her eyes clouded with pain. When the wagon train reached Washington-on-the-Brazos, she must send a letter to Ireland. Her sisters must be told of their father's death.

Thoughts of her sisters brought an overwhelming sense of aloneness. Johanna would give anything to see them. But she had known when she left Ireland that it would not be safe for her to return. Too many stories had been circulated, too many people had guessed her secret, and she had been in grave danger from the authorities. Had she been taken for questioning, her secret could have been exposed.

Johanna had begged her sisters to journey to the new world with them. But they were married and had families. And they all knew they would be safe if she left. No one could accuse them of witchcraft. Only herself . . . she who had been born at the wrong time.

Johanna sighed. It did no good to relive the past. It was over and nothing could change it. The future lay ahead. And her reactions to the present would determine that future. Six years ago she had fled her homeland with her father. Now, she had fled New Orleans. How many times would she be driven from her home? Was there nowhere in this world that she could live in peace? Even now, she could not count herself safe.

"You can't blame them for being afraid, Johanna," her father had told her time and again. "People fear what they don't understand."

But Michael Durant hadn't been afraid. It would have been better if he had.

Forcing memories of Durant from her mind, she concentrated on putting one foot in front of the other. The hardships she had encountered on this trip were minimal compared to what she had already been through. Whatever lay ahead, she would utter no complaint.

Her eyes went to the sun hanging low in the west. Day was nearly at an end. Her gaze swept the area to her right, searching for the thicket of willow trees and sycamores that would mark the passing of the Brazos River. Emmett Rogers, the burly wagon master of the train, had said they would stop for the night when they reached the river. Even then, there would be work to be done, for the wagons would have to be pulled into a circle, the oxen would need to be unhitched, the mules and horses tethered, firewood gathered, a meal fixed, and dishes washed.

From the start, the journey had been ill-fated, plagued with sickness, flooded rivers, and broken equipment. But even through all the hardships she had endured, Johanna counted herself lucky to have found passage in the Hoffmans' wagon.

The wagon train, made up of eleven families, had left Galveston three days ago and was still several days out of Washington-on-the-Brazos. Emmett Rogers had told the travelers there would be a stopover there to replenish supplies and make necessary repairs on the wagons before going on to Austin.

Johanna hoped she could find a position in the next town. She felt she couldn't impose on the German family any longer. During the trip she had become well acquainted with them and knew she would miss them when they continued their journey to Fredericksburg.

She pushed a dark curl back from her face with a work-roughened hand, and tucked it behind her ear. A movement on top of a hill caught her attention and she narrowed her eyes on the object. It appeared to be a horse and a rider. She frowned. She had heard it wasn't safe to travel alone. Comanches had been sighted in the area.

The very thought of the dreaded Comanches sent a chill creeping through her bones. Since the wagon train had left Galveston, she had heard many stories of the Mexicans who were still raiding in the area, and even worse than that were the painted warriors who swept down on unsuspecting travelers and massacred whole families.

A distant shout near the front of the wagon train told her others had spotted the rider as well.

"What's happening, Johanna?" Called Frieda Hoffman from her place on the high wagon seat.

"It's a horse and rider," Johanna replied, pointing to them. She saw a man on horseback move out to meet the rider. "Cole is riding out to meet him."

The two men spoke together for a moment and then rode toward Emmett Rogers' wagon. Johanna stumbled over a large rock on the trail and nearly fell. Deciding the man posed no threat to them and becoming aware that she was falling behind, Johanna picked up her long skirts and hurried to catch up with the Hoffman wagon.

The setting sun painted the sky with long ribbons of lavender and pink as the weary travelers topped a rise and saw the river spread out before them. They greeted the sight with cheers and it wasn't long before the wagons had been pulled into a circle near the banks of the river. Despite the weariness of the travelers, there was much good cheer as they went about the duties of settling in for the night. Campfires glowed in the thickening twilight as women bustled around preparing the evening meal.

Gunter and Herr Hoffman took the stock to the river for water while Frau Hoffman searched through the supplies in the back of the wagon for the makings of their evening meal.

On learning there was a spring nearby, Johanna picked up the water bucket and set out to fetch a bucket of fresh water. As she dipped her bucket into the cool water, her eyes found a bunch of watercress growing at the edge of the spring. She put her bucket down and began to gather the watercress, knowing Frieda would be delighted to have a fresh salad with their meal.

When Johanna had gathered all that was near,

she searched for more of the greens. A patch of green farther on caught her eyes. If she wasn't mistaken, it was poke salad. Deciding to have a closer look, she left the watercress near her bucket and made her way to the spot.

She had been right. It was poke salad. But it proved to be only a small patch, not nearly enough to serve four people. She needed more. She scanned the area and, farther on, past a deep gully, she spied a larger patch of the greens. Johanna skirted the gully, picking her way past loose rocks and gravel. She was nearly there when she heard the warning rattle.

Johanna jerked around quickly, having already learned the sound came from a rattlesnake. Her movement caused a large rock at her right to move. At that very moment, she saw the rattler.

A cry escaped her lips at the same time the rock hit her ankle. Johanna lost her balance and found herself tumbling backward, sliding down the loose shale in the gully.

A moment later she was lying at the bottom of the trench, her heart beating wildly against her ribcage.

Pushing herself to her elbows, she looked frantically around. Had the rattlesnake tumbled down into the ravine with her? Was she still in danger from it?

Johanna's green eyes skittered to and fro, searching for the deadly reptile. A moment later she saw it, coiled not more than eighteen inches away. At the instant it struck, a shot rang out, severing the head from the body.

Had anyone been watching, they still wouldn't have seen the man draw. It was done as fast as a man could blink; he had pulled his gun, cocked the hammer, and squeezed the trigger of his right hand Colt, killing the rattlesnake that lay writhing at her feet.

Johanna let out a long breath, her startled gaze flying to the man at the top of the gully. Although he looked vaguely familiar, Johanna knew he wasn't traveling with the wagon train. During the past few days she had come to know each and every one of the travelers. None of them wore buckskins.

Even from where she sat, she could see he was tall, more than six feet. He hurried down the gully, slipping and sliding until he came to a skidding stop near her. His beaded buckskin shirt covered massive shoulders and the soft leather of his pants encased powerfully muscled thighs.

"Are you hurt, Miss?" he asked, kneeling beside her.

Johanna lifted her eyes to the stranger, feeling a sense of recognition as she looked into his unfathomable black eyes. Her heart skipped a beat, then picked up speed as she realized why he was so familiar. He was the man she had seen in Galveston, just before she had met Frau Hoffman. From his look, she felt he remembered her as well.

Her heart began to pound loudly in her ears. "I'm all right," she mumbled, scarlet staining her cheeks. For she had been caught staring at the man in buckskins again.

"What happened?" he asked gruffly.

The question brought her fears back. "The rattlesnake startled me," she said. "I lost my balance."

"You shouldn't be out here alone."

She pointed toward the poke salad up the hill. "I was just going to pick some of those greens when I heard the rattle and . . ." She shivered. "Like I said, the snake startled me. I slipped and fell."

"You probably scared the snake as much as it scared you," he said. "They're skittish creatures. Don't like people much."

She grinned ruefully. "The feeling is mutual." Pushing herself to her knees, she slowly regained her feet. Agony shot through her ankle and she cried out with pain.

His expression became concerned. "Where does it hurt?" he asked.

She remained silent, gritting her teeth against the pain. He repeated the question. "It's my ankle," she muttered. "I must have turned it."

Kneeling beside her, he pushed her skirt aside and picked up her right foot. "This one?"

She nodded, then realized he couldn't see the action with his head bent over her foot. "Yes," she said huskily. His fingers on her ankle were doing curious things to her stomach. She wondered if she was going to be sick.

He remained bent over the ankle, examining it closely. "It's swelling," he said. "You can't walk on it."

Before she could protest, he had scooped her into his arms and lifted her against his chest.

"Please," she said, avoiding his eyes. "I can make it on my own. There's no need for you to carry me."

He ignored her protests, carrying her easily out of the gully. She was all too conscious of his arms wrapped around her, one circling her waist, the other beneath her knees. This was the first time she'd ever been in a man's arms and she found the experience almost overwhelming.

Johanna lowered her eyes, staring at his brown throat. Against her will her eyes traveled upward again, noticing for the first time the scar that marred the left side of his forehead, running from the hairline down to the top of his ear.

She wanted to ask his name but found herself almost tongue-tied. And the man's arms around her, holding her against his chest, didn't help matters one bit. She tried to think of something to say, something that would ease her embarrassment at the situation she found herself in, but nothing came to mind.

Neither of them noticed the old man approaching until he spoke. "What happened to Johanna?"

Looking up, Johanna recognized Saul Porter, a frequent visitor at the Hoffman wagon. He was going to his brother's farm near Fredericksburg.

"The young lady had an accident," the stranger said gruffly. "She injured her ankle."

The grizzled farmer clucked in sympathy for Johanna's plight. "Hurt bad?" he asked.

"Just a sprain," came the answer.

"Don't recall seein' you around before, Mister," the old man said, his faded-gray eyes studying the

50

man in buckskin. "You got a name?"

"They call me Hawkeye."

"Saul Porter here," the old man said, sticking out a gnarled hand before remembering Hawkeye had his hands full.

Johanna could have been a sack of flour being toted to the wagon for all the attention they gave her, but her humiliation at her situation was so great that she felt only gratitude.

"You a buffalo hunter, mister?" queried a young voice near Johanna's elbow.

Turning her head, she saw the red hair and freckled face of ten-year-old Johnny Malone. Her cheeks flushed scarlet as she saw several children trailing along beside them.

"No, son," Hawkeye said gruffly. "I'm a trapper."

"What do you trap?" asked Sally May Edwards, her blond braids flopping up and down as she skipped along beside them.

"Some beaver. Some weasel. And a few other varmints as well." Even though he carried Johanna, he did it effortlessly, as though she were weightless.

"Mr. . . . uh, Hawkeye," Johanna said timidly. He turned his dark gaze on her. "Y-you can put me down now. I think I can make it the rest of the way."

He remained silent, ignoring her words.

"You ever kill any Injuns?" Johnny asked.

Hawkeye's fingers tightened on her flesh, and Johanna caught her breath at the pain. Instantly, his fingers loosed.

51

"Did you?" young Johnny persisted. "You ever kill any of 'em?"

Realizing the stranger was bothered by the boy's question, Johanna interfered. "Don't be so bloodthirsty, Johnny," she chided.

At that moment she realized they had reached the Hoffman wagon and she breathed a sigh of relief. The wagon swayed as Frau Hoffman appeared in the opening, her arms loaded with foodstuffs. An expression of concern crossed her features as her gaze fell on them.

"It's all right," Johanna hurried to reassure the woman, explaining what had happened.

"Hawkeye said it's only a sprain," Sally May piped up. Even though the child knew Frau Hoffman understood very little of what she said, it didn't stop her from talking. "He's a trapper," Sally May added, throwing the buckskin-clad man a glance that held something akin to awe. "He had to carry Johanna 'cause she couldn't walk. And he don't even breathe hard." Her blue eyes studied the stranger's muscled arms.

Frau Hoffman clucked in sympathy, set the foodstuffs she had collected down and cleared a space for Johanna to sit on a box. After being told his name, she held her hand out to Hawkeye and gave him a hearty handshake.

"Guten Tag, Herr Hawkeye," she said. *"Bitte essen mit uns."* Without waiting for a reply from the man who obviously didn't understand a word she'd said, she turned and examined Johanna's ankle.

"You've been invited to eat with us," Johanna

said, meeting his dark gaze over the woman's head.

"I'd be pleased to accept," he said gruffly.

The Hoffman men arrived and she introduced the men and made the necessary explanations. Instantly a conversation began between the men, translated in part by Gunter, since Wilhelm was still learning to speak English.

"Did you see any Injuns up ahead?" Saul asked.

"Saw a party of hunters at a distance," Hawkeye replied. "It's my guess they were scouting for buffalo. The beasts aren't as plentiful since the hidehunters have been slaughtering them."

"Daddy said the Injuns use the buffalo hides to build their houses," Sally May said. "Did you know that, Mr. Hawkeye?"

Hawkeye nodded. "The Indians use the buffalo for other things as well. They eat the meat and use the hide for clothing and lots of other things. There isn't a part of the buffalo that's left to go to waste."

"Heard that before," said Saul. "Mebbe the best way to get rid of the Injuns would be to kill all the buffalo."

"That would be an awful thing to do," Johanna said. Her eyes found Hawkeye's. "Are they really as bad as what I've heard?"

"Depends on what you've heard," Hawkeye said, probing her with his dark gaze. "They aren't happy about being pushed off land they feel is rightfully theirs. And they take steps to drive settlers out. Some of the steps they take may seem harsh to some. But it's the only way they know."

Johanna had a feeling he was trying to tell her something, but she had no idea what it could be.

"It ain't their land," Johnny piped up. "It don't belong to nobody."

"Afraid they don't see it that way," Hawkeye said. "Since they were here first, they figure they have more right to it than the settlers."

"You seem to know a lot about the way the Injuns feel," Saul growled. "Hope you ain't one of them Injun lovers. This land's here for whoever can hold onto it. My brother's already at Fredericksburg and it's all he can do to keep them thievin' Injuns from stealin' him blind. They run off more'n fifty prime horses and slaughtered a bunch of his herd. It's a fact them Injuns is a gettin' bolder and bolder all the time. We don't watch out, they'll be ridin' in an' stealin' our kids like they done at Parker's Fort."

Johanna had heard about the raid on Parker's Fort two years ago. She had listened to the men as they talked around the campfire at night. During the raid the Comanches had killed several adults from the Parker family and carried off several people, among them a young girl. One could only wonder at her fate.

Hawkeye stayed late in the evening, talking quietly with the men. Johanna was aware that his dark eyes strayed to her often, probing, seeming to strip her right to the core and bring to light all her weaknesses. And yet, his face remained expressionless, revealing nothing of himself and his thoughts about her. As the evening passed, her self-consciousness increased and she found herself getting more than a little miffed at him. And yet, when he rose to leave she watched him go with mixed feelings.

She had a deep-down feeling that they would meet again in the wilderness somewhere ahead.

Chapter Four

It was late when the wagon train reached Washington-on-the-Brazos. The travelers camped that night on the east bank of the Brazos River, and Johanna, eager for a sight of the town that would surely be her new home, was disappointed to find it was hidden from view by the dense forest. The only indication of civilization was the ferry and the road that left the river and continued up the banks into the thick foliage.

Early next morning, Johanna bid the Hoffmans farewell and boarded the ferry that would take her across the river to her new home. She wouldn't allow herself to think otherwise.

Until she topped the rise and saw the town.

Johanna stared at it in dismay, her spirits taking a downward plunge. How could she hope to find a position in such a place?

From where she stood, she could see the whole town. It was laid out in the woods and had only one well-defined street. Even that had stumps in it.

Log buildings were lined up along both sides of the street. The businesses were bunched together in the center of town while cabins lined both ends.

Worry creased her brow as she began her search for work. She felt no surprise when each proprietor shook his head at her request for a position.

By mid-morning Johanna had exhausted all possibilities and her rumbling stomach could no longer be ignored. She was debating about returning to the wagon train when her gaze fell upon a cabin she had missed.

It was set farther back into the woods than the other buildings, and the sign above the door read MARY'S CAFE.

Intent on filling her empty stomach, she pushed open the door and stepped inside.

The cafe smelled like soup and fresh baked bread, like cloves and cinnamon and strongly-brewed coffee.

The walls had been whitewashed to brighten the interior and the floor was made of smooth planks. A long table with benches placed on both sides dominated the room while several smaller tables paired with hide-bound chairs were placed in the corners.

There were only a few patrons—an elderly couple just finishing a meal—two rough-looking men seated nearby and beyond them, a grizzled old man with his head bent over a steaming cup.

"Set yourself down anywhere," called a cheerful voice from across the room. "I'll be with you in a minute."

Johanna had only a glimpse of a blue calico dress before the woman disappeared through a door that obviously led to the kitchen area.

Her thoughts troubled, Johanna pulled a chair out from the nearest table and seated herself. She had counted on finding work, had not allowed herself to believe she might fail. Now what was she to do? The Hoffman family had made it clear she could continue the journey with them, but she refused to take advantage of their kindness. They had done enough already.

Johanna sighed heavily and looked up, straight into the eyes of a man seated at the long table.

She looked away from him.

"Come sit with us, honey," he called.

"No, thank you," she said stiffly, flicking him a brief glance. He was on the lean side, dark-skinned, with close-set eyes. A shock of black hair fell over the right side of his sharp-featured face. She placed him in his early twenties.

He eyed her with a slow thoroughness that made her flesh crawl, and a wide grin spread across his face. "Don't be unsociable," he said.

"You botherin' my customers, Luke?" The voice was sharp and belonged to a leathery-thin middle-aged woman with dark hair bundled into a knot on the nape of her neck.

"Now, Mary," the sharp-featured man said, "I wouldn't do a thing like that."

"Best you don't," she retorted sharply. "One

58

more time and Sam won't feed you no more."

Grinning, he pushed back his chair and stood up. "Time for us to be leavin'," he said. "I ain't wantin' to make that husband of yours sore again." He tossed a coin on the table, then his eyes raked Johanna. "I'll prob'ly be seein' you again if you stick around these parts."

Johanna didn't like the look in his eyes. It was half malicious amusement, and half threat.

"Don't pay no attention to him," the woman said. "He talks a lot, but so far ain't caused no real problem."

Johanna remained silent, wondering if the other woman really believed that.

"What can I get for you?" Mary asked.

"I'm not very hungry." Johanna said hesitantly. "Do you have any suggestions?"

"Sam made some potato soup. How's that sound?"

"Perfect," Johanna replied.

Mary looked up at the grizzled man who had entered from a back room. He was tall and hefty with a bulbous nose, lined with dozens of broken blood vessels. He strode toward them, and his ambling walk reminded Johanna more of a bear than a man.

"You hear that, Sam?" Mary asked. "This young lady wants some of that potato soup you made."

"You wantin' me to fetch it?" he asked gruffly.

"Figgered you could," Mary said with a grin. "Seein' as how you don't have nothin' else do do."

"What're you up to?" he asked.

"I ain't up to nothin'." Her dark eyes twinkled with mischief. "I'm just gonna take me a little rest." She pulled out a chair and sat down across from Johanna. "This young lady's a stranger here. She might have some questions 'bout our town."

"You ain't foolin' me woman," he growled. "You know she's from the wagon train. You're tryin' to beat Bessie Pearl outta the latest news from Galveston."

"Bessie Pearl," Mary sniffed. "That ol' woman thinks she's gotta be the first to know ever'thin'. An' you know I don't like gossip."

"Not if you don' tell it your ownself," he agreed. "Just go dish up the soup, Sam."

He grunted. "Thought I was supposed to be the cook around here. You never said nothin' 'bout all these other jobs you 'spect me to do."

Mary winked at Johanna. "What other jobs?" she asked mildly.

"You know what other jobs. I gotta cook, an' keep the peace in this place, an' half the time I gotta wash the dishes. Now you're wantin' me to wait on the customers. It ain't fittin' a man's wife should always be tellin' 'im what to do."

She shooed him away with a wave of her hand. "Stop grumblin'," she said. "You know you don't mind." As the big man left the room, she turned her attention back to Johanna. "I'm right 'bout you travelin' with the wagon train, ain't I?"

"Yes," Johanna replied. "At least I was. I'm hoping to find work here."

"What kind of work you lookin' for?"

"I can't afford to be too choosy," Johanna said.

"My money won't last long."

"Saloon's always lookin' for girls."

"I'm not that desperate yet."

Mary nodded thoughtfully. "Figgered as much." Her eyes left Johanna, fell on Sam, who was approaching the table with a bowl of soup. "Think you could handle waitressin'?" she asked.

A look of puzzlement crossed Johanna's features. She had just told Mary she wouldn't work at the saloon.

"Not at the saloon," Mary said, guessing her thoughts. "Here."

Johanna's eyes widened and she swallowed hard. "Are you offering me a job? she asked, her voice was husky with hope.

"Sure am," Mary said.

Johanna was distracted as Sam carefully set the bowl of soup and a plate of cornbread on the table.

Mary's eyes gleamed with mischief as she watched her husband. "Sam, here, was just gripin' about havin' to carry a bowl of soup. An' things get mighty busy around here sometimes." Her lips curled into a wide smile, and she leaned back in her chair, her eyes still on her husband. "We just hired us some help," she told him.

"We have?" Sam's expression was confused. "But, Mary, we don't need . . ."

"Now, you just hush up, Sam. You don't know what we need." Her eyes returned to Johanna. "We can't pay nothin' right now, honey," she said apologetically. "We ain't been open very long, but we got an empty cabin back yonder in the woods we could throw in with the job. You could eat all your meals here. All the cash money you'd get would be tips. An' they don't 'mount to hardly nothin'. But if you want it, the job's yours."

Johanna's green eyes moistened and she swallowed around a lump in her throat. "I want it," she breathed huskily. "And I don't know how to thank you."

"No need," Mary said gruffly. "You're the one doin' me the favor. Go ahead an' eat up. When you're done, I'll show you the cabin."

Johanna, anxious to get settled, didn't linger over her meal. Since she was the only customer in the cafe, Mary left her husband in charge and followed the younger girl outside.

The cabin was only a short distance away and Johanna felt a sense of belonging the moment she saw it. It stood nestled back among the trees. Heavy grapevines had entwined themselves around the building, completely covering the roof, making the cabin blend with the woods.

They stepped inside and Mary flung the shutters wide to allow the sun's rays to penetrate the shadowy interior of the cabin.

"Needs cleaning," Mary said, wiping a palm across the windowsill, and frowning at the dirt she'd collected. "Ain't been nobody here for a spell."

Johanna hadn't moved since she stepped inside the room. Her gaze dwelt on the four-poster bed covered by a patchwork quilt, slid to the dresser beside it. The bright colors of the quilt were picked up in the braided rug on the floor. At the other side of the room was a rocking chair, placed before a stone fireplace, with shelves built on both sides for storage space. Near it stood a table and two hide-bound chairs.

Johanna turned to find the older woman watching her with a curious expression.

"Reckon it'll do?" Mary asked.

Tears glistened in Johanna's eyes. "It'll more than do. Who lived here, Mary?"

"My mother." The tone of her voice told the younger girl it wasn't needed any more.

"Are you certain you don't mind me living here?"

"Course not," Mary said briskly. "Wouldn't've offered if I did." Her voice softened. "Momma would want you here. 'Specially if it kept you outta the saloon. Where'd you leave your things?"

"I don't have much," Johanna said. "All I have is in my reticule."

"Guess you could use a few things then," Mary said, sparing a brief glance at the small bag. "We'll do somethin' about that later. Right now you can get settled in. After we close the cafe, me an' Sam'll bring some sheets and dishes."

"You've done so much already," Johanna protested.

"No such thing," Mary said. "There's times a body needs help. 'Pears to me, this's one of 'em." With a smile at Johanna, the older woman left.

Johanna emptied the contents of her reticule in a dresser drawer, hiding the gun beneath her nightgown. Then, feeling as though a great weight had been lifted off her shoulders, she sank down in the rocker and began to rock back and forth, back and forth.

As she rocked, she contemplated her circumstances. They had drastically changed in the last month. Her father was dead and she was alone, having fled her home to make her way in the wilderness.

And it was all due to Durant.

Rage surged forth and her eyes blazed emerald green. Michael Durant had a lot to answer for. He had thought to break her will, to own her, body and soul. But he had failed. She had escaped him. And even though she wanted to see him punished, she knew her limitations.

She must put the past behind her, build a future for herself in this wild Texas land. And above all, she must keep her secret hidden. For therein lay the cause of all her pain.

Hawkeye sat alone at a table in the shadowy corner of the room, the same table he had occupied for the last four days. On the table in front of him sat a glass of whiskey, but he had not taken a drink. Nor would he, for he had no use for whiskey; it was the white man's poison, and he had had occasion to see its effects many times over. He knew how it could dull his brain, slow his thought processes, and he could not afford for such a thing to happen, especially not now. If anyone even suspected who he was and why he had come, his life would be worthless.

A shriek of laughter from across the room drew

his attention and he stiffened, his hand moving automatically to his knife. Then, when he saw it was nothing more than a slightly tipsy barmaid escaping from a customer's fumbling hands, his body relaxed again.

His black eyes slid around the room, skimming lightly over the dark-haired girl in the flaming red dress who had offered to keep him company earlier. Even had he not been waiting for his contacts, he would still have refused.

A vision of another dark-haired girl rose in his mind.

Johanna.

Damn! Why couldn't he keep her from his thoughts? Perhaps it was his body's way of telling him he had been too long without a woman. If that was the case, one of the saloon girls should suit his purpose. But for some reason, the thought of going upstairs with one of them was completely abhorrent to him.

He remembered the way Johanna had felt in his arms, the soft, womanly smell of her, and most of all, he remembered how she'd looked when he bid her goodbye . . . with the wind blowing through her dark hair, the firelight on her sun-kissed skin.

Giving himself a mental shake, he allowed his dark gaze to roam around the saloon. His face revealed none of the anxiety he felt at the continued absence of Jude and Cremp. His gaze touched lightly on the four men nearby who were hunched over the cards held tightly in their hands, then returned to the door to resume his silent vigil.

Although Jude and Cremp were two days late,

he felt certain they would come. He had known men like them before, and although they were untrustworthy, they were also greedy. If they exposed him they would lose the gold.

Yes. They would come. But after he delivered the gold he carried, he would have to watch them carefully. He knew they would just as soon kill him as not.

But right now, all he could do was wait.

Suddenly the saloon doors opened and Cremp walked in. The girl in the red dress made a bee-line for him.

Hooking her hand around Cremp's arm, she smiled invitingly up at him. But the man ignored her. When his sweeping gaze spotted the man he was searching for, he spoke sharply to the girl. She shrugged, released him, and returned to her position at the bar.

Cremp headed for the table where the man dressed in buckskin waited.

"You're late," Hawkeye said as Cremp pulled out a chair and seated himself.

"Couldn't be helped," Cremp said. "It took a while to locate enough drivers we could trust." He grew silent as the barmaid approached. After ordering whiskey, he waited until she was out of hearing before he spoke. "You bring the gold?"

Hawkeye nodded. "Where's Jude?" he asked.

"He stayed with the wagons. Wasn't sure how far we could trust them drivers we hired."

Hawkeye's lips curled at the corners. "You certain you can trust Jude?"

"Hell, yes!" the man exclaimed. "Me an' Jude

go back a long way. I'd trust him with my life."

The girl came back with a bottle of whiskey and a glass. She poured a hefty swig, then started to leave. Cremp caught her wrist. "Leave the bottle," he said, slapping down a silver dollar.

Hawkeye waited impatiently while Cremp lifted the glass and tossed it down his throat.

"You ain't drinkin'?" Cremp asked, eyeing the glass in front of Hawkeye.

"Had enough already," Hawkeye said. "I've been waiting two days. I'd like to see what I'm paying for."

"Sure," Cremp grinned. He corked the bottle of liquor, picked it up by the neck and pushed his chair away from the table. "I'm ready whenever you are."

Hawkeye followed Cremp from the saloon into the night. The town seemed almost deserted as they walked down the darkened street. Hawkeye felt a sense of unrest, and that should have warned him. But when the attack came, it took him by surprise. Jude waited until he passed the alley, then he struck. Hawkeye had only a glimpse of him before Cremp pushed him into the alley and Jude brought the knife stabbing down. Hawkeye felt a sharp pain in his chest, then another and another. His legs crumpled beneath him and he slumped to the ground.

Johanna sighed with relief as she finished stacking the dishes. She had completed her fourth day at work. The cafe was closed and it was time to go home. It was usual for Sam to walk her home, but tonight he had left early. Since it was dark when they closed, Mary offered to walk Johanna home, but Johanna refused. She knew that Mary was tired — they had had an unusually large crowd that day.

After checking to make sure the windows were locked up tight, Mary followed Johanna outside and locked the door. Heavy storm clouds filled the sky, completely obliterating the stars, though they thinned out around the moon to create a curious ghostlike haze around it.

"Looks like rain," Mary commented.

Johanna nodded in agreement and they bid each other goodnight. A few moments after she'd left Mary, she was passing an alley and heard something, a sound so slight she wasn't sure if it was really there. Her first thought was to hurry on, but she hesitated a moment. The sound came again . . . a groan. Was someone injured?

Her heart fluttering wildly, she entered the alley . . . and stopped.

A shaft of moonlight illuminated his face; even at a distance she could see the coppery cast to his skin. He lay crumpled in a heap against the wall. And there was something about him . . . Could it be . . . ?

Cautiously, she moved closer, her eyes widening with recognition. It was Hawkeye. And there was a dark patch of blood on the ground surrounding him. A lot of blood.

She knelt beside him, horror-struck. There was so much blood on him she didn't see how he could still be alive. She pulled open his shirt, her face paling as she saw the three gaping wounds in his chest. Each one of them seemed bad enough to kill him. How could he still be alive? She felt ill as she studied the damage done to him. He moved slightly and she started, lifting her eyes to find his dark gaze on her. Although he uttered no word, his pain was evident.

"I'll get a doctor," she said shakily. "And the sheriff."

His throat worked convulsively as he tried to speak, and the croaking sound he made was barely intelligible. "No sheriff," he muttered. He closed his eyes for a moment and as she watched a shadow passed over his face. When his lashes fluttered open again, she saw the knowledge of his own death written there.

She swallowed raggedly. "You must at least have a doctor," she protested. "You're badly wounded."

"It's too late," he said. "Your doctor can not . . . help . . . me." Each word cost him a shuddering effort. "I have seen death before," he whispered, "but never so near."

Fear for him tightened her throat. Who had done such a thing to him? Who hated him enough to want him dead?

Swallowing around the lump in her throat, Johanna used the edge of her skirt and wiped the blood away. His chest lifted with the effort he expended as he tried to fill his lungs with air.

Compassion filled Johanna. And something else, something she couldn't, or wouldn't put a name to. She didn't know who had stabbed him, or why. She only knew he would die if he didn't have help.

Suddenly she became aware of a change in the rhythm of his breathing. He was no longer conscious.

Opening his shirt, she stared at his bloodied chest, found the knife wounds, the dark holes surrounded by torn and puffy skin. God! Could anyone live after sustaining such wounds?

She had to help him, and there was no time to waste. She'd worry about the consequences later.

Placing a spread hand on his breastbone, she closed her eyes. *Please, God,* she prayed silently. *Don't let me fail. Not again.* Then her head fell forward and she loosed the healing energy.

Time passed; she didn't know how much. Then, his breathing changed, became easier, his violated body relaxed. She felt drained when she opened her eyes. Bending over, she examined the wounds again. Although the cuts were still visible, there had been a dramatic change. They seemed little more than flesh wounds now, as though the knife had barely penetrated the skin.

She made to rise and fell back weakly on her haunches. There she remained, her arms hanging limply at her sides, feeling as though she had drained a sinkhole of pollution and barely escaped with her life.

Chapter Five

A loud crash woke Johanna and she sat up gasping, feeling totally disoriented as she fought against the covers that seemed intent on holding her captive.

Moonlight filtered between the curtains, only slightly dispelling the dark shadows within the cabin. Her gaze swept the shadowy interior of the room searching for the source of the noise, finally coming to a stop on the figure in the bed.

Hawkeye!

Memory flooded swiftly back to her sleep-dazed mind and she struggled free of the confining quilt.

He was sitting up, holding one hand to his head, while balancing himself on the bed with the other. For some reason he looked out of place in her bed with the patchwork quilt, almost alien, as though he was unused to such civilized trappings.

71

Johanna's steps were reluctant as she slowly approached him. When he looked up and saw her, his eyes widened in astonishment.

"Are—" She stopped, cleared her throat. "Are you hurt?" she asked huskily.

"No," he said. "But I think I knocked the lamp over."

Bending over, she picked up the broken lamp, placed it on the table and turned back to him. His coal black hair fell across the coppery skin of his forehead, and his thick black lashes veiled his dark eyes. His eyes traveled over her, taking in her fragile figure clad in a cotton nightgown, the way her raven locks framed her face, flowing softly past her shoulders to fall upon the gentle swells of her breasts. His eyes lingered there a moment too long, making Johanna suddenly aware of how revealingly she was dressed.

What am I thinking of? she wondered, blushing to the roots of her hair and snatching her wrapper from the back of the chair where she had flung it the night before.

Turning her back to him, she slipped her arms in the garment and fastened it with trembling fingers. She found it difficult to breathe properly as she reluctantly turned to face him again.

Hawkeye studied her silently for a moment before his puzzled gaze left her to travel around the unfamiliar room. Where was he? he wondered. And how did he come to be in here? He returned his gaze to the girl who waited quietly before him. Although his memory was hazy, it had not hampered his recognition of her.

She was Johanna, the girl with the spring-green eyes who had haunted his dreams. And although she'd told him she was bound for Washington town, he'd not expected her to stay, having been almost certain she would be unable to secure a position.

"So you're finally awake," she said, her voice betraying a slight nervousness.

What did she have to be nervous about? he wondered. His eyes searched her face as though he would find the answer there.

"What am I doing here?" he asked gruffly.

She shifted uncomfortably, as though bothered by the question. "I . . ." She stopped, looked beyond him, and continued. "Do . . . don't you remember what happened?" she asked huskily.

His dark eyes narrowed as he continued to watch her. "No. Suppose you refresh my memory," he suggested.

"I . . ." She swallowed hard. "You're in my cabin," she said.

He studied her thoughtfully, certain she was hiding something from him. Otherwise, why would she display such unrest? "How did I get here?" he asked.

She smiled at him but her smile seemed forced. "You—someone attacked you," she said. "I found you in an alley. A friend helped me bring you here."

A friend? His body stiffened. "And your friend's name?" he barked.

She frowned, wondering at his tone, then her expression cleared. "You don't have to worry," she

73

said softly. "Sam Sheppard is my employer as well as my friend. He won't tell anyone you're here."

Although Hawkeye was relieved, he gave no outward sign. His eyes never left her as he tried to shift the cobwebs from his mind. A half-forgotten memory slowly emerged. He had been in the—

"Saloon." The words slipped through his lips as he caught the memory and sifted through it. He had been at the saloon . . . waiting for someone.

Her?

Try as he would, he couldn't remember. He sensed the tension in her as she waited for him to speak. Tension? Perhaps that wasn't quite the word. She seemed almost on the verge of panic. The question was, why?

And why had she brought him here? Although he had been raised by the Comanches, he knew enough about the white man's ways to know she had acted in a most immodest manner by doing so.

Disappointment flowed through him. The answer was obvious enough. The girl was not the innocent he had believed. She must have met him at the saloon, perhaps even worked there. His expression darkened, becoming almost a scowl. He didn't like the conclusion he had drawn, but it would explain everything. She *must* be employed at the saloon, must have bewitched him into drinking the whiskey, and when his senses had left him, had brought him here.

But for what purpose?

Fool! chided an inner voice. There could be only one purpose!

Realization set in and anger boiled up from deep within his body. Since he could remember nothing that had occurred, then he had not got his money's worth. He reached out a hand and his fingers fastened like a steel band around her slender wrist. He gave a quick jerk forward, throwing her off balance and tumbling her across his body.

"What — what are you doing?" she gasped, staring up at him fearfully. *No,* he corrected himself. That wasn't fear in her eyes, it was something else, something completely undefineable. "L-let me go," she whispered huskily.

His eyes were hard as he gazed down at her. "What's the matter?" he asked derisively. "Didn't I pay you enough last night? If you're holding out for more gold, then consider it done."

"More gold?" He could have sworn her puzzlement was real. "What do you mean?" she asked.

"Don't pretend," he said savagely. "We both know what I mean." His lips lowered to claim hers, and with a horrified gasp, she pushed against him, squirming frantically beneath him, trying to twist out of his grasp. Scorn swept through him. He had met women like her before. Apparently she liked to play games. Well, he had no objection to giving her what she wanted. His lips ground hard against hers until the coppery taste of blood flowed in his mouth. Suddenly, his tactics changed, his lips softened, became coaxing, his palm cupped the fullness of her breast.

She stilled instantly, opening her mouth to suck in a sharp breath. Hawkeye was quick to take advantage and slid his tongue into the moist recess. She moaned low in her throat, whether from passion or protest, he couldn't say.

As his fingers found the neck of her robe and slid it back, she began to fight again. Her fists pounded against his chest and he grunted in pain and turned her loose.

She bounded quickly away, breathing heavily. "How dare you," she hissed. "You have no right to touch me that way!"

He ignored her, dropping his gaze to search for the source of his pain. His eyes narrowed on the puckered skin of his wounds. Feeling totally confused, he looked at her for an answer. "What happened to me?" he asked slowly.

Something undefineable flickered in her green eyes, then was quickly gone. "I told you," she said angrily. "You were attacked. And I'm beginning to think your attacker had ample reason for doing so."

He sensed she was holding something back. Did she know his attackers? "It seems I was wrong," he said. "I thought you were . . ."

Her lips tightened, and her voice dripped ice when she spoke. "It's obvious what you thought. And I'd appreciate it if you'd leave my cabin."

"Of course." He pushed himself to a sitting position, but he was totally unprepared for the weakness that swept over him. Gripping the mattress tightly, he said. "I won't impose any longer if you'll hand me my trousers."

A red flush stained her cheeks as she snatched his buckskins off the back of the rocker and tossed them on the bed. "Sam undressed you," she said stiffly.

He nodded, then wished he hadn't, because the act caused the room to whirl in a kaleidoscope of colors around him. Closing his eyes, he tried to force back the nausea.

"What's the matter?" she asked, her voice seeming to come from a long distance.

"Don't know," he muttered, laying his head back against the pillow. "Feel . . . weak."

She laid a cool palm against his clammy forehead. "You've lost a lot of blood," she admitted slowly.

Hawkeye opened his eyes and stared at her in confusion. "The wounds don't look bad enough to affect me that way." He drew a ragged breath. "If you'll just give me a minute, I'll get out of your way."

"Do you have a place to stay?" The words seemed forced from her.

"No."

"Then you'd better stay here," she said grudgingly. "Only don't try anything like that again."

Hawkeye's grin was weak. "Lady," he said. "I don't have the strength." He closed his eyes again. "If it's all right with you," he said. "I'm going back to sleep."

Johanna knew any attempt to go back to sleep would be in vain. She couldn't forget the way his lips had felt against hers . . . the way he'd touched her so intimately.

A warm flush stained her cheeks when she

remembered how she'd responded to him. He had awakened feelings in her she hadn't even realized she possessed.

Like any other young girl, she had often dreamed of love and marriage, but she sensed that the man asleep in her bed was a loner who would find such a relationship cumbersome.

Another possibility suddenly struck her. Hawkeye had told her nothing of himself. He could already be married.

At that moment, the man who occupied her thoughts shifted on the bed and groaned. She turned her head to look at him. In his sleep, he seemed so vulnerable.

Feeling totally impatient with herself, and needing to get away from the close proximity of the man who occupied her thoughts, she dressed and left the cabin.

The streets were empty in the half-light before dawn. It gave Johanna a feeling of complete aloneness, and she didn't like the feeling.

A light in the cafe told her that Sam had arrived early to start the bread, and her footsteps turned in that direction.

Sam looked up in surprise when she entered the kitchen. "Up early, ain'tcha?" he asked.

"I couldn't sleep," she admitted.

He nodded his grizzled head, looking at her keenly. "Worryin' 'bout your friend," he guessed. "How's he doing'?"

"He's sleeping." She picked up a red-checked apron and tied it around her slender waist. "Thanks again for helping me, Sam. I couldn't have managed without you."

"He's a big man all right," he agreed. "Reckon he's wanted by the law?"

"I don't know," she answered. "But it makes no difference. He saved my life when he shot the rattler. I had no choice except to help him."

He nodded in agreement. "Feller's gotta do what he has to," he muttered.

"Does Mary know about him?"

"You said nobody was to know, didn'tcha?"

"Yes," she said. "But she's your wife, and I wasn't certain . . ."

"Mary's a good woman," he said. "None better. But she's as big a gossip as her friend, Bessie Pearl. Neither one of 'em knows how to keep a secret." He looked hard at her. "Best you keep that in mind," he added.

Johanna's lips twitched. She had learned Bessie Pearl and her husband, Abe Turner, were the owners of Turner's Mercantile, and the Sheppards' closest friends.

After pouring herself a cup of coffee and refilling Sam's, she took out the salt pork and began to slice it in strips. They worked in companionable silence until Mary arrived.

The day proved to be a scorcher, and by midmorning damp tendrils of hair clung to Johanna's skin, curling softly around her face.

Johanna arched her back, stretching aching muscles and wiped the perspiration from her brow with the back of her hand. Sam, who had been working beside her, looked up and frowned at her.

"Why don't you take the dishes out front?" he

asked. "It'll give you a break from this hot kitchen."

"And what about you?" she asked wryly. "Aren't you hot too?"

"I'm used to it," he said gruffly. "Been a cook for so many years I lost count. Cooked for many a trail drive, and they ain't much shade to be found out on the prairie. I've got it easy since me and Mary decided to get hitched an' open the cafe."

"How long ago was that?" she asked.

"Three years."

She looked at him in surprise. "I thought you two had been married much longer."

He grinned at her. "Nope." He rubbed the side of his bulbous nose with the tip of a finger. "Took me a long time to find Mary," he said. "But when I did, I grabbed 'er an' hung on tight."

"Did Mary object?' Johanna laughed.

"She sure did," he growled. "Objected mighty hard, too. I knew right away Mary was the stubbornest woman I ever laid eyes on. An' I'd have to do some mighty tall talkin' afore she'd come aroun'."

"You two talkin' 'bout me?"

They looked up and saw Mary standing just inside the swinging doors. "Sam was telling me how you two got together."

Something flickered in Mary's eyes. "He tell you I worked in a saloon? Didn't figger I was good enough for the likes of him."

Johanna felt surprise, but allowed none of it to show on her face. "No. He didn't tell me that," she said softly. "But where you worked is no

80

business of mine. Nor should it concern you. You are a lovely person, Mary. If you hadn't given me a job and a place to live, then I could be in the same situation."

Mary's eyes were suspiciously bright. "I don't believe that for one minute, Johanna. You'd have found some other way to live. But it's awfully nice of you to try and make me feel better."

Sam put a muscled arm around his wife and squeezed her shoulders. "Johanna means it, honey," he said gruffly. "You're a mighty nice woman, and you're beatin' a dead horse bringin' all that up again."

Deciding the two of them needed to be alone, Johanna loaded a tray with clean dishes and said. "I'll just take these out to the dining room."

She pushed the swinging door open with her elbow and carried the heavy tray of dishes out onto the breezeway. Her gaze fell on a man intent on tying his horse at the hitching rail. Something about him seemed vaguely familiar. Johanna was trying to place him when he swung around. In that moment she saw him clearly, and a sprinkle of gooseflesh crept up her arms as the color drained from her face.

It was Carl Fowler! One of Durant's henchmen. *Don't let him see me!* Johanna prayed silently, taking a backward step into the kitchen, her eyes never leaving Fowler. She felt the odd sensation of trying to walk underwater as she took another backward step and released the door. As it swung shut, the man looked up . . . in her direction.

Johanna's breath seemed stuck in her throat as

panic poured through her. Had he recognized her? Or had the door shut fast enough to hide her from the man's view? What could he be doing in this wilderness town? Had Durant sent him to find her?

Waves of nausea swept through her. *God! He must not see her! She couldn't go back to the hell that waited for her at Durant's Institute. She wouldn't!*

"What's the matter?"

She swung around, startled, and found Mary watching her with a peculiar intensity.

"What's the matter?" Mary repeated. "Your face has gone pure white, Johanna. Like you mighta seen a witch out there."

Johanna's thoughts had been totally absorbed with Fowler, and her desperate need to hide from him, but Mary's word struck her with the impact of a knife. In spite of the heat, she felt a cold chill dance between her shoulder blades.

Why had Mary mentioned witch?

What little color Johanna had left fled from her face.

Sam looked up from the pie he was crimping. "Don'tcha mean ghost?" he laughed. At Mary's inquiring look, he said, "Folks usually say you seen a ghost." His glance traveled to Johanna and the laugh died on his lips when he saw her pale face.

"Not where I come from," Mary retorted smartly. "Back in the Appalachian mountains a ghost don't hold no candle to the evil powers of a witch. Us mountain folk learned that the hard way."

"Ain't no use arguin' with you," Sam growled.
"But be that as it may, Johanna's gone plumb
white. And you stand there yappin' on 'bout
witches and evil powers." His look at the girl was
concerned. "What's troublin' you, girl?"

She dared not tell him. Although Mary had first
spoken in jest, there had been real hatred in her
voice when she spoke of witches and their evil
powers.

Johanna knew she couldn't go into the dining
room. Not with Fowler in there. For whatever
reason he had in Washington, if he saw her, he
would report back to Durant.

Her pulse hammered in her temples as her
frantic gaze fell on the two people who faced her.
"Mary," she whispered. "I—I've got a splitting
headache. Could you take over for me?"

"Sure thing," Mary said. Her expression was full
of sympathy, completely unsuspecting. "You go
on home and lie down for a while. And don't
came back until you're feeling better."

"Thank you," Johanna said. Even though her
nerves were stretched and tingling, she allowed
herself a sigh of relief. Mary had just given her the
way to hide until Fowler left town.

Peering cautiously out the side door, she stared
at the emptiness. Fowler was gone; more than
likely he had entered the dining room. She would
have to hurry before he grew tired of waiting and
came looking for service.

Stepping outside, she hurried toward the cover
of the woods. Her heart fluttered wildly against

83

her ribcage as she made her way toward the safety of her cabin.

It seemed she had come full circle. In Ireland, her neighbors had believed her a witch and she had fled her homeland. In New Orleans, she had seen the hatred and fear directed at those who stood accused as witch. Now, here, in this wild Texas town, she had encountered the same feelings of hatred.

It seemed people were the same everywhere and she was destined to live her life alone . . . forever set apart from fellow beings.

Was there no place she could go?

Chapter Six

Hawkeye woke with total recall . . . or almost.

He remembered meeting Cremp in the saloon and going with him on the pretext of examining the rifles. And he remembered Jude, springing out of the alley, driving the knife deep into his chest.

What a fool he'd been! he chastised himself. He had no excuse for such carelessness, could very well have been killed by it.

And that's where his memory went awry.

He had been certain his wounds were mortal, thought he was dying when Johanna found him.

With brows drawn into a puzzled frown, he ran a hand over his chest, pausing when he felt the puckered skin beneath his palm. Although the wounds seemed of no consequence, his strength had completely left him. It was something he couldn't understand and he was still puzzling over his weakened condition when the door opened and Johanna walked in.

Johanna stepped into the cabin and closed the door behind her. She was hardly aware of the other occupant until he spoke.

"What has happened?"

She drew an audible intake of breath and her head jerked around to see him sitting up in the bed, his chest naked, the coverlet falling around his waist.

"What has happened?" he repeated, his dark eyes narrowed on her pale face.

"Nothing," she said, lowering her lashes to avoid his gaze. "Merely a headache. We weren't busy, so . . ." She broke off as a dark shadow flitted by the window, startling her.

Frozen, Johanna stared at the window. Could Fowler have followed her? Could he, even now, be prowling outside the cabin, waiting to catch her unaware?

Her lips had suddenly gone dry and she moistened them with the tip of her tongue, unaware of the man who watched her from the bed, of the tension that stiffened his body, the eyes that shifted, searched, and found the weapons she had draped across the rocking chair a few feet away.

Johanna's thoughts were totally absorbed as she moved on leaden feet, crossing the room to the window, drawing the curtain carefully aside.

At that moment a red cardinal swooped by and landed on a bush outside the window. It was quickly joined by another. Johanna sighed with relief and her body relaxed as she let the curtain fall back in place.

Chiding herself for her foolishness, she turned around, and met the probing eyes of Hawkeye. Silence spread around them like ripples from a pebble dropped into a pond. How could she have forgotten him? Even for a moment. Her dark lashes fanned against her cheeks as her eyes dropped away from his, and she found herself staring, instead, at his naked chest.

She remembered how she had felt when he had carried her, remembered, too, the breathlessness she'd experienced, the feeling of being safe, protected. Remembered as well the feelings she'd experienced when he'd kissed her. How could a comparative stranger make her feel that way? she wondered.

Lifting her eyes, she met his head on and a flush of color tinted her cheeks. She shifted her gaze, staring at a spot above his left shoulder. "Are you hungry?" she murmured.

"Yes."

Was that laughter in his voice? Her eyes flew to his, accusing. But there was no humor there, instead, she encountered something else, a softness that seemed completely alien to his nature.

"Johanna." Although spoken softly, the word thundered through the silence. "I owe you an apology."

She nodded, still unable to meet his gaze.

"Please consider it given."

"And accepted," she murmured, forcing herself

to meet his gaze. After all, she wasn't the one at fault.

He smiled at her. "Could I ask one thing of you?"

"What?" she asked, eyeing him warily.

"Would you bring my weapons over here?"

His answer was totally unexpected, but she did as he asked, hanging the holstered pistols on one post of the bed. He checked his weapons, making certain they were still loaded while she prepared the meal.

Hawkeye waited until she placed a plate filled with biscuits, gravy and salt pork on the stand beside the bed before he spoke again. "You said your employer brought me here."

Although it was more a statement than a question, she found herself nodding her head. "Sam Sheppard," she explained. "I found work in a cafe."

Mention of the cafe reminded her of Carl Fowler and her reasons for returning to the cabin. Her green eyes flew to the window as though she expected to see him staring in at her. Even though there was no one there, she felt jittery again.

Was Fowler still in town? Was he, even now, waiting outside, hoping to catch her unaware?

She paced restlessly around the cabin, unaware of Hawkeye's quiet gaze following her every step of the way.

The silence grew and thickened, but she remained unaware, her thoughts totally absorbed by the danger represented by Fowler, and ultimately, by Michael Durant.

How could she protect herself from his poison? She should have killed him!

Feeling suddenly stifled, she rose from the chair. She refused to hide any longer. Where was her courage anyway? Her father would be ashamed of her!

Crossing to the dresser, she opened the top drawer and her fingers closed around the barrel of the pistol Patrick had given her. She kept her back to the bed, as she shoved the weapon deep in her pocket, hiding the bulge it made in the folds of her skirt.

If Fowler was still in town, she would confront him now. After muttering, "I'm going for a walk," to the man in the bed, she left the cabin.

She saw at a glance that Fowler's horse was gone. But he could still be hanging around town. A quick word with Mary told her otherwise.

"You missed the excitement," the woman told her.

"Excitement?" Johanna queried.

"Luke picked a fight with a stranger." She grinned. "He didn't fare so well."

Luke had been a frequent customer since Johanna had been working for the couple. And she liked him less each time she saw him. Although he was a bully, he considered himself a ladies man as well and usually made a pest of himself whenever he came in.

"We have a stranger in town?" Johanna asked. "Did the stagecoach arrive?" She knew the stagecoach wasn't due to run for two more days.

"No," Mary said. "Rode through on his horse.

Said he was headin' fer 'is sister's place somewhere close to Austin."

"You said he rode through," Johanna said casually. "Has he already gone then?"

"Uh huh. He only stopped for a bite to eat. Said he was tired of his own cookin'." She laughed. "Reckon he was right. He put away a steak thet'd choke a horse. Not to mention two helpings of potatoes and beans. Finished it off with some of Sam's peach cobbler. It's a wonder he didn't sink the ferry when he went across the river."

Relief was a tangible thing, flowing through Johanna. She felt as though a great weight had lifted off her shoulders. "Do you need me here, Mary?" she asked.

Mary refused, telling her to get some rest. After thanking her, Johanna turned her steps toward the cabin. She was preoccupied when she opened the door and stepped inside the shadowy interior.

The door slammed shut behind her.

Johanna screamed, whirling around to stare with terror-stricken eyes at the armed man who confronted her.

Hawkeye!

His fierce expression left him, became one of concern as he noticed her stricken state. Laying his gun aside, he gathered her shivering body into his arms.

"It's all right," he murmured, holding her against his chest and stroking her silky hair. "There's nobody here but me. No one to hurt you."

Wrapping her arms around his waist, she clung tightly to him, badly in need of the comfort he offered after the tension of the last several hours. His lips brushed her cheek and she clung tighter, her body shaking hard.

Hawkeye lifted her chin with a gentle finger and wiped the tears away from her face. Then he kissed her softly on the mouth. Her arms seemed to move of their own accord, winding around his neck and pulling him closer. She needed what this man was offering, needed it desperately.

Suddenly, the kisses that had been meant as comfort, changed. His lips became harder, demanding, leaving her breathless, wanting more.

She had no thought of protest when he lifted her, carried her to the bed and lay down beside her. *I must be dreaming,* she told herself. This couldn't be happening to her. She felt as though she was in an emotional minefield, in danger of making a complete fool of herself.

Hawkeye's head lifted, his dark eyes glittering down at her, hot with ancient sensuality.

"Please let me go," she whispered, but even as she uttered the words, she knew she didn't mean them. His hold was rough but she was caught in a spell, too helpless to resist him.

"Tell me you don't want my touch," he said harshly. Even while he spoke the words, his fingers gently circled around her taut nipples. His touch lanced through her with white-hot pleasure that made her tremble. "Tell me you want me to stop."

She heard the challenge in his voice and tried to

say the words, but they wouldn't form on her trembling lips. Her eyes were glazed with passion as they stared into his.

"Tell me quickly," he said. "Do you want me to stop?"

She knew it was madness to continue. She meant nothing to him. She was only a convenience. But no matter how she tried, she couldn't say the words to make him leave her.

Her sense of decency should make her demand to be released. She should be rejecting the sensuous, lingering hands that continued to create magic on her breasts and to stir feelings that had lain dormant, buried deep within her body, feelings she'd never had for anyone else before. But she hesitated, for she felt as though he were a missing piece of the puzzle she realized herself to be. And somehow, she was consumed with the rightness of the two of them together.

Then there was no more time. For the lips that had hovered tantalizingly, mere inches above her own, descended and closed over hers again.

How could such a thing happen? she wondered feverishly, lifting her hands to clasp him tightly around the shoulders and pull him closer against her. He made a satisfied growl deep down in his throat and his mouth left hers.

Her fingers dug into his shoulders, and she uttered a soft moan of protest that changed to a gasp of passion when the tip of his tongue traced its way down the soft curve of her neck, over her bare flesh until it reached the swell of her breast. She was vaguely aware of him pushing aside the fabric of her gown. Then his mouth captured one taut peak and her head fell back and she uttered a startled cry. His mouth scorched her with its heat, as his lips nursed the swollen, throbbing nipple. She had never felt such an intense longing before as the one that shot through her now.

He found her hip with his hand and impatiently pushed her gown aside, sliding his fingers, hot on her bare skin, caressingly up her thigh. Johanna's breath came in short gasps; she was caught in an agony of fierce excitement, the anticipation for something unknown building like a violent storm deep within her being.

His finger found the moistness between her thighs and she quivered breathlessly as he began to stroke softly. An inferno began to ignite deep within, an inferno that he continued to stoke with his movements.

Suddenly, as though impatient with the garments separating them, he stripped them away from her and tossed them aside.

When he pulled away, she uttered a protest. But he was gone for only a moment, and then she felt his naked flesh against her own. She lay against the warm, muscular length of his urgent body and her shy hands seemed to move of their own volition, exploring and caressing his flesh as he was touching hers.

What she was experiencing was so far removed from anything she had ever felt before that she could hardly comprehend it. His fingers moved, gliding over each hollow, each curve of her body, tracing a slow erotic spiral across the flat plane of her stomach. Johanna's body burned and ached for more, and as though sensing her need, he poised himself above her.

Holding her with a stark, compelling demand, he slid his hands beneath her hips and lifted her toward him. As he entered her she felt a quick stab of pain and uttered a cry, a cry quickly drowned beneath his lips.

His movements gentled the pain as he began the age-old rhythm, coaxing her past it until she began to move with him. She could feel his will reaching out, seducing her.

Soon his movements grew bolder, faster, as he plunged harder, deeper into her body, carrying her higher and higher with him until they seemed to be soaring together among the clouds.

Suddenly he gave a hoarse cry and collapsed against her. He lay there, breathing raggedly, his face buried against her neck.

Johanna clutched him tightly against her. She wouldn't even try to analyze her feelings for this man. Later perhaps. But not right now. The tension she had experienced throughout the day had taken its toll. She closed her eyes and was soon fast asleep.

She wasn't sure what woke her, but she was instantly aware of the man beside her. The dim light of the moon cast shadows across his cheekbones, seeming to highlight the scar that marred his face. Impulsively, she reached out and touched it lightly, tenderly, careful not to waken him for he slept the sleep of the totally exhausted.

How had he come by the scar? she wondered.

Her gaze dropped lower, to his bare chest, moving past the heavy cross he wore around his neck, to study the flat male nipples with interest. A smile flitted across her face. In all her wildest dreams she had never imagined herself this way, lying in bed with a man and daring to study his body so intimately.

The quilt had been pushed aside and she had an ample view of his masculinity. She indulged her curiosity and studied it boldly. To her surprise, the flesh that had been quiescent, grew, hardened. Her startled eyes flew to Hawkeye's face and her breath stopped as she found his eyes open and watching her.

With a low growl of passion, he covered her body with his own, leaving Johanna with no time for thought as their bodies merged and they became as one. Moving together, they searched for the place among the clouds they had found only a short while before.

Hawkeye woke several times in the night and reached hungrily for the girl beside him. He couldn't seem to get enough of her, and she seemed almost as eager as himself. Finally, exhaustion took its toll and he fell into a deep sleep that lasted the rest of the night.

Gray light filtered through the curtains when he woke again. He lay beside Johanna, listening to her even breathing, knowing he must leave her.

Jude and Cremp still had the rifles and he had to find them. He could not allow the weapons to slip through his fingers.

Rising from the bed, he put his shirt on and fastened it. Then he donned his trousers and moccasins.

Turning back to the bed, he looked down at Johanna, sprawled in wild abandon on the sheets, her hair a dark cloud on the white pillowcase. His gaze lingered on her mouth, soft and red, swollen from his kisses.

For a moment, he wondered if he should wake her, then decided he wouldn't. If things went well, he would return for her. If they did not . . . words would do no good and were better left unsaid.

With a sigh of regret, Hawkeye left the cabin and closed the door softly behind him.

Chapter Seven

The town seemed deserted in the half-light before dawn. Hawkeye's moccasin-clad feet made hardly a sound as he strode up the dirt street onto the raised plank sidewalk that ran beside the log buildings. It took only moments to reach his destination, and he pushed open the swinging doors of the saloon and stepped inside.

Smoke hung low in the ceiling, and despite the early hour, four men were seated around a table playing cards and drinking whiskey. The saloon-keeper leaned against the bar, conversing with a blond girl wearing a scanty green silk dress trimmed with black lace.

When Hawkeye approached the bar, the bartender left the girl. "What'll it be?" he asked.

Hawkeye let his gaze roam the room before returning to the man behind the bar. "I'm looking for two men," he said. "One called Jude, the other, Cremp."

"Never heard of 'em," the bartender replied.

Hawkeye described the two men, but the bartender shook his head. "Description fits a lotta men," he growled. "Been busy lately. Too busy to take much notice of the customers. Long as they pay," he added. "They don't . . ." He reached beneath the counter and pulled out a rifle.". . . I got ol' Betsy here to take care of them that don't."

Nodding, Hawkeye turned away from the bar. He had hoped for some kind of lead in the saloon. Now he would have to look elsewhere and he couldn't afford to attract attention to himself.

"Is one of 'em the guy you was with t'other night?" inquired a voice beside him.

Hawkeye turned to the speaker, a grizzled old man with a white, tobacco-stained beard, a red nose and faded, red-rimmed eyes.

"Yes," Hawkeye agreed. "That was one of them. Have you seen him?"

"Might be I did," the old-timer said. "And might be I didn't." He pointed to a bottle behind the bar. "A little o' that whiskey might help me recall."

The barman snorted, but Hawkeye signaled him to pour the old man a drink while he dug in his buckskins for the few coins the men had missed when they took his money belt. The bartender set a filled glass in front of the old man, then took the coin Hawkeye dropped into his hand.

Lifting the glass to his mouth, the old-timer swallowed the whiskey down in one gulp. After wiping his mouth on his sleeve, he muttered. "He come in an' bought a bottle of whiskey 'bout an hour after ya'll left here. Had 'nother man with 'im. Big man like you described. Don't recollect hearin' no names mentioned, though."

"Do you know where they went?"

The old man picked up his empty glass and frowned darkly at it. Hawkeye, taking the hint, reached for the bottle and refilled it.

"Thankee," the old-timer muttered. "Don't mind if I do." He drained the glass and gave a pleasures sigh. "I heered them two fellers talkin' 'bout joinin' the wagon train thet was camped up the river. Fer some reason, they seemed in a mighty big hurry to get outta town. Didn't sound like they was 'spectin' to be here this mornin'. Much less meet nobody."

Hawkeye dropped a silver dollar into the old man's hand. "Buy yourself another drink."

He felt inquisitive eyes on him, knew he was attracting attention that he could ill afford, and yet, he also knew it was imperative that he locate the two men as soon as possible.

Pushing open the saloon door, he spared only a brief glance toward the cabin where he had left Johanna. Then his steps turned in the opposite direction. He felt an urgency to reach Jude and Cremp before the wagon train continued on its way.

Upon reaching town, he had left Diablo at the stables. Now he made his way there, opened the wide door and stepped into the darkened interior. The stallion, recognizing his scent, nickered softly from a nearby stall. It was only a moments' work to saddle the stallion. Another moment and they had left the town behind them.

It was mid-morning when he found the place where the wagons had been camped, but one look at the cold campfires told him they had been gone for at least twenty-four hours. His lips stretched into a thin line. No matter. They were miles ahead of him, but the wagons would be slow and easily trailed. Eventually, he would find them, and he would have the rifles.

Or their lives.

It was mid-afternoon when he spotted the wagons from a hilltop. Pulling up the stallion, he watched the wagon train crawl slowly across the prairie, like some great turtle that had lost its way.

His dark eyes were hard as he studied the intruders who had invaded Comanche land. The war chiefs were certain they could be driven back, but Hawkeye was not so sure. He had lived among the Texans, knew them well, and he was afraid nothing could stop them. Not even the rifles he sought. But at least by obtaining the firearms, he would deprive the Texans of them.

He curbed the urge to ride down and confront Jude and Cremp with their treachery. If the facts were known, the settlers would side against Hawkeye. He knew he would have to catch them alone and make them tell him where the rifles were.

His lips tightened grimly. He would take their rifles and recover his gold as well. For there was no need to honor a bargain that had already been broken.

Johanna didn't know what time it was when she woke, but she was instantly alert, remembering what had happened the night before — Hawkeye's lovemaking, and her total abandonment.

A blush spread across her cheeks.

How could she face him this morning?

With the thought came the sudden knowledge that she wouldn't have to face him.

She was alone in the bed.

Her eyes moved to the door, then to the clock on the dresser. *How long had he been gone?*

And more to the point, *where* had he gone?

Her heart began a slow, painful thud, as her eyes returned to the clock and she watched the minutes tick slowly away. And with each tick of the clock came the certainty that he would not be returning.

Pain dimmed her eyes and a chill swept over her and with it came a sense of betrayal, of having been used. Why she harbored such a feeling she didn't know, because she had wantonly surrendered herself to him, had shamelessly abandoned her virginity without a second thought.

Tears of shame filled Johanna's eyes and slid down her cheeks. Her lips tightened and she wiped them away with the back of her hand.

No use lying here feeling sorry for myself.

She tried to close her mind to the memory of Hawkeye and what had happened, but found it impossible. How could she forget when her lips were still swollen from his kisses, and her body still ached with the proof of his possession?

God! she had been such a fool!

Dragging herself from the bed, she built a fire and heated some water. After filling the tin bathtub, she got in and bathed herself. At first, her movements were slow, almost languorous. She washed her face and hair as though taking part in a ritual cleansing ceremony. But when she began to wash her body, the memory of Hawkeye's hands caressing her body surfaced, and she began to scrub harder and harder until her flesh was bright pink, as though intent on scrubbing away his touch.

When she had finished bathing, she stepped from the tub and wrapped herself in a towel. Then, standing before the long dresser, Johanna studied herself in minute detail. Outwardly, she looked the same, it was impossible to tell how much she had changed, for there was nothing to show what an abject, appalling fool she had been. She must have taken leave of her senses to allow such a thing to happen. She knew very well what the results of such an action could be.

Would Mary allow her to hold her position if she became pregnant?

She stared into the mirror with eyes that were filled with pain. She had often wondered how a well-bred girl could find herself in such circumstances, could allow such a thing to happen to her.

Now she knew.

Johanna opened the side door to the cafe and

slipped inside. Mary was sitting at a nearby table, humming softly as she filled sugar bowls. She looked up and, with a frown and a little click of concern, hurried forward.

"You look terrible, Johanna," she said. "Sit yourself down while I get you a cup of coffee."

Johanna stretched her lips into a smile. "Don't trouble yourself," she said. "I'm here to work, not to be waited on."

Ignoring her words, Mary pushed her into a chair and studied Johanna's wan face, taking particular note of the dark shadows beneath her eyes. "Looks like you didn't have a good night," she said. "You forget about work today and go back to the cabin and rest."

"Don't be silly," Johanna said, attempting to rise and finding herself pushed firmly back down. "No. Really," she muttered. "I'm fine. There's no need to worry about me."

"You're not fine," Mary insisted. "You've got dark circles under your eyes and you don't have any color about you at all."

Johanna felt near tears. She didn't want to go back to the cabin, didn't want to be alone with her thoughts. Work was what she needed. "Please, Mary," she whispered. "I need to work today."

Mary was silent for a moment, then she gave a long sigh. "All right," she said. "If you insist. But first you're going to eat."

"I'm not—" Johanna began, but found herself cut off.

"Don't say you're not hungry," Mary said shortly. "I'm not going to have you fainting and

103

ruining my customers' appetites. You either eat or get yourself back to the cabin."

Knowing from the tone of her voice that Mary meant business, Johanna subsided. She watched the older woman leave the dining area and enter the kitchen. Moments later, Sam's burly frame filled the doorway.

"Everything okay?" he asked, wiping his hands on the towel tied around his waist which served for an apron.

Johanna nodded, wondering what Mary had told her husband.

Although he seemed unconvinced, he pulled his grizzled head back into the kitchen, leaving her alone with her thoughts.

She wasn't aware Mary had returned until the older woman set a plate filled with ham, biscuits, and gravy in front of her. "You eat that up," she said with forced heartiness.

"Thank you," Johanna said, looking at the food with repugnance. It was the last thing she wanted. But she knew she would have to force it down in order to ease the minds of both her employers.

Johanna tried to put thoughts of Hawkeye out of her mind as she forked the food into her mouth and chewed. Each bite she swallowed was an effort, but she persevered until it was gone.

From that moment on, Johanna had no time to herself. She had just finished setting the tables when the door opened and several customers arrived, intent on filling their empty stomachs.

"Coffee over here," one man yelled as he sat down at the long table with two other men.

Johanna had no more than taken care of the first batch of customers when another group came in. There was a steady stream of hungry men and women all morning long, each demanding service at once. But instead of feeling harassed, she felt relieved. She had no mind to be thinking of the man who had used her and then cast her aside.

It was late in the afternoon before the crowd emptied out. The Sheppards decided to take advantage of the slow period to pass the time of day with their friends, Abe and Bessie Pearl Turner. They suggested Johanna take a breather while the cafe was empty. A suggestion she heartily approved of.

She seated herself just as the door opened and two men walked in. She recognized Luke instantly. Johanna had never seen his companion, a heavy-set, middle-aged man, before.

"Wal, now," Luke said, a wide grin spreading across his sharp-featured face. "Just lookee who's here." His close-set eyes scanned the empty room, and satisfaction glinted in them when they returned to Johanna. "Who's mindin' the cafe?" he asked.

"I am," Johanna said calmly. She pushed back her chair and stood up. Although dreading to wait on him, she had a duty to her employers. "Would you like to see a menu?" she asked calmly.

"Yes, m'am," supplied the middle-aged man.

Johanna felt Luke's eyes on her as she crossed to the bar and took two menus from beneath the counter. Keeping her face expressionless, she placed the menus in front of the two men, took

105

her pencil and pad from her pocket and stood waiting quietly for their orders.

Luke leaned back in his seat, ignoring the menu in front of him, his eyes boldly studying her feminine form from head to toe.

Johanna felt a surge of rising anger, but tried her best to suppress it. Her knuckles showed white as her fingers clutched the pad tighter. She knew Luke was intent on causing her embarrassment, and she refused to allow him the satisfaction.

Luke's companion cleared his throat, and Johanna looked at him with a raised eyebrow, poising her pencil just above her pad.

"Have you decided what you want?" she asked him.

"Yes," he said "I—"

"Guess," Luke interrupted. His eyes held a mean, cunning look, and he gave her a wide smile, displaying broken, tobacco-stained teeth.

"I don't have time for guessing games." Johanna's voice crackled with distaste as she fixed him with a cold stare.

"Knock it off, Luke," the older man said, shifting uneasily in his seat. "Sam ain't gonna like you pesterin' his help. "If'n you don't look out, he'll likely not feed us any more."

"Why not?" Luke asked. "Ol' Sam ain't gonna refuse us. Our money's just as good as anybody else's."

The other man looked uneasy. "That ain't the impression I got the last time you caused trouble in here. He seemed mad as hell 'bout you pesterin' his customers."

"She ain't a customer," Luke grinned, reaching out and gripping Johanna's wrist with cruel fingers. "Bring us some coffee," he said. "And you can join us."

"I don't have time," Johanna said coldly, twisting her hand free of his grip. "If you'd like coffee, then I'll bring it, but my duties don't include entertaining the customers."

Luke let his eyes circle the room that was empty except for themselves. "Seems like you got plenty of time for coffee and whatever else I got in mind," he said. "Ain't nobody here but us."

Fury surged through Johanna. Her eyes glittered with rage and her skin paled to the color of alabaster. She had been used by men like this one too often. First, there was Durant who thought to use her for profit. Then Hawkeye, who used her body for his own pleasure. Now, this lout of a cowboy thought to use her as well. It was past time that she stood up for herself, made Luke, and men like him understand that she had no intention of letting herself be intimidated . . . ever again.

She would serve Luke the coffee. But that was all he would get from her.

With a swish of skirts, she crossed to the bar, picked up the coffeepot and two cups, and returned to the table where the men waited. She had no more than filled the cups when Luke grabbed her wrist again.

"You can set the pot and yourself down," he growled.

The glitter in her green eyes should have warned

him, but it didn't. Her action was completely unexpected. Her hand tilted the pot, and the hot liquid spilled out . . . onto Luke's lap.

Uttering curses, Luke released her wrist and sprang to his feet. His face was mottled with rage as he looked at her. "You bitch! You did that a'purpose!"

He drew back his fist as though to strike her but his companion caught it in a tight grip.

"Hold on, Luke," he growled. "You ain't gonna hit 'er."

"Like hell I ain't," Luke replied. "You saw what she did. I ain't lettin' 'er get away with burnin' me with that coffee."

"What'n hell is goin' on here?" a deep voice roared.

Hawkeye!

Johanna's head jerked toward the door, her heart in her mouth. But the light died from her eyes when she saw Sam Sheppard standing on the threshold.

"That bitch spilled hot coffee in my lap," Luke snarled. "And she done it a'purpose."

Sam's gray eyes were shrewd as he looked at Johanna. Her green eyes were still glittering angrily, her breasts rising and falling with her quickened breathing.

"That right, girl?"

"Yes," she said, holding herself rigidly erect and staring defiantly at Sam. "That is exactly right. And with good reason too. Luke seemed to think I should provide entertainment with his meal."

"Figgered as much," Sam growled. His eyes

108

were the color of gunmetal as he turned them on Luke. "I warned you afore about causin' trouble in my place. If'n you're lookin' for entertainment, they got plenty of it at the saloon down the road. We don't sell nothin' here but food."

Luke glared at him, his hands knotted into fists. "You ain't gonna be able to stay open long with that attitude," he snarled. "I aim to tell folks what happened here today. If'n I was you, I'd get rid of 'er, 'cause you cain't do bus'ness if you ain't got no customers."

Sam let out a roar of laughter. "You must be crazy if you think you can convince my customers to stay away. Now either sit down and drink your coffee or leave it on the table. Either way, you pay for it."

"After she scalded me?"

"Sit down, Luke," his companion said. "You know you had it coming." He turned to Johanna. "I'm plumb sorry, miss," he said gruffly. "I'll see he don't bother you no more."

Reaction had set in and Johanna began to tremble. Sam noticed her condition and took her to the kitchen with him.

"You go on home," he said kindly. His hand was awkward as he patted her on the shoulder. "Mary's still at Bessie Pearl's. But I'll take care of things here till she comes back."

When she would have refused, he gave her a small shove toward the door. Knowing she couldn't take any more from Luke or his kind today, Johanna gave in and went to her cabin.

Chapter Eight

Hawkeye waited in a quiet place deep in the woods. It was a cheerful spot by day; sunbeams pierced the leaves of the cedars and oaks, falling in golden patterns on the leaf-strewn ground where bluebonnets and wild phlox swayed in a gentle breeze and the song of the whippoorwill could be heard.

But when night fell, it changed; the woods became still, forbidding, and since the moon's pale light failed to penetrate the dense growth of trees, darkness reigned supreme.

It was a warm evening, the kind that usually induced nocturnal creatures to forage. But, although Hawkeye listened carefully, no such sound broke the stillness. It was as though the creatures of the wild knew of the rage that boiled inside him at the thought of the two men who had cheated him and left him for dead.

Deciding he'd waited long enough for the travelers to settle down for the night, Hawkeye left his place of concealment and made his way closer to the camp. Now he could hear the hum of conversation and an occasional burst of laughter.

Hawkeye worked his way silently through the cedar and underbrush until he was close enough to observe without being seen. Then he settled down to wait.

Before long, his vigil was rewarded. For as his gaze searched the camp, he spied Jude and Cremp playing cards with a couple of the travelers.

As he watched, Jude slapped his cards down and rose from the makeshift table. "Damnit to hell!" he growled. "Ain't never had such a run of bad luck before." He glared at the man sitting on his left. "An' I ain't so sure it's just bad luck neither."

A silence fell over the group and several of the travelers nearby turned to stare at the four men.

"You sayin' what I think you are?" the man Jude had addressed asked.

"Now, Roberts," Cremp said placatingly. "Jude was just spoutin' off. He didn't mean nothin'. You know how it is when—"

"Let him speak for hisself," the man called Roberts said, never taking his eyes off Jude's face. "Was you meanin' what I think you was?"

"You damn right I was," Jude snapped.

Cremp put a hand on Jude's shoulder and Hawkeye watched him squeeze tightly. Hawkeye's eyes glinted. If Jude didn't back down, Roberts might be taking care of Jude himself. Hawkeye didn't mind. One of them would be enough to tell him where his gold and the rifles were.

Hawkeye could tell the exact moment when Cremp's silent message penetrated Jude's thick skull. Jude's eyelids flickered. His mouth that had been drawn into a thin line went slack and his fists relaxed.

"Aw hell," he blustered, his gaze shifting away from the other man's. "You know how it is, Roberts."

"No," the big man said softly. "Suppose you tell me."

"Well, a man gets mad at a run of bad luck. But I ain't accusin' nobody of nothin'," he said. He tried to grin, but his lips were more a snarl. " 'Specially you, Roberts."

A shard of humor flickered in Hawkeye's eyes. Jude wasn't used to backing down, which made it obvious the two men intended to keep out of trouble.

Hawkeye watched the two men stride away from the card players and move closer to the fire. They sat down and began to talk quietly together. Somewhere in the night an owl hooted, and farther away a coyote howled at the moon. And Hawkeye, the Comanche warrior, settled down to wait.

As the hours passed, the travelers began to drift away, one by one, and make ready for bed. But still Jude and Cremp sat beside the fire. Hawkeye remained where he was, hidden behind a tree as he waited for the two men to retire to their wagon where he could at least have some privacy for what needed doing.

Suddenly, Cremp rose from the log he had been using for a seat and jerked his head toward where Hawkeye waited. The warrior stiffened. Had he somehow given himself away? He drew his knife, determined to be ready for them this time. But they turned aside before they reached him and took the path to the creek. He followed closely behind and was only a few feet away when they stopped.

"What were you doin' back there?" Cremp demanded. "We agreed we had to keep from attractin' too much notice."

"You saw what was happenin'," Jude growled. "He was cheatin' me!"

"Roberts ain't smart enough to cheat nobody," Cremp said, "but that don't make no difference. Even if he'd a' been doin' it, you was a fool to say so."

"I ain't gonna play cards with no cardsharp."

"You'll do whatever I say!" snapped Cremp. "There's more at stake here than a few dollars won in a card game."

"I could 'a killed 'im," Jude growled.

"An' been hung for it!" Cremp replied, his lips curling into a sneer. "Then the money we're gettin' from them rifles wouldn't a' done you no good."

"And that would have been too bad," Hawkeye drawled, stepping out from behind the tree. "Especially since you went to all that trouble to get me out of the way."

Whirling around, the two men stared at him as

though they had seen a ghost.

"We killed you!" Jude gasped, backing away from him. "You cain't be here. We killed you!"

"You only thought you did," Hawkeye said. "Now we've got some talking to do."

Cremp had been sidling away while Hawkeye was watching Jude. But Hawkeye knew the trick, had used it many times. They thought to keep him diverted while they split up and took him unaware. When Cremp made his move, Hawkeye was ready for him. As Cremp leaped for him, Hawkeye struck the man in the heart with his knife. He watched Cremp crumple to the ground, then leapt lightly over his body. Before Jude could recover from his surprise, Hawkeye's knife was at his throat.

"You cheated me," Hawkeye hissed, his ebony eyes glittering with fury. "You stole my gold and tried to steal my life." He looked every inch the warrior he was.

"Wait a minute," Jude said, trying to back away, but with each backward step he took, Hawkeye took one forward, and the knife remained pressed tightly against Jude's throat. The man swallowed thickly, his adam's apple bobbing rapidly. A drop of blood appeared on the blade. "It wasn't none of my doin'," he babbled. "The whole thing was all his idea. I was goin' to give you the rifles."

"Where are they?" Hawkeye asked coldly.

"Cremp sold 'em to Carlos Mendoza. He loaded up and left Galveston when we did."

"And the destination?" Hawkeye pressed the knife harder and another droplet of blood appeared.

Jude's expression was panicked. "Enchanted Rock," he babbled. "He's meetin' another Mex there."

Hawkeye knew the place. "How many guards with the rifles?" he growled.

"Four," Jude said hurriedly. "And two wagons." His face was white. "Hey feller, ease off on thet knife, will ya? I'll tell you anything you want to know."

Hawkeye eased the knife up slightly. It wasn't his intention to kill the man before he had gathered all the information he needed.

"It ain't too late for you to go after them rifles," Jude said. "I'll give you back half of the gold and help you get the rifles."

Hawkeye held the other's gaze for a long moment, pretending to consider the proposition. "Where is the gold?" he asked.

"Under my wagon seat in a strong box," Jude said.

Hawkeye released Jude. "We'll go after it," he said. "Just remember, one false move and I'll slit your throat."

"Sure. Sure," Jude mumbled. He turned away from Hawkeye, as though taking the lead, but instead of walking away, he bunched his fist and swung around, knocking the knife aside and lunging for Hawkeye's throat.

The move took Hawkeye unaware, but he recovered quickly. For a moment the two men grappled with the knife, then Jude slipped and the advantage was Hawkeye's. He drove the blade deep into

Jude's chest. For a moment Jude's mouth hung slack, his eyes wide with shock, then his legs crumpled beneath him and he slumped to the ground.

Hawkeye was breathing heavily from the exertion. And he waited a moment to catch his breath before stepping over the two dead men and making his way swiftly to the circle of wagons. As he reached his destination, his footsteps slowed. Although the travelers had retired for the night, a lone man stood guard.

Hawkeye watched the man stoop over and add another log to the dying fire. The guard stirred a stick among the coals, raking several glowing pieces beneath the log. He remained there for a time watching the log catch fire and burst into flames, then, rising, the guard began his rounds, his footsteps carrying him toward Hawkeye's place of concealment.

Hawkeye dropped to the ground behind a bush and lay still. He didn't want to kill the sentry. It could prove dangerous with the other travelers so near. But he had no intention of leaving this place without the gold. Hawkeye was an honorable man and, if Cremp and Jude had honored their agreement, he would have left the precious metal with them, feeling they had earned it.

But they had not, therefore, the gold was still his, and he would do whatever it took to retrieve it. If lives were lost, then, so be it. The white men had stolen enough from the Comanches already, leaving them little to bargain with for their needs. *No.* He definitely would not leave without the gold, but he would rather obtain it without killing the sentry, if possible.

The guard was closer now, standing only a few feet away from Hawkeye.

The Comanche warrior gripped the handle of his knife tightly. If the guard came a few more feet he would see him. But he would kill the sentry before a cry escaped his lips. He must, or the travelers would awaken. Hawkeye's muscles bunched as he readied himself for the attack.

Suddenly the fine hairs on the nape of his neck prickled. He had had the feeling before and knew exactly what it meant. He was being watched.

Slowly he turned his head, his narrowed gaze searching the darkness. He found nothing. His eyes moved lower, sweeping the area, stopped and moved back to a small bush.

A rabbit.

He breathed a sigh of relief.

But too soon. The rabbit stood frozen for only a moment, then he made a dash out of the underbrush, straight across the boots of the sentry.

"What the hell?" the man growled.

He had brought his rifle up and it was aimed straight at Hawkeye.

Certain he had been discovered, Hawkeye gripped the handle of his knife and bunched his muscles to spring upon the guard, but the man lowered his rifle and swung around.

"Nothin' but a rabbit," he muttered. "Must be gettin' jumpy with all thet Injun talk." His boots thudded against the hard ground as he went on his rounds.

Hawkeye waited until the man was hidden from view before he made a silent dash for the wagon. It swayed slightly as he entered it, and moments later he held the box that contained his gold. He waited until the sentry had passed the wagon again, then made a dash for the forest. In the cover of the dense woods he stopped long enough to take his money belt from the box, then he fastened it around his waist and mounted Diablo.

When he came to the fork in the road, he pulled the stallion up. One road led back to Washington-on-the-Brazos. The other led toward the western horizons.

Johanna was in Washington, the rifles were on their way to the dark-skinned people whom the Comanches hated even more than they hated the Texans.

Hawkeye was reluctant to leave Johanna behind, for she belonged to him now and had no further place among the white men. On the other hand, he knew he had to follow the trail of the rifles without delay. If they fell into the hands of the Mexicans, they would be used against his Comanche brothers even more viciously than the Texans would ever dream of.

Hawkeye spared only a short glance toward Washington-on-the-Brazos. He already knew he had no choice in the direction he took. From the day the Comanches found him wandering alone beside the river, his loyalty had been decided.

He urged Diablo up the western trail.

The loneliness Johanna felt was as real as a bubble of cold air in her chest, but as the days crept by, slowly turning into weeks, she found herself able to put Hawkeye out of her mind for longer periods of time.

She began to know the names of the regular customers who frequented the restaurant and of one man in particular, Sheriff Eli Wade, who had developed a habit of stopping in for coffee late in the afternoon during their quiet period. Invariably, he coaxed her into sitting down with him for a cup of coffee and quiet conversation.

Johanna came to look forward to their time together, and Eli made it plain from the beginning that he held her in high regard. It was one such occasion when he surprised her by asking her to a box social.

"That's very nice of you," she replied, smiling gently at him. "But I think perhaps not."

"Would you mind telling me why?" he asked gruffly, his gray eyes steady on hers.

Pink stained her cheeks. How could she answer him? *I've been hurt by men too many times?* No! she couldn't tell him that. She lowered her eyes and stared into the amber liquid in her coffee cup. "I'm rather tired after I leave here," she said, intent on letting him down easy. "Especially tonight." She lifted clouded green eyes to him, silently begging him not to press the issue.

He was not to be so easily dissuaded. "It's not tonight," he said quietly. "The town council is holding it a week from Saturday."

119

Sighing, she set her cup down on the table, and said, "Eli, I really don't think it would be wise to —"

He laid a warm hand over hers and squeezed it lightly. "Johanna," he chided. "The city council is trying to raise enough money to build a school." His gray eyes glinted with humor. "You should consider it your civic duty to help."

Despite herself, a bubble of laughter escaped her lips at his reasoning. "Eli Wade, you're a perfect scoundrel," she accused. "I don't know anyone else who would ask a girl out, and then tell her it was her duty to the community to go with him."

"A scoundrel, perhaps," he agreed. "But not perfect by any means. Thing is, I don't believe in wastin' time when I find something I want."

Johanna's smile died on her face. "Eli," she said slowly. "Please don't think I don't appreciate —"

"I'm not askin' for anything," he said casually. "All I want is your company at a box social given to benefit the people in our town. Now, is that askin' too much?"

Put that way, how could she possibly refuse?

Chapter Nine

Hawkeye was sorely troubled as he watched the sun sink below the horizon. It had been almost three weeks since he had taken up the trail of the rifles and from the start, it had seemed as though fate was against him.

There seemed no end to the troubles he'd had. First a heavy rain had caused the Canadian River to swell beyond its banks, and he'd lost precious time waiting for the waters to lower enough to allow his safe passage. Then the stallion had gone lame and he had spent several days walking beside him.

And all the time he worried.

He worried that the wagons would reach Enchanted Rock before he could stop them. Worried the Mexicans would grow tired of waiting and ride out to meet them. If they did, he would have little chance against such odds.

And he worried about the girl he had left behind him. What had she thought when she had wakened to find him gone? He had been in such a rush to retrieve the rifles, he had forgotten Johanna had been frightened by something—or someone. Suppose something happened to her while he was gone. His mind instantly rejected the thought, finding it too painful to bear.

And so it went. Minute by minute. Day by day.

He continued to follow the trail, finding it remarkably easy to follow the ruts the wagons left on the ground, until one day, as the setting sun splashed the horizon with shades of gold, red, and purple, Hawkeye topped a rise and spotted his quarry.

His gaze narrowed against the sun, settling on the two wagons lurching across the prairie. As he watched them, a plan began to take form in his mind. The fact that he was one man pitted against the four armed guards and two drivers made not the slightest difference to him. He could easily follow them and pick them off one by one with his rifle. But he would not do so. Neither would he use his pistols. Instead, he would use the white man's fear of the Comanches as his weapon. And when the six men lay dead upon the prairie, there would be no mistaking who had killed them. And their deaths would serve as a warning to all who dared steal from the Comanche people.

He had no doubts about his ability to kill them and take the rifles. Hawkeye knew he had an edge on the men who transported the weapons. Except for Carlos Mendoza, the contents of the wagons were only goods to be delivered. Not so with Hawkeye. The rifles could mean the difference between life and death for his people. And, if it was required, he would fight to the death for them.

The camp was shrouded in a blanket of darkness as Hawkeye cautiously approached the camp. Overhead, gray clouds scudded across a star-studded sky, dimming what would otherwise have been a bright glitter.

Through the dense brush surrounding the camp, Hawkeye could barely make out the two men who stood guard over the sleeping men.

That makes four in the bedrolls, he silently told himself. A movement near the fire caught his eye and he shifted slightly, narrowing his gaze on the man who had been hidden from view. *Three asleep,* he corrected himself, watching the man at the fire lift a cup to his mouth, take a long swallow and toss the dregs onto the hard, dry earth. Then, setting the cup down, the man rose to his feet, and came toward the brush where Hawkeye lay hidden.

"Carl," one of the men standing guard called.

The man stopped, turned back. "Yeah?"

"Watch yourself out there. Remember what Carlos told us 'bout them Injuns."

"I remember," Carl replied. "But they ain't no Injuns aroun' these parts. If'n they was, we'd a' seen 'em before now."

"A body can see you ain't had no dealin's with the Comanch," the other man growled. "By the time you hear 'em, it's already done too late."

Carl nodded abruptly and continued striding away from the camp. He stopped near Hawkeye's hiding place and fiddled with his trousers. Then there was the sound of water splashing on the hard-baked earth.

The man was fumbling with the buttons on his trousers when Hawkeye rose from the ground and reached for the man with his knife. A moment later Carl sank to the ground, his throat slit from ear to ear. A gurgling sigh was the only sound he made to indicate his passing.

But it had been too much.

"You say somethin', Carl?" The words came from the guard who had spoken before.

Hawkeye circled around in the darkness, putting distance between the fallen man and himself.

"Carl?" The voice came again, wary, questioning.

"What's the matter?" growled a deeper voice.

"Don't know, Carlos," came the first. "Carl left to take a leak. He ain't come back yet. What's more, he ain't answerin'. Reckon he's just out of hearin' range?" The last words asked for reassurance.

A muttered curse came from Carlos. "We cain't take no chances," he said. "Get ever'body up, an' tell 'em to spread out and look for Carl."

Hawkeye could hear the mutter of voices as the men were wakened, then the sudden quiet that said they had been alerted to the possibility of

Indians about.

He knew the exact moment when they found the body.

"Jesus!" a voice muttered. "Carl!" A moment later, the same voice came again, panic-stricken. "Carlos. I found him! He's just lyin' there with his throat sliced right open. And there's blood all over the place."

Much shouting followed those words, then suddenly there was quiet. As though everyone became aware at once that they, themselves, might be the next target. A few minutes later Hawkeye identified the thud of approaching footsteps. Then the man appeared. He was tall and whipcord lean. Hawkeye wasted no time in making his move.

The guard sensed his presence at the same moment Hawkeye lunged for him. A cry of warning escaped his lips, just before the knife sliced through his jugular vein. The cry became a gurgling sound as his knees buckled and he went down with a thud.

Seemingly aware that one of their numbers had been attacked, a volley of shots rang out and the whine of bullets passed near Hawkeye's head, striking a boulder nearby and ricocheting with a loud ping. He wasted no time in making his escape. But he didn't mind leaving. He had accomplished what he had come for. Even though the guards had been alerted, their numbers were now four, instead of six.

Knowing it would be suicide to tangle further with the rifle guards since they had been alerted, Hawkeye found a good hiding place beneath an overhanging ledge that was concealed by large boulders. Then he settled down into his bedroll and a moment later had fallen asleep.

He trailed the wagons for the next two days, killing two more guards with well-placed arrows, leaving only two men left alive. If one of them had not been Carlos Mendoza, they might have abandoned the rifles and run for their lives. But not Carlos. He was too greedy. The promise of the gold that awaited him on delivery of the goods was too tempting. And Hawkeye especially wanted him. He knew Carlos from the past. It had been Carlos Mendoza who had led the raiders who had killed his parents and burned their house. He was a snake that had long needed exterminating.

And Hawkeye was the man who would do it.

But he was running out of time. Enchanted Rock was only a day's ride away. Hawkeye rode ahead to the place he had selected earlier where large boulders rose from the earth as though flung there by some giant hand.

Urging Diablo behind them, he began to prepare himself for the final assault on his enemies. When he attacked them, Carlos would know his enemy. As he should. Hawkeye stripped down to his waist and painted his face with garish hues of red and green. Then he waited for the wagons.

His muscles were knotted with tension as he saw the horses and wagons. It seemed to take hours for them to move past his place of concealment. When they did, he rode out after them.

He recognized Carlos in the first wagon. At that same moment, the man jerked his head around, staring at the rider who appeared from behind a jagged rock formation. An expression of fear crossed his face as he stared at the Comanche warrior riding a big black stallion. Man and horse seemed almost a streak as the muscular animal galloped alongside the last wagon.

"Aaa-ii—ee!" Hawkeye shrieked, waving his tomahawk fiercely above his head. The horses, startled by the shrieking warrior and the black stallion thundering down on them, leapt forward, jerking the heavy wagon behind them. The wheels hit a deep rut, and the jolt tumbled the driver from the seat. The traces snapped as the wagon turned over, the wheels spinning freely while the animals ran away.

Hawkeye ignored the fallen wagon and raced after the other one that contained Carlos Mendoza. A bullet whizzed by his ear and Diablo began a zigzagging course to make Hawkeye a harder target. When Hawkeye drew close enough, he threw the tomahawk. It struck the pistol and sent it flying from the wagon. A look of desperation crossed Carlos's face as Hawkeye made a wild leap for the wagon from the back of the running stallion.

At the same moment the wagon wheel hit a gopher hole and gave a lurch, causing Hawkeye's heel to slip. He went down on his hands and knees. Instantly, Carlos was on him, pushing roughly against his body, attempting to shove him off the swaying wagon.

But Hawkeye resisted his efforts, lifting his large hands and wrapping them around Carlos's neck. Carlos's face turned red, then purple. His eyes bulged out and he gave a strangled cry, attempting to dislodge the warrior's fingers from his neck. The wagon wheel hit another hole, throwing Hawkeye off balance. The two men fell hard against the wagon bed and Carlos used the moment to wrench free from Hawkeye's grip.

Carlos rose to his feet and sent a savage kick into Hawkeye's side. Hawkeye grabbed the other man's leg and yanked it hard, causing Carlos to lose his balance again. His arms flailed the air as he tried to regain his balance. The wagon gave a lurch and Carlos went over the side, striking the ground with a heavy thud.

Breathing hard, Hawkeye grabbed the reins and pulled on them. The wagon ground to a halt. He turned it around and returned to where Carlos still lay on the ground. One look was all he needed to tell him that the man's neck had snapped upon impact with the hard-baked ground.

Hawkeye, realizing he would be unable to drive both wagons, searched for a place to leave the rifles until he could return for them. It didn't take him long to find what he was searching for. Behind a huge boulder that was thrusting skyward, lay an even larger one with a cliff overhang. Together, they formed a perfect hiding place large enough to hide both wagons.

But first, he had the job of righting the overturned wagon. A job that proved time-consuming, as well as hard to accomplish. But by persevering, he did accomplish it and by noon of the next day, he was using broomweeds to sweep the area clean of all sign. When he had finished the task, he urged Diablo down the trail and began the long journey back.

Hawkeye gave a heavy sigh as he pulled Diablo up at the ferry. It had been a hard month. The longest one he had ever known. But he had found the rifles, and now they were stashed away, just waiting until he could get some help to fetch them. First though, he had some unfinished business in Washington town.

A smile crossed his face as he thought of Johanna. He curbed the urge to forget about a bath and find her. He had a month of trail dirt on him and needed a bath before he saw her. He couldn't possibly greet her looking the way he did now.

His dark eyes glinted with anticipation. He would have a bath at the stables, then he would go to her cabin. He smiled as he imagined her surprise when she saw him. But he had not one single doubt that her reaction would be a joyous one.

We won't leave right away, he silently told himself. *Tomorrow is soon enough.* He wanted the time to breathe in the womanly fragrance of her, to taste her warm sweetness once again before taking up the trail.

He could feel his body's reaction at just the thought and thought about forgetting the bath and going straight to her cabin. Although the idea greatly appealed to him, he quickly dismissed it, deciding to stick with his original plan and take time for a bath. *After all,* he consoled himself, *a bath won't take long. And we will have all night to enjoy each other.*

He reined Diablo up in front of the stables, dismounted, and led Diablo inside the shadowy interior.

"Howdy," a grizzled old man said. Hawkeye recognized him as the stabler. "Need a stall and some hay fer your hoss?"

"Yes," Hawkeye replied, sliding the saddle off the stallion's back. "Just for tonight. I'm leaving at first light." The old man watched Hawkeye rub Diablo down with some straw. "I need a bath," Hawkeye told him. "I've been on the trail the past month."

"Want your water heated?" the old-timer asked.

Hawkeye inclined his head. "I'd be obliged," he said. "And I'll need an extra mount when I leave in the morning."

"Reckon I can help you there. Got an old nag out back you can have fer fifty dollars gold. Don't know how fer she'll go afore she gives out." His eyes glinted with amusement. "But if you happen to be lookin' fer a good horse, I got one comin'. Just bought a mare not more'n an hour past. She ain't here, but I seen 'er right enough. Seen 'er plenty of times. She's a rare beauty, that one. Feller'll be bringin' 'er come daylight. I could let you have 'er fer two hundred." His gaze was shrewd. "Not Texas currency neither. That stuff ain't worth the paper it's printed on since the Big Panic set in."

Hawkeye grinned inwardly. These Texans were something else. They printed currency, then refused to use it. He couldn't really blame them though. The banks had dealt in too much land speculation last year, lending money without security to any and all and the results had been disastrous. Bank after bank began to close, rendering currency notes worthless. Some places in Texas had even returned to the barter system.

After a deal was made on the mare, Hawkeye took his bath. The old man sat on a crate and kept him company.

"We got us a box social tonight," he said. "They'll be some singin' and dancin' and some mighty fine eatin' in some o' them fancy boxes. Feller might even get lucky and find hisself a purty lady to go along with 'is supper."

"I don't need to go looking for a pretty lady," Hawkeye said with a grin. "There's already one waiting for me as soon as I'm cleaned up. But thanks all the same."

"Hope she knows you're comin', son," the old-timer said. "Ever'body in town's gonna be there. Ain't much chance in gettin' a decent meal nowheres else. Mary's place is already closed up."

"Closed already?" His eyebrows lifted and a gleam of anticipation lit his dark eyes. If the cafe was closed, then Johanna would likely be at the cabin.

"Yep," the old man said. "I was down to Mary's a while back. Figgered on havin' me some of Sam's blackberry cobbler." He smacked his lips. "Sam makes the best cobbler around these parts. Ain't nobody makes one better. Sure was disappointed when I found that cafe locked up tight as a drum. An' all on accounta thet there box social. Seems like ever'body in town's gonna be there."

Everybody? Could Johanna be attending the box social? What, exactly, was a box social? Hawkeye voiced the thought to the old man.

The old-timer chuckled. "Thought ever'body knew what a box social was, son. Well, let me tell you, it's a sight to behold. The ladies cook up a mess of vittles. The finest they can make." He licked his lips at the thought. "An' they tie 'em up with fancy ribbons and such. Then them boxes get auctioned off to the highest bidder. That's when the fun really begins." His faded eyes gleamed as he leaned forward. " 'Cause them ladies thet brought the boxes, they gotta share the supper you bought with you. An' when you finish eatin' all thet fried chicken and fried pies they cooked up, then the benches and tables is moved and the fiddles is tuned and the dancin' starts." He let out a cackle of laughter. "Boy, when I was younger, I really swung them ladies around. I . . ."

Hawkeye let the old man ramble on, his thoughts turning to Johanna. Would she be at the box thing? Perhaps he shouldn't have wasted time taking a bath. He wondered what time it started and if he could reach the cabin before she left. *Damnit!* He had not the inclination nor the time to go to some box something-or-other to find her. Surely the old man was wrong. Johanna didn't seem the socializing type. At least he hoped not.

Hawkeye's movement were irritated as he reached for the towel and stood up, hurriedly drying his body off and donning fresh clothing. He felt a need to hurry and reach the cabin . . . and ultimately, Johanna.

"Decided to go, huh?"

Hawkeye's gaze narrowed on the old man. He had been so distracted with his thoughts that he had forgotten the old-timer's existence. "Go where?" he queried.

The old man's grizzled brows pulled into a frown. "To the box social," he growled. "What'n hell we been talkin' about here?"

"Damned if I know," Hawkeye said shortly. He tossed the old man a silver dollar and left the stables, intent on finding Johanna.

Chapter Ten

Johanna stood before the mirror, watching her reflection twine a green ribbon through the mass of glossy curls arranged high on her head.

She wondered, not for the first time, if she was making a mistake by attending the box social with Eli, and she regretted the impulse that had led her to accepting the invitation.

All day she'd been plagued by thoughts of Hawkeye, remembering every detail of their time together. She remembered the way he held her so protectively against him, the feel of his warm lips against her own, so tender, as though he really cared for her.

But it was all pretense, she reminded herself silently. No doubt he'd been attracted to her, but only in a physical sense. And, fool that she was, had been easily assuaged. Had her innocence disappointed him? *Yes. That must be the answer.* Otherwise, he'd have wanted her longer than one night. *Wouldn't he?*

Johanna studied her reflection carefully, looking for outward signs of her pain. The girl in the mirror looked back calmly.

Deciding she'd pass inspection, Johanna gave her hair a last pat. A quick glance at the clock told her that Eli would be arriving soon, so she hurried to the bed and picked up the dress Mary had generously helped her make for the festivities. When she finished dressing, she studied herself in the mirror again. She knew she had never looked better. The green silk twill gown enhanced her pale skin and brought out the color of her eyes.

A knock on the door announced Eli's arrival and she opened it.

"How beautiful you look," he said, his admiring eyes sweeping over her.

She smiled her thanks at him, picked up the gaily wrapped package she had already prepared and followed him from the cabin.

The sun was sinking below the horizon, painting the sky with glorious shades of orange and purple as they made their way down the street toward the town hall.

Neither of them noticed the buckskin-clad man step from the stables and stop short at the sight of them. They didn't see the anger that flared in his eyes, or the way his knuckles turned white as his hands clenched into fists.

The town hall was already filled to capacity with folks intent on having a good time. Old Ben

Keller was busy tuning his fiddle and the screeching whine followed them as they worked their way through the crowd toward the long bench lining one wall.

Eli saw her seated, then took the gaily wrapped box from her. "I'll see the auctioneer gets this," he said solemnly. "With instructions he's to sell it to no one but me."

"You can't do that, Sheriff," came the deep voice of a man nearby.

Turning her head, Johanna met the amused gaze of Bill Hobbs, a local rancher, who frequented Mary's Cafe.

"That auctioneer's got no choice but to sell them boxes to the highest bidder," Hobbs continued. "If Jenny here wouldn't skin me alive," he tempered his words with a grin at the little woman beside him, "then I'd give you a run for your money."

"You best think twice before you go biddin' on another box, Bill Hobbs," said the feisty little woman beside him. "Now you quit flappin' your lip and take my box to that auctioneer."

"You tell him, Jenny," Eli said, winking at the rancher's wife. "With a wife like yourself, he ain't got no call to stray in nobody else's pastures. And this box and the lady that goes with it belongs to me."

Although Johanna knew Eli spoke in jest, she felt slightly uneasy at his words. They only served to reinforce her worry about his intentions. She liked him well enough, and he had been nothing but respectful in his attitude toward her, but she knew, with a certainty, they could never be anything but friends.

The two men continued to joke back and forth as they carried the gaily wrapped boxes up front and added them to the growing stack on the table. Neither they, nor Johanna, saw the man in buckskins who stood near the door, his dark eyes cold and forbidding.

After all the boxes had been collected, the auctioneer, a portly middle-aged man in a gray suit, held his hands up for silence. Gradually, the voices quieted, and the room grew still.

"Any more boxes out there?" the auctioneer asked.

Silence.

"All right," he said heartily. "We've got a lot of entertainment here tonight. Old Ben Keller is over yonder with his fiddle. Guess most of you heard him tunin' it up." Scattered laughter greeted this remark. "I understand Casey Johnson brung his guitar too." Heads craned as people tried to locate the young man and his instrument. "Now them two cain't hardly wait to play us some foot-stompin' tunes." He paused, let the silence draw out, then said, "But first, there's other more pressin' business to be took care of. It's what this box social is all about. An' that's raisin' money for a schoolhouse in our town."

Reaching down, he picked up a square box tied with yellow ribbon. "It's time to start the biddin', folks." He looked at the box in his hand, hefted it as though weighing it, then said, "This here box is mighty heavy. Whoever buys it, oughta be gettin' a mighty fillin' meal." He looked out over his audience. "And by the looks of this purty yaller ribbon, I'd say he's gonna get to eat it with a mighty purty lady as well."

"Is that it, Annabelle?" came a loud whisper from the audience.

"No tellin' now," said the auctioneer, unable to miss the quick nod the lady in question had given the young man. "This here's a secret auction. Nobody's s'posed to know who the box belongs to."

A titter of laughter came from the ladies in the audience.

"Now, who'll start the bidding?" the auctioneer inquired, his eyes roaming around the room.

"I bid a quarter," said the young man who had spoken earlier.

"Fifty cents," yelled an older man.

"Six bits," said the young man.

"Who'll make it a dollar?" the auctioneer shouted. When there was no response, the auctioneer said, "Going once . . . going twice." He struck his gavel on the podium. "Sold to Jesse Young for the sum of six bits. Hope you enjoy the eats and the young lady who goes with it," he added as the young man paid his money, accepted his goods and returned to his lady friend.

Johanna smiled often as she watched the pile of boxes grow smaller and smaller. She found the enthusiasm of the crowd contagious, and was really enjoying herself. Her box was the last one to be auctioned off. The auctioneer held it aloft, extolling its beauty and its worth. The bidding started and there were a few good natured bids against the sheriff but most everyone could see very shortly that he was determined to buy the box and Johanna's company as well. Finally, when the other bidders had all dropped off and it looked like the sheriff was going to get the box for two dollars, the auctioneer asked for a last bid.

"Twenty dollars!"

Heads turned to see the man who had spoken from the back of the room, Johanna's along with them. Her face drained of color as a big man in buckskins stepped from the shadows.

Hawkeye! He had returned!

Although she wanted to run to him, fling herself into his arms, shock held her still. She met his eyes and flinched from the impact, feeling as though she had run over hot coals.

Was he angry with her?

Indignation was like a flame; once lit, it began to burn brightly, leaping and twisting until it was out of control. If anyone had cause for anger, it was her. After all, he was the one who had left.

The auctioneer's voice seemed to come from a long distance when he spoke. "I got twenty dollars here, folks. Yonder's a man who knows what he wants and how to get it. The bid's at twenty dollars now. Anybody out there want to raise it?"

The sheriff's body was suddenly stiff with tension beside Johanna. "Twenty-one," he said gruffly.

"Thirty!" growled Hawkeye.

"Who the hell does he think he is?" Eli asked, looking grim. Before Johanna could speak, he countered. "Thirty-one."

"Fifty dollars!"

Instantly, a hush fell over the room. From the start the bidding had been high over the small box supper. But now it had reached outrageous proportions. The sheriff looked at Johanna with helpless rage. Fifty dollars was more money than most had seen in a long time, including him.

"It's all right, Eli," Johanna assured him. Although she spoke quietly, her green eyes glittered with fury when they shifted to Hawkeye. "He's not a stranger to me," she said, forcing herself to speak calmly. "I really don't mind sharing the meal with him."

"Well I do mind," Eli muttered grimly. "Damnit, Johanna. This was supposed to be our night together. I didn't plan on some drifter comin' to town to spoil it. Who is he, anyway?"

She had no time to answer before the auctioneer claimed Eli's attention. "Are you finished bidding, sheriff?" The auctioneer's voice betrayed a slight unease as though he had picked up on the sheriff's mood and was afraid he would be held responsible for the sheriff's failure to secure the box.

Eli gave the auctioneer a surly nod. His eyes were cold with rage when he turned back to Johanna. "I'll see you later," he growled. Then, pushing his way through the crowd, he left her standing alone.

Johanna's lips were tight as she waited for Hawkeye to pay for the box and join her. He took her arm and she jerked it away as though stung by a wasp.

His lips thinned, tightening as he stared grimly at her. "You lead the way," he growled.

Although Johanna's back was rigid with disapproval, she held her silence until they found a comparatively quiet spot to eat. She seated herself at a small table, then rounded on him. "What do you mean by pulling such a stunt," she asked, her voice fairly dripping with ice.

Hawkeye reacted instantly, his eyes smoldering as he reached out and gripped her arm. She could actually feel the strength in his hard frame. Every ligament and muscle in his body seemed taut with anger when he spoke. "I had no wish for you to eat with him. You shouldn't have come here. Have you no loyalty at all?" The cutting edge of his voice cut into her, hurting, but she refused to allow her feelings to show. Instead, she covered them with anger.

"Loyalty!" she hissed. "You're a fine one to speak of loyalty. You walked away from me over a month ago. And now you have the unmitigated gall to show up again and speak of loyalty." She leaned toward him. "Get this, mister," she said, tapping the table with a fingertip. "What I do is none of your business. Nor whom I do it with," she added.

"I left here because it was necessary," he said shortly. Then, as though tiring of the subject, he sat down opposite her, took out a piece of fried chicken and bit into it.

Johanna studied him angrily. He obviously intended to tell her nothing more. Not what he had been doing all this time, nor why he had considered it necessary. "Did you know Eli is the sheriff here?" she asked.

"I saw the tin star," he growled. "But the badge means nothing to me. No man takes what belongs to me."

A part of her mind registered his heavy breathing. She ground her teeth together and glared at him. "You're insane!" she snapped. "I belong to no man, especially not to you."

"You're wrong, Johanna," he said coldly. "You gave yourself to me willingly."

She sucked in a sharp breath. "How dare you speak of that night," she raged. "You used me and when you were done you cast me aside." She knew she was sounding like some heroine out of a melodrama, but the hurt had gone deep and would be a long time mending.

"I have no need to explain my actions," he said. "I did what needed doing." He took another bite of chicken. "That's good," he said conversationally, casting a glance into the open box. "I see you made fried pies as well."

Johanna's hands clenched into fists and her nose was pinched with the effort of control. Her body trembled with rage as she fought the urge to strike him. But he seemed not to care one whit about her feelings.

Was she of so little consequence to him?

Suddenly, she saw the sheriff across the room. Even from this distance, she could see his hands clenching and unclenching at his side. His eyes were on them, dark and forbidding. "The sheriff is interested in you," she said.

"I noticed," he replied, keeping his eyes on the chicken leg he was bent on tearing asunder with his teeth.

Although he continued wolfing down the food, she sensed he wasn't as uncaring of the law man's attention as he seemed.

"I thought you didn't want to attract the attention of the law," she said, her voice dripping honey.

"Did I say that?"

"Not in so many words." She watched him closely. "But you certainly didn't want the sheriff notified when you were attacked."

He tossed the chicken bone in the box and reached for another piece. "You should eat some of this," he said.

"I've lost my appetite," she said coldly, her gaze roaming around the room, looking anywhere but at him. She saw the sheriff approaching. "He's coming over here."

Hawkeye's eyes lifted, narrowed on the man striding toward them, and he let the chicken fall back into the box.

"Don't start any trouble," she said quickly.

"I won't have to," he said grimly. "He's going to do it for me."

She silently agreed with him. Eli looked about ready to explode. She felt apprehensive. Was Hawkeye wanted by the law? Even though she was furious at him, she didn't want him locked up. She had to prevent a confrontation between the two men.

When the sheriff reached them, she pushed her

chair aside and gripped his arm with her fingers. "Will you see me home, Eli?"

He looked at Hawkeye. "He botherin' you?"

Recognizing the menace in his tone, she hurried to say, "No. It's all right. But I have a bad headache."

Although she knew he didn't believe her, he kept his silence. She didn't look back as she left the town hall with Eli, but she felt the heat of Hawkeye's eyes on her all the same.

After bidding Eli goodbye, Johanna entered the cabin and lit the lamp. The silence was oppressive and she sighed heavily, realizing she had been spending far too much time alone. She was restless and had a feeling she would be unable to sleep. She tried to put thoughts of Hawkeye from her mind but they kept intruding as she prepared for bed. After blowing out the lamp, she crawled into bed and pulled the covers up to her chin. But sleep proved elusive. She lay there, watching the curtains billow in and out with the night breeze. Her nerves were wound up tight. She pushed back the covers, allowing the cool breeze to wash over her, willing herself to unwind. But to no avail. Sleep proved increasingly distant.

A shiver ran over her as she remembered the scene with Hawkeye. Suddenly reaction set in and her teeth began to chatter. She pulled the covers up to her chin again and huddled into a tight ball. It seemed hours before she began to relax and succumb to the arms of Morpheus.

The sound of knocking at the door woke Johanna. She lay there for a moment, wondering if she had imagined the sound. Then she heard it again. Knock-knock-knock.

Someone was knocking on her door, softly, as though her visitor were unwilling to attract outside attention.

Sliding out of bed, she grabbed her robe off the chair and crossed to the door. "Who's there?" she asked, leaning her ear against the door.

"Hawkeye."

She recognized his voice immediately, and stiffened. He had a nerve, coming here. "What do you want?" she asked tightly.

"Open the door," he commanded.

"I've nothing to say to you," she said. "Go away."

He was silent for a moment, then he said, "Open the door, Johanna. We have to talk."

"I have nothing to say to you," she said stubbornly.

Another long silence. Then he said, "I have no time to argue with you. Open this door right now, or I'll break it down." His voice had risen dramatically, as though he no longer cared who heard him.

She contemplated refusing again, but her fear that some passerby would see him and come to investigate, thereby learning of their relationship and damaging her reputation, had her lifting the bar from the door. She would allow him to say his piece and then order him to leave. She had not the slightest fear of him—until he stepped inside and

145

closed the door behind him.

There was a leashed energy about him, turbulent in its impact. He resembled a caged panther about to break loose from his confines and spring. She stood stunned. Except for the heavy gold cross lying against his bronzed skin, Hawkeye's chest was bare. His buckskin trousers fit snugly across his hips, emphasizing his muscular leaness; a beaded headband held his hair back from his forehead and two feathers hung from the side. She licked suddenly dry lips and his eyes were caught and held by the movement.

"Why-why are you dressed like that?" she stuttered, blinking rapidly at him. "Y-you look like a—a—"

"Comanche warrior?" he suggested softly.

Comanche warrior? His words echoed in her mind, but her expression remained confused. What did he mean? She had never seen a warrior of any kind, much less a Comanche one. What was he suggesting? she wondered. Her eyes lifted, met the brooding intensity of his gaze, then moved to the feathers fastened in the beaded headband.

Comanche warrior? No! What he was suggesting was impossible! Wasn't it?

She stared at him, her quickened breathing heightened by the rise and fall of her breasts, afraid to believe what her eyes told her.

His dark eyes traveled over her, taking in her bare feet just peeking beneath the hem of her nightdress. She was unaware of the seductive picture that she presented with her tousled hair fall-

146

ing in soft waves against the fabric of her robe.

"Why did you lock the door against me?" he growled.

"You—" She stopped, licking lips that had suddenly gone dry. "You have no right here. Why have you come?"

"I came back for you. And as for rights, I have every right, Johanna. You are my woman."

Comanche warrior. The words still lingered like a distant echo, but her mind still refused to accept the possibility.

He must be mad!

She didn't know she had voiced the words until he spoke. "No more than any man who has been deceived by his woman."

"I haven't deceived you," she said, her green eyes growing wider as her mind tried to deal with the truth. *Comanche.* "And . . . I'm not your woman," she said slowly.

"I don't have time to argue with you," he said, his voice low and dangerous. "There are things I must do that are far more important." His anger was a tangible thing, a beast that needed soothing, but, even though she had finally accepted his words, she had no intention of appeasing him. Regardless of who his people were, he was still the man who had taken her virginity, then abandoned her.

"Then go do them!" she snapped, her indignation and hurt covering her momentary fear at finding he was one of the dreaded Comanches. "I didn't ask you to come back."

Ignoring her, he strode to the dresser and began

147

pulling the drawers out and dumping the clothing on the bed.

"What are you doing?" she asked.

"If you wish to take anything with you, get it now," he said, grabbing a pillowcase and stuffing the contents of the drawers into it.

"Stop that!" she said, grabbing a petticoat just before he stuffed it into the makeshift bag. "What do you think you're doing?"

He ignored her and continued filling the pillowcase with her clothing.

Her green eyes glittered with rage. He had no right to treat her this way. *No right at all!*

Taking him completely unaware, she grabbed the pillowcase from him, threw it down on the floor and stomped it with her foot. "I've had enough of this," she snapped. "I'm going for the sheriff."

Immediately, his hand snaked out, his fingers wrapping around her wrist and he yanked her hard against him. "The only place you are going is with me," he growled savagely. "Make no mistake about that, Johanna."

She struggled furiously with him, her face suffused with anger. "No," she gritted, trying to wrest her wrist out of his grip. "Damnit! Let me go!"

"Don't make me force you," he said tightly.

She kicked out wildly, connecting with his shinbone. He flinched, but didn't release his grip. Slowly, but surely, he subdued her, pulling her against his lean hard body, his eyes hard and taunting.

"Let me go!" she cried, despising herself for the

way her body was reacting to his. "You . . . you . . . *Comanche!* she yelled. "You have no right to do this."

"I have every right," he growled. "You gave yourself to me freely. That made you mine." His mouth lowered, ground savagely against hers, kissing her ruthlessly until she was breathless and pale, leaning against him for support. "I won't let you go, Johanna," he said softly. "Not ever."

Wordlessly, she stared up at him, her knees threatening to buckle beneath her.

His hand slipped down her arm, reached around her waist, while the other wound around her hips. Then, with one swift movement, he lifted her off her feet and tossed her across one broad shoulder.

The action caught her by surprise and he was across the room before she regained her senses. "Put me down," she gasped, furiously pounding small, white-knuckled fists on his broad back. "Let me go!"

Ignoring her, he picked up the filled pillowcase, carried her out the door and threw her into the saddle with a jolt that took the breath from her body. Before she could gather her wits together he was sitting behind her. It was then that she really panicked. *This couldn't be happening. It couldn't!*

She opened her mouth to scream and he clamped a big hand across it, shutting off the sound along with her air. She struggled and wiggled and twisted, but he held her clamped tightly against him and no matter how hard she tried, she couldn't break his hold.

Touching his heels against the flanks of the black stallion, Hawkeye urged Diablo out of the town called Washington-on-the-Brazos.

Chapter Eleven

Hawkeye headed the stallion in a northwesterly direction. He spoke no word to Johanna, giving her no indication of where they were going or what was going to happen once they got there. He seemed almost oblivious to her presence as her overactive mind raced with unvoiced questions.

Where was he taking her? Johanna asked herself. *And for what reason?* Her mind imagined all sorts of things, some too horrible to even contemplate.

The farther they rode through the night, the more she worried. But there came a point in time when anger covered her fear of the future. Her drooping shoulders squared, her eyes glittered and her lips tightened, all outward signs of her determination. A determination to be rid of him at the first opportunity which presented itself.

151

She would be damned if she would let him get away with his actions. She had had enough of being treated like a possession. She belonged to no man, nor would she ever. Her fate lay in her ability to form her own destiny. And she was determined she would be the one to control it. Whatever this madman had in mind, he would not find her a biddable piece of fluff.

It was true that she had been attracted to Hawkeye, had even thought she was in love with him. And yet, if he was to be believed, he was one of the dreaded, much-feared Comanche Indians. She still found it hard to believe. How could she have let him make love to her? How could she have been such a fool?

She found no answers to her questions.

As time passed, Johanna's anger cooled. As did her body, for she wore nothing but her nightdress and robe which offered scant protection from the chill night air.

The gait of the stallion unavoidably threw their bodies in close contact and it was only the warmth of Hawkeye's body against her back and his arm circling her waist, that kept her from shaking with cold.

Just when Johanna had decided Hawkeye meant to travel all night, he pulled the stallion up beside a shallow stream.

After dismounting, he pulled her off the horse's back, and helped her to a fallen log when her legs would have crumpled beneath her. She sat on the log, watching him with hard eyes and shivering with cold.

"You should put something else on," he said. "That . . . *garment* you're wearing—" His eyes settled on her heaving breasts, taut against the thin fabric. "—can't be very warm."

Instantly, her hackles rose and she shot him a look of immense dislike, her cheeks flushing crimson. "It wasn't my choice to leave my cabin in this manner," she said, her voice dripping ice.

Unfastening the pillowcase from the saddle, he tossed it at her and it landed with a thud near her foot. "See if you can find something in there to wear," he growled.

She dug into the makeshift bag and extracted a blue, cotton day dress that needed mending. Laying it aside, she checked the rest of the pillowcase's contents, finding nothing except undergarments. Her lips tightened. She had no choice except to wear the torn dress.

A shudder shook her small frame and she quickly dismissed the rip in the garment. It was unimportant. She removed her robe, then donned the dress, putting it on over her nightgown for added warmth. After she had smoothed it over her hips, she turned her attention back to the man who had abducted her. He had unfastened a rope from the saddle and was uncoiling it.

His gaze was dark and brooding as he approached her. "Give me your word you'll stay put," he growled.

"I'll do no such thing," she muttered, her eyes glittering dark green. Almost immediately she wished the words unsaid, because he grabbed her wrist and yanked her hard against him.

"What are you doing?" she asked breathless.

Instead of answering, he looped the rope around one of her wrists, secured it, then reached for the other one. She stared at him, feeling too stunned by his actions to think of stopping him. "What are you doing?" she repeated.

"Tying you up," he said gruffly, flicking her an amused glance.

"I can see that," she snapped, belatedly jerking at her wrists in an attempt to free herself. "But why?"

Ignoring her, he took the other end of the rope and bent to tie her ankles together. She recovered her wits enough to kick out at him, catching him on the side of his head. He growled in anger and grabbed at her ankle. Her breath came in short gasps as she kicked out again, and he jerked back to avoid the blow. But she had only delayed the inevitable for his fingers wrapped around her feet and pulled her off balance.

She hit the ground with a heavy thud, knocking the breath out of her. Hawkeye took advantage of her position and bound her ankles together.

Then, as though nothing untoward had happened, he got to his feet and slid the bridle from the stallion. He spared only a brief glance for the girl who lay panting on the ground before he began rubbing the stallion down. When he was finished, he left the animal to graze nearby.

Johanna lay on the ground, hating him with every breath she took. Her eyes were sullen as she watched him remove the blankets from the saddle and toss one in her direction, before wrapping the other around himself.

"Better get some rest," he said, stretching out on the ground and closing his eyes.

She stared at him. He was going to sleep. *Damnit! Just like that, he was going to sleep.*

"Why have you done this?" she asked angrily. "Where are you taking me?"

"We're going to my village," he said.

"Your village?" she squeaked. "An *Indian* village?"

"That's the kind," he growled. "Now be silent."

Be silent? She stared at him mutinously. "You're not going to sleep and leave me trussed up like a Christmas turkey," she gritted. "Turn me loose!"

"Be silent, damnit!" he snarled. "I'm doing my best not to beat you."

"Beat me?" Her voice raised hysterically. "I don't know why that should surprise me. After you've gone to the bother of kidnapping me, why should you balk at beating me?"

"How the hell should I know?" he snapped, rolling over to stare at her. "Why should I try to make it easy on you? You've done everything possible to make me angry."

"You—you savage!" she snarled. "You haven't the brains of a—a—pea-brained possum! If I had a gun, I'd use it to shoot you!" Her body was actually quivering with her fury.

He sat up suddenly, throwing his blanket aside and moving toward her. "You're askin' for it," he growled.

She glared at him. "Well, go ahead! Just go ahead!" she shouted. "Don't hold back on my

155

account! You've already taken my virginity! What else is there?"

He pushed her back down against the ground, and savagely covered her mouth with his. His lips ground into hers, hurting, bruising the tender flesh against her teeth. She could feel his heart beating in a fast, savage rhythm as he held her crushed tightly against him. Despite herself, her nipples grew taut against the fabric covering them. There was a labored edge to his breathing and she remained still, frightened of what she had aroused in him. He was like the savage she had accused him of being.

A bittersweet feeling of sadness welled into her throat. His desire for her was evident, and yet there was no emotional involvement in his desire. If there had been even the slightest bit of love on his part, he couldn't treat her in such a manner.

A tear slipped from beneath her eyelid and was quickly followed by another.

When he felt the wetness on her face, he drew in a sharp breath and pulled back to stare into her anguished face. Then with an angry oath, he left her alone and strode off into the dense woods.

She lay there a moment trying to recover from the assault on her senses. How could he have treated her so? It was obvious he had lost all respect for her. And, damnit, she didn't deserve his contempt.

Fury surged forth and she began to work on her bonds with her teeth. A feeling of elation swept through her as she felt a strand loosen, then another. It was only a matter of moments before her bonds were loose enough to free her hands. then she bent over and untied her ankles, keeping a wary eye out for Hawkeye.

When there was no sign of the man, she rose to her feet and approached the stallion who was grazing a short distance away, talking softly to him all the while.

The horse lifted his head as she neared, but made no sound, not even when she slipped the reins over his head. She walked on silent feet until she was clear of the camp, then, pulling the horse over to a stump, she mounted him and rode away from the camp.

Hawkeye stood among the woods near the edge of the creek, his thoughts in turmoil. Johanna's tears had affected him strangely, causing a heavy pain in his chest. Had he been wrong to bring her against her will?

Although she protested loudly, he had thought she would give in when confronted with the completed act. It was the way of the Comanche women to accept whatever their mate decreed, and he had seen enough of the white men's way to know it was the same in her world. There might come a day when women had some say in their future, but at present, the men of their family held complete control over them.

And that was the way it should be.

But was he really in control of her? It took only one look from her grass-green eyes to make him go all soft inside.

Did he treat her unkindly? He knew he had not. He had shown her every consideration. And yet, she had cried. Usually a woman's tears had never stirred him, but the sight of hers had caused a curious ache in the region of his heart.

Even so, he would not return her to Washington. She was his. And he would not let her go. Could not let her go. Even the thought caused him pain.

Hawkeye gave a deep sigh. They would go on to his village. And in time, she would come to accept what she couldn't change. But he had wanted more than acceptance from her. Although he hated to admit it, he knew he wanted her love.

Hawkeye had begun to retrace his footsteps when, suddenly, he froze. Had that been the pounding of hooves? Was someone approaching?

Realizing he had left Johanna alone and undefended, he hurried back toward the camp. When he reached it his heart plunged down to his belly.

She was gone!

Johanna's heart was heavy as she dashed through the brush and forest, clinging tightly to the stallion's mane as though it were a lifeline. Through the pounding of her heart and the brambles that tore at her clothing, she was too panicked to contemplate what lay ahead, feeling only the need to put distance between herself and Hawkeye.

She dug tight with her knees, her body moving in rhythm with the horse with the easy skill of a seasoned rider. She allowed herself little time to think as she rode, concentrating on guiding the stallion past the fallen logs and bushes.

As the sun begun to creep over the horizon, painting the forest with fingers of gold, she came to a creek and pulled the stallion up, knowing the animal and herself both needed to drink and rest for a few minutes. After she had quenched her thirst, she allowed the horse to drink, then ground-reined him a short distance away where the grass was in plentiful supply.

Sitting down beneath the shade of a tree, she drew her knees up and rested her chin upon them. She was so discouraged, so physically and emotionally exhausted at this point that she wished she had never run away from Hawkeye.

Knowing she must rest, she closed her eyes and willed her body to relax.

Suddenly, a scrabbling noise jerked her head up. She listened closely, heard a faint rustling of dry brush. A moment later a rabbit hopped into the clearing and she breathed a sigh of relief.

Her relief was short-lived, for she saw what had startled the animal, and a feeling of cold dread came over her.

"Aaa-i-yee!"

The blood-curdling sound was followed by four savages, naked to the waist, their faces painted in bright, garish colors. They erupted from the bushes, waving their weapons and giving a hard, coughing war cry.

For a moment she stood rooted to the spot. Then Johanna's heart began to thud wildly in her chest and shivers trembled the length of her spine, like melting bits of ice trickling down a window-pane.

The nearest warrior was almost on her before she gathered her senses about her. Fear gouged into her, touching a deep, primitive level.

Her terror-filled gaze flashed to Diablo, but she knew the stallion had wandered too far away to do her any good. She'd never make it before they were upon her.

Lifting her long skirts up and tucking her arms close to her sides, she sprinted up a deer trail, then, veered to the right, leaping over the narrow stream, instinctively heading for the woods as she ran for her life with a speed she never knew she possessed.

As she ran, her panic swelled. She jumped over a dead log, then ducked under a low-hanging branch, dashing madly through the underbrush with the howling savages close behind her.

But there, leaping directly toward her, was another of the painted warriors, and he was so close that she could see the red paint gleaming across his eyes and the black slashes across his lower face. He was only a few feet away, holding a hatchet up to strike.

And behind her came the other warriors.

Terror spurred her on and she swerved sideways, dodging around the warrior who blocked her path.

Thud, thud, thud.

Her heart pounded loudly, beating so fast she thought it would surely burst as she crashed through the brush with the Indians chasing after her. She knew in her heart that she had no chance to escape them, knew also, that she could do no less than try. It came as no surprise when she felt the blow on the back of her head. It knocked her forward, slamming her against the trunk of a large oak, knocking the breath out of her. She lay face down on the ground, gasping for air, aware of the Indians looming above her. Rolling over, she stared up at the savages through a tangled mass of dark hair, her green eyes wide with terror.

God in Heaven!

Was it her time to die?

It seemed not yet, for one of the Indians reached down, and dragged her to her feet. He was so close that his fetid breath made her gag and she turned her face away from him. With a grunt of annoyance, the warrior grabbed her chin and forced her to look at him.

Don't show your fear! she told herself. She had heard somewhere that Indians admired courage and despised weakness, so she made herself return his look boldly.

Something glinted in his dark eyes, and unbelievably, a grin spread across his face. Deliberately, his fingers slipped down to her neck and he began to squeeze tightly.

He was going to choke her to death!

Raw terror filled her eyes as she kicked and clawed, her breath wheezing in her throat, but she might as well have been a rabbit fighting a snarling coyote, for all the good it did her. She knew she was no match for his bestial strength.

Although hope had shriveled up into a tight knot in her chest, she lashed out, raking her nails down the side of his face.

She felt his skin tear, saw the warm spurt of blood that flowed from the wound.

He howled in pain and dealt her a blow that sent her senses reeling. Another blow sent her sprawling to the ground. And as darkness closed around her, she wondered if she would ever see Hawkeye again.

Chapter Twelve

Hawkeye, fearful of Johanna's safety, wasted no time in following her. She had made no efforts to cover her trail, but he knew his chances of catching her were slim. Although he had been trained as a long-distance runner as a child, traversing four-mile courses over rough country while carrying a mouthful of water without swallowing it or spitting it out, he was on foot and Johanna rode astride Diablo, the mount that had been chosen for his speed and endurance.

He ran swiftly, breathing evenly as he went, covering a distance of miles in only a few short minutes without any signs of strain.

Hawkeye knew he could run all night, and all the next day if need be. For, as part of his training, he had been made to stay awake for long periods of time to learn how to deal with exhaustion, and now he could cover eighty miles a day on foot in the most forbidding terrain.

Farther and farther he ran, trying to keep his fears for Johanna at bay, but he found it impossible, for he knew better than most the dangers that could lie ahead for a woman alone on the trail.

The sun came up in a blaze of glory, casting its golden rays across the forest and meadowland. Robins and meadowlarks chirruped cheerfully as they flitted from branch to branch, paying scant attention to the man kneeling on the ground, his dark eyes riveted to the tracks of five unshod horses.

A feeling of cold dread shuddered through Hawkeye. He had known instantly the meaning behind the tracks. Indians had come across Johanna's trail . . . and altered their original direction. Now they were following behind her.

His mouth tightened grimly as a picture rose, unbidden to his mind; Johanna, her fragile body bruised and broken, her face frozen in the agony of death. He forced the image from his mind, finding it too painful to be borne.

It was another half hour before he found the place where she had been attacked. His heart pounded with unnamed fear as he searched the area for blood . . . and found it.

Someone had been wounded. And he was almost certain it wasn't one of Johanna's pursuers.

Rage, more terrible than he had ever known before, flowed through his being. He would find them . . . and he would rend her attackers limb from limb.

Moments later, his nostrils twitched at the smell of woodsmoke and he knew he was nearing a deep draw that was hidden well enough for the Indians to feel safe from intruders.

He slowed his steps, his muscles knotting with tension as he inched his way closer, ever alert to the sounds of the forest around him. Even without the smoke to guide him, he would have known he was close, for the creatures of the forest were silent. The only sound that reached his ears was the wind sighing through the branches above, and the gurgling of the water in the creek as it flowed downstream. He knew there should be other sounds along the creekbank; frogs croaking, a squirrel chattering . . . something.

Suddenly, he heard the hum of voices, accompanied by the stamp of horses' hooves and a short nicker. His blood began to pound furiously as he circled the area where rope had been drawn across a gully, making a corral for Diablo and five other horses.

From a vantage point behind a large boulder, he could see the camp. He took in the three warriors sitting around the fire in a glance.

Apaches!

They were the dread enemies of the Comanches, the fiercest tribe of warriors, known for their cruelty to their enemies.

His gaze searched farther and he drew a deep breath of relief when he saw Johanna.

Her wrists were bound behind a sapling, and her head lolled to one side. A dark bruise marred

165

her forehead, and blood ran from a cut on her arm. Fury surged though him, and his first thought was to charge into the clearing, to draw his guns and kill the warriors. But caution bid him proceed slowly. Five horses usually meant five riders.

Which meant two were missing.

His gaze returned to the warriors. One of them tore off a strip of meat from a small carcass, probably a rabbit, hanging above the embers. Another was staring morosely into the fire, while still another held a stick in the live coals.

The Indian with the stick pulled it out and looked at the end. It smoked, but had not yet caught fire.

He said something to his companion that sent a chill through Hawkeye. They were getting ready to torture Johanna.

Pain stabbed through Johanna's head, and she groaned softly and opened her eyes. For a moment nothing registered; she was only conscious of the excruciating pain that throbbed in her temples as the light hit her eyes. She closed them quickly, waited a few seconds for the pain to ease, then slowly opened them again.

Suddenly she caught her breath and panic flowed through her. Three war-painted warriors were sitting around a campfire, their eyes on her. When she tried to move, she discovered her hands were tied behind her back. She licked her dry lips, squinting against the pain that throbbed in her temples, narrowing her eyes on the Indians who stared silently at her.

She tried to speak, but only a thick croak issued from her parched throat.

She swallowed heavily, and tried again.

"Please," she croaked from her dry throat. "Could I have some water?"

They ignored her words and began talking among themselves. One of the warrior's eyes moved boldly over her slender body. He said something to the others and laughed, and the sound sent cold chills racing down her spine.

Hawkeye, she cried silently. *Help me.*

But she knew he couldn't.

In her foolishness, she had run away from Hawkeye, a man who had surely meant her no real harm. Now, she longed for him with every fiber of her being. But, foolishly, she had not only run away from him, but taken his means of pursuing her as well.

Suddenly, one of the warriors took a burning stick from the fire. He looked at her and a wide grin spread across his face.

Please God, she prayed silently, *don't let them torture me. Let them kill me quickly.*

Her eyes were riveted to the burning stick. As though he sensed her terror, the warrior stood and came toward her, the stick held out in front of him.

Inserting a dirty hand between her neck and her clothing, he gave a mighty tug that ripped her dress and nightgown down the front, exposing the creamy swell of her breasts to his malevolent gaze.

167

Johanna clenched her teeth tightly together, determined to show no fear. But when he touched her with the point, the pain was unbearable and all her determination flowed away. As agony seared through her body, she could hear someone screaming, over and over again . . . and then, a merciful blackness overcame her.

She woke as water splashed in her face and ran down her clothing. One of the warriors stood over her, a tomahawk raised threateningly.

Her green eyes opened wide with horror.

Was he going to dismember her?

Drawing back his arm, he swung at her . . . She was conscious of a hard whack beside her and it took a moment to realize that, rather than her head, he had struck the tree behind her.

Johanna found it hard to believe that she was still breathing.

Although she knew in her heart it was useless, she struggled against the rope that bound her hands, succeeding only in chafing the fragile skin of her wrists even more.

Dread filled her soul and her green eyes searched desperately for something . . . some *one* to help her.

As her gaze swept the dense woods, a low-hanging branch moved gently in the wind.

Her gaze moved on, searching, her fear-ridden mind looking desperately for some way out. Some way to . . .

Suddenly, she looked again at the woods, narrowing her eyes on the limb that had moved. There had been something about it that wasn't quite right, but she couldn't put her finger on what it was.

She lifted her face, tilted it toward the sky . . . and, suddenly the answer came to her.

There was no wind.

Not even a slight breeze.

What had moved the branch?

Her gaze returned to the tree, zeroed in on the spot. She held her breath . . . and waited. As she watched, the limb moved again and a bronzed face appeared in a small opening. She had only a moment's glimpse before it was gone.

But it had been enough. For in that instant, that one timeless moment, she had recognized Hawkeye. Hope burst forth, sparking into a flame that burned brightly, swelling into enormous proportions.

He had come!

She didn't know how it could be possible, only that he had found her. And somehow . . . Someway, he would save her.

Rage surged through Hawkeye as he worked his way behind the tree. His chest still throbbed with the pain he had felt when the stick had burned Johanna's soft breast. The Apache dogs would die for what they had done to Johanna. He would see to it personally, and he would take great delight in their deaths.

Drawing his knife, he began cutting away the leather strips that bound Johanna's wrists together. It was in his mind to kill her attackers, but he must be sure she was free to escape in case he failed. If worse came to worse, she could make a run for Diablo while he kept the Apaches busy.

He forced back a curse as the leather bonds parted and he saw what they had done to her fragile skin. But he knew there was no time to dwell on it. He would make them pay for what they had done . . . and intended doing . . . to her.

Johanna hardly dared to breathe as she felt a tug on her bonds. Her heart beat madly against her ribcage, thrumming loudly in her ears. A moment later and her wrists were free. The ache, as she tried to move her arms, was almost unbearable.

Something hard pressed against her hand and her fingers were closed over it. It took a moment to realize Hawkeye had given her his pistol.

Her mind whirled furiously as she tried to decide what he wanted her to do. If only he could tell her, but she knew to utter one word would alert the Indian warriors.

While she stood, rigid, something shirred next to her ear. A moment later one of the Indians fell over with an arrow protruding from his back. Another arrow felled another warrior and Hawkeye appeared beside her, his eyes glowing like hot coals of fire.

"Run, Johanna," he said harshly, bounding forward to face the remaining warrior with his knife.

Johanna stared at him in confusion. Where did he want her to run?

She remained rooted to the spot as the two men struggled silently over the knife. As Hawkeye raised the knife above them, his foot tripped over a fallen branch and the two men fell heavily together. Hawkeye's body beneath the Apache's.

Johanna's eyes widened with horror as she saw blood pooling up around the two men. One of them had been stabbed, but she couldn't tell which one.

Her breath was caught in her throat as she watched the Apache warrior push himself off Hawkeye's limp body and stumble to his feet. Although his upper body was bloody, she was sure the blood belonged to Hawkeye and she swallowed hard, her chest tight with sorrow, as she raised the pistol and pointed it at the savage. Even as her finger tightened on the trigger, the warrior stumbled, his knees buckling beneath him and he slowly crumpled to the ground.

"Why the hell are you still here?" Hawkeye growled, feeling a bump on his head even as he climbed to his feet. "I told you to run. Don't you realize there are two more?"

With a curse, he grabbed her hand and pushed her behind him.

"I couldn't leave you," she choked, unable to believe he was still alive.

With a muttered curse he grabbed her wrist and pulled her along with him, half-dragging her until they reached the horses. Pushing her atop the stallion, he bounded on the back of one of the other horses and with a yell drove his mount toward the herd, sending them galloping in front of them.

Johanna could hear the Apaches behind them

and her heart thundered loudly, beating fast with fear.

The forest had never seemed so dense or close before and each branch that swayed in the breeze seemed to be a savage warrior to Johanna's mind.

That night, they camped in a small cave Hawkeye found.

"Shouldn't we keep on the move," Johanna inquired.

"No," he said. "They won't attack at night. They'll hole up somewhere and wait for first light."

"How can you be so certain?" she asked.

"Apaches believe it's bad medicine to fight at night. If a brave is killed at night, he'll never be able to find his way to the happy hunting ground. His spirit will be doomed to forever wander the land."

"Do you believe that?" she asked

He lifted his shoulders into a shrug. "Who can say what happens when we die?"

She looked at him with puzzled eyes. He was a man caught between two worlds and she wondered if he would ever fit in either one.

The fire that night was fueled by buffalo chips. Hawkeye told her they were hot and smokeless and a fire built with them could not be seen for more than ten feet. He brewed a pot of coffee and cooked a rabbit he had killed.

After they had eaten they sat together in silence. Night cloaked the land, shrouding it in darkness. Far away an owl hooted, its mellow cry blending in with the night sounds, the croaking of frogs and the sounds of the crickets in the bushes.

Hawkeye's gaze traveled over Johanna. She had mended her bodice with a thorn from a mesquite tree, using it as she would have used a pin. His eyes lifted to her face and he studied her profile, the way the firelight cast a bronzed glow across her face. She was the most beautiful woman he had ever seen. And the Apaches had thought to mar that beauty.

Remembering the cut the warrior had inflicted on her arm, his gaze lowered, narrowed on her pale skin and his eyes became puzzled.

Reaching out, he took her arm between his fingers and examined it closely. *There was no sign of a wound.*

"What's wrong?" she asked, flicking a quick glance at him.

"The cut is gone," he said, smoothing a finger-tip across her creamy flesh. His dark eyes lifted, probing hers.

"Cut?" although her voice was questioning, he sensed she knew exactly what he meant. Why was she being evasive?

"Your arm was cut," he explained gruffly. "It was bleeding. Now there's no sign of a wound."

"The blood you saw belonged to one of the Indians," she muttered, looking away from him. "I scratched him with my fingernails."

Reaching out, he pulled aside her bodice, ignoring her outraged cry, and examined the smooth skin of her left breast. Although she had been burned with a heated stick, her skin was un-marred.

"Did I imagine the burn as well?" he asked

"There is no burn." Her words came out clipped and cold. She tried to soften the effect by adding. "The stick wasn't hot enough to burn me. It only reddened the skin."

He released her, feeling completely baffled. He had been so certain she was injured, and yet, she was not. Something was not as it should be. He turned his gaze toward the flames, watching them leap and dance, as he tried to fit the pieces of the puzzle together.

After a moment, Johanna sighed, then leaned her head back against the wall of the cave.

"Why did you run away from me?" Hawkeye asked, startling her.

She turned her head toward him. His expression was as gentle as his voice, and her traitorous body quickened beneath his gaze. "Surely you already know the answer to that," she said, trying to keep her voice level. She chastised herself for melting every time he showed her a little kindness.

"No. Tell me."

She caught her bottom lip between her teeth. "Did you really think I would go with you?" she asked. "Did you really think I'd be willing to spend my life among savages like those we've just barely escaped?" Her green eyes sparkled with sudden anger. "You saw what those Indians had planned for me. They were getting ready to torture me."

"They were Apaches, Johanna. My people are Comanches."

"They were *Indians!*" she said. "As far as I'm

concerned, there's no difference in Apaches and Comanches. They're all savages."

His lips tightened with anger. "You are quick to put names to a people you know nothing about," he said.

"I learned all I wanted to know back there."

He turned his head away from her.

She was silent for a moment, then she said softly, "Hawkeye. Please take me back home."

"You have nothing to return to," he said harshly. "Or were you thinking of the good sheriff."

"No," she denied. "I wasn't thinking of him. He doesn't mean anything to me."

"You need someone to help you," he said. "A woman shouldn't live alone, Johanna."

"I like living alone," she said, her cheeks pinking slightly as she told the lie.

"Do you?" he asked softly.

Reaching out, he touched the side of her neck with tender, arousing fingers.

She swallowed hard.

"You're very beautiful, Johanna," he said in the gentlest of tones. "A woman like you is made for love."

She stared up at him, completely mesmerized, unable to stop the thrill that flowed through her at his touch.

"I knew the moment I saw you that you were going to mean trouble," he muttered.

Her breath seemed stuck in her throat as she held his gaze. "What do you mean?" she whispered raggedly.

"I've always been a loner," he said. "Even after the Comanches found me. I was adopted by the tribe and accepted as one of them, but there wasn't any one person for me . . . not anyone who belonged to me alone."

"You were adopted by the tribe?" she asked. "You're not really a Comanche?"

"I think my parents were Creole," he said gruffly. "But in every way that counts. I'm a Comanche warrior." He stared at her, a level, unblinking look that made her heart race.

She barely heard his last words. Her heart was overjoyed. He wasn't an Indian. She gave a sigh of relief.

Reaching out, he gathered her into his arms. "Does it make a difference?" he asked, his mouth hovering over hers, so close that she could feel his warm breath on her parted lips.

Did it make a difference that his people had mixed blood? Of course not. Now that she knew he wasn't one of the dreaded Comanche Indians, then nothing could make a difference.

"No," she whispered, her body hungry and aching for him. "Why should it? My people are both Irish and Scotch. Does that make a difference to you?"

He gave a low laugh. "Not the slightest," he said.

His lips found hers in the gentlest caress she'd ever known. Then they slid down to her throat and she arched it to allow him greater access.

The scent of him filled her nostrils, excited her senses.

Pushing aside the shoulder of her gown, he kissed her shoulder. As a wild savage hunger tore through her, she wound her arms around him, pulling him close against her.

His tongue touched the soft corners of her mouth, and without the slightest hesitation, her lips parted under the deepening urgency of his. This was what she wanted, what she needed. His heartbeat quickened, and she could feel his masculinity throbbing with unrestrained passion; pulsing as though it had a life of its own.

Her tongue dueled with his, tasting the inner warmth of his mouth as a golden tide of passion curled through her body. Spreading her hands over the rippling muscles of his back, she delighted in his strength.

There was a labored edge to his breathing as he pushed her down against the hard earth, his hands shoving and tugging at her gown until they rested on her bare thigh. The feel of his body, hard against her own, was doing shocking things to her. Her mind was whirling, her body almost in a torment of desire.

She drew in a sharp breath when his hands began to caress the flesh of her inner thigh. His tongue tangled with hers, probed the inner moistness and she shuddered with the intense passion that flowed through her.

He grew impatient with their clothing and moved away, stripping her garment from her, then casting his own aside.

Then he entered her and she felt as though a missing part of her had returned.

They began the age-old rhythm of love, and he carried her to heights that she had never known before, even when they made love the first time. Then, she had been an inexperienced girl; now she was a woman who knew what she wanted. And it was this man.

They floated through spirals of ecstasy until they reached the peak. And then they soared through the clouds together.

Chapter Thirteen

Johanna stirred, opened sleep-fogged eyes, blinked, then closed them again, intent on getting a few more winks of sleep. But sleep was elusive. Her bed was incredibly hard, as though it were filled with rocks.

Rocks?

Her eyes popped open again and she took in the unfamiliar surroundings.

The walls were covered with bumpy green paper. She narrowed her eyes, concentrating on one spot . . . and caught her breath.

The green paper resembled *moss*. And the walls seemed to be rock. Turning her head, she stared up at the ceiling. The *rock* ceiling.

A cave!

The sleep-clouds were swept away as memory suddenly returned. Hawkeye had found a cave and they had taken refuge in it. No wonder her bed was hard. They were sleeping on the ground.

At that moment her pillow moved beneath her head.

"Are you awake?" The husky whisper stirred the hair beside her ear.

She became aware of the delicious warmth pressed against her back, and of the arm circling her waist, holding her firmly clamped to his body.

Her lips lifted into a smile and she wriggled around to face Hawkeye. Her green eyes were tender as they met his. "Good morning," she murmured softly.

"Yes," he agreed. "It is a good morning." He pushed a silky curl away from her face and kissed the end of her nose. "A very good morning to travel."

She groaned loudly. "Must we leave right now?"

His lips touched hers with a kiss as soft as a butterfly's wings. Then, to her chagrin, he released her. "Yes," he said. "We must. We have a great distance to ride today."

Feeling a surge of disappointment, she sat up, reaching for her chemise and pantaloons. She slid the pantaloons past her legs and hips and tied the strings in a bow, then put her arms through the straps of her chemise.

Becoming aware of Hawkeye's gaze on her rounded bosom, she paused in the act of fastening the garment and met his eyes. "You're certain we must leave?" she asked mischievously. "This is your last chance."

His lips twitched. "I have a mind to make love

to you again."

She arched a dark brow, her emerald eyes widening. "Is that a promise?" she asked, leaning over to wind her soft arms around his neck.

He shook his head regretfully and unwound her arms. "No," he said firmly, putting her away from him. "We must leave now." His dark eyes became serious. "You forget the Apaches, Johanna."

A shadow crossed her face. "Do you think they're still searching for us?"

"I'm certain of it."

"How far are we from Washington?"

He reached for his buckskins. "Two days' ride," he said, pulling them up over his hips. "But it makes no difference. We aren't going there."

She paused in the act of pulling her gown over her head. *Not going to Washington?* She worked her head free from the gown and stared up at him. "If we aren't going to Washington, then where are we going?"

His eyes were level on hers. "To my village."

His village? Not the Comanche village? He couldn't mean that!

"I thought we were going to Washington-on-the-Brazos," she said, trying to keep the panic from her voice, concentrating instead on slipping her arms into the sleeves of her dress, then smoothing it down her hips.

"What made you think such a thing?"

She thought back. And could not remember one word he'd said that had led her to reach such a conclusion. "You said . . ." she faltered, stared up at him. "You're not a Comanche."

His dark eyes hardened, his lips thinned as he held her gaze. "I am, Johanna," he said harshly.

"No!" she held up a hand, as though she would physically ward off his statement. "You said—you said your parents were Spaniards. You said the Indians found you . . ."

"So they did," he said in a hard voice. "They raised me from boyhood . . . to be a Comanche warrior." His gaze was unrelenting, forcing her to hear his words. "They are my people, Johanna. My loyalties lie with them."

"Your loyalties?" She swallowed around a lump in her throat. "Are you saying you would fight with them? Against our own kind?"

"Now you have it."

"I can't believe you mean this," she said. "The Comanches killed your parents."

"No," he said. "You're wrong. Renegade white men killed them. The Comanches found me wandering beside the Brazos River. They took me in and gave me a home. They made me one of them, Johanna."

She couldn't take it all in. She refused to believe he had cast his own people aside for the sake of a tribe of savage Indians. But one look at his stony expression was all it took to convince her. He meant what he said.

Her heart thudded with dread. Where did that leave her? But she already knew the answer to that question. He meant to take her with him. He meant . . . Her eyes widened. "I heard—" She swallowed hard. "Indians take more than one wife," she whispered. "Do you have . . ." She couldn't finish the question, didn't want to hear the answer.

He took her resisting body into his arms. "I have no wife," he said softly. "You will be the only one."

"For how long?" she asked harshly, pushing against his chest, unwilling to be consoled. "How long before you grow tired of me? Before you want another woman to share your bed?"

"Hush," he said gruffly. "You are becoming upset."

"Let me go!" she said, struggling against his greater strength. "Let me go!"

"Stop it," he grated harshly, shoving her head against his chest and stroking her silky hair. "Try to understand, my love. Your place is with me. The Comanches are no more to be feared than your own people. Don't ask me to give you up. I would find it impossible."

As his words penetrated, she stopped trembling and began to relax in his arms. He had called her his love, said her place was with him. And it was. Wherever he was. The Comanches had been kind to him, had adopted him into their tribe.

The Comanches are no more to be feared than your own people, he'd said. He didn't know that she had reason to fear her own. She raised her head and looked up at him. "Are you sure they will accept me?"

Relief was in his eyes as he stared down at her. "You are my woman," he said. "They will accept you as such."

The sun had risen when they left the cave, and

yet dark shadows lingered beneath the trees. The air was cool and tasted sharp upon her tongue.

Hawkeye saddled the stallion and helped her astride, then he mounted the other horse and they rode away. It was only a short time before a crashing noise in the brush snapped her head up fearfully, but it was only an armadillo followed by two young ones.

It was midday when the attack came.

They were passing through a sunlit glade when three war-painted warriors rode out of the forest, straight toward them.

Johanna's mount reared, his hooves flailing the air and she felt herself slipping. Before she could regain her balance, the animal humped his back and came down on all fours, tossing her from the saddle like a sack of potatoes. She hit the ground with a bone-jarring thud.

Hawkeye had reacted instantly. His hand streaked to his pistol and he cleared leather faster than the eye could blink. The weapon spat flames and the nearest warrior screamed out in agony. He tumbled off the horse near Johanna and lay still.

Johanna, groggy from her fall, shuddered at the sight of the dead Indian. She was aware of the thud, thump, of fists striking flesh, knew that Hawkeye and one of the Apaches were fighting, knew also, there was another to be accounted for.

Her gaze found the rifle beside the fallen Apache and she scrabbled for it . . . almost had it in her hand when her leg was grabbed and she was dragged violently away.

She kicked out savagely, connecting with a chin.

A loud grunt of pain accompanied the action. Then fingernails were digging into her ankle as she struggled to reach the rifle again. Her fingers closed over it.

Suddenly, Hawkeye was beside her, his knife slicing toward the Indian who still held Johanna's ankle in a tight grasp. The Apache released her foot and made a dive for Hawkeye.

The two men fought desperately while Johanna lay breathless, horror-stricken. They rolled over and over, the sun glinting off the tip of the knife. Johanna screamed when it began its downward course. She heard flesh striking flesh, and then the two men were still.

A minute later, Hawkeye pushed the Apache warrior off and climbed groggily to his feet.

Johanna's heart was beating fast as she huddled on the ground. *Was it all over?*

"Are you hurt?" Hawkeye asked, his eyes on her.

She shook her head, averting her gaze from the dead Indians. Her eyes fell on the Apache warrior who stepped from the forest and loosed his arrow . . . straight toward Hawkeye.

The arrow struck his chest with a dull thunk and his knees buckled beneath him as he slumped to the ground, his eyes still on her.

"Run," he groaned. "Get away while you can."

She stared at him in horror, unable to move.

Suddenly, something moved in her peripheral vision and she turned to see the warrior bounding toward her, his knife raised high in the air, poised to strike.

"The gun, Johanna," Hawkeye gasped. "Shoot

185

him!"

She fumbled for the rifle, tried to bring the barrel up to bear on the warrior. He was too close. She rolled away, barely avoiding the warrior, aimed the rifle at his chest and squeezed the trigger.

Nothing happened. She had forgotten to cock the rifle.

She scrambled away as the warrior struck with the knife. Her actions deflected the blow, instead of entering her chest, it sliced a long streak in her arm. Before he could strike again, she had cocked the hammer and squeezed the trigger.

The weapon roared, the warrior's body was flung backward from the impact. He struck the ground with a violent thud.

Breathless, her face drained of color, Johanna turned to Hawkeye, crumpled on the ground. The arrow had struck deeply. His eyes were closed and he looked lifeless, his blood running out onto the ground around him.

She had eyes for no one but him as she dropped the weapon and crawled to his side. She didn't see the Indian with the knife in his back crawl away into the underbrush.

Chapter Fourteen

A feeling of dread swept over Johanna as she picked up Hawkeye's wrist and felt for a pulse. She was unaware of her own wound, her thoughts totally absorbed with the man she loved. She found a faint pulsebeat with her thumb, and her throat worked convulsively as she expelled a sigh of relief.

Johanna tried to separate herself from her feelings, dispassionately studying the arrow buried in his chest. The shaft had penetrated deep and it would have to come out before she attempted to heal him.

Her gaze left the arrow and fell on his pale face. Would he die before she could help him? She pushed the thought away, but it promptly returned, refusing to be ignored.

Suppose she was unable to help him? She

187

hadn't always been successful.

A picture of her mother, lying dead upon the heather, rose in her mind. Johanna had tried so desperately to save her mother but she had been too young, too uncertain, and she had failed.

"Please, God," she breathed. "Don't let me fail again. I couldn't bear to lose him now."

Swallowing around the lump in her throat, she rolled Hawkeye on his side, hoping the arrow had gone completely through.

It hadn't.

Dear God. She would either have to pull it back out or push it on through. She realized it would be hard to pull it out, and yet, if she pushed it farther into his chest, it might do even more damage.

"I don't have a choice except to pull it out," she muttered.

Gripping the arrow with her right hand, she pulled hard on it. Hawkeye groaned loudly.

Tears streamed from Johanna's eyes, flowing down her pale cheeks at the thought of causing him more pain. But she knew she had no choice. The arrow must come out and as quickly as was humanly possible.

Closing her eyes to the pain she was inflicting on the man she loved, she pulled harder on the arrow and was rewarded with a slight movement. Tears blurred her eyes and she swiped at them with the back of her hand, then commenced pulling on the arrow again. It came out an inch or two, then stopped as though something were holding it firm.

Her breath came in harsh gasps as she strained

with the effort to pull the arrow from his body. It seemed as though his muscles and tendons worked against her, trying to impede her progress. She had no way of knowing if she was doing the right thing or not, knew she had no choice except to continue.

Her eyes found his face, noticed the big droplets of sweat that had formed on his forehead. Uncertainty filled her. Was she doing him more harm than good?

"God! Don't let me hurt him," she whispered.

Then, suddenly, she felt flesh and muscle yield. The arrow came out in a warm rush of blood. Her gaze flew to Hawkeye's face. His skin had turned a pasty-gray color, and she knew, with a certainty, that she must waste no time if she was to save his life.

Sitting back on her haunches, she closed her eyes and touched the lacerated, bleeding flesh . . .

The effort of healing left Johanna weak, spent, hardly able to hold herself upright. Yet she went on until she had no strength left. Then faintness overcame her and she crumpled upon the forest floor.

Unconscious, she lay beside Hawkeye, lost to the world around her, unaware of the warrior watching, with silent awe at what he had witnessed, from the bushes nearby.

Hawkeye's eyelids fluttered softly and he groaned, stirred, then turned his head to see the inert figure of the girl beside him.

"Johanna!" His voice was sharp, anxious.

He sat up, staring at the dead warriors nearby. Had they killed her?

Anxiously, he reached for her, unaware of the watcher who crept silently away to return to his people and inform them of the girl sent by the Great Spirit to heal the people.

Hawkeye gathered Johanna into his arms. His gaze traveled over her, searching out her injuries. There was a long cut on her arm and blood flowed freely from it. But it wasn't bad enough to render her unconscious.

He placed a hand lightly on a bruise on her cheek, then ran it down her jawline. It didn't seem to be broken. His eyes narrowed on a trickle of blood near the base of her skull that he had missed. Gently, he pushed back the dark tresses and sucked in a sharp breath as he saw the jagged, two-inch gash at the base of her skull.

Laying her back on the ground, he tore a strip from her bedraggled gown and wiped at the blood. The cut would need stitches. It looked as though it was caused by a hard blow on the head. He suspected it was caused by the fall from her mount.

Knowing there was little he could to for it, he turned his attention to the slash on her arm. Blood continued to drip from the cut and he knew he must bind it before resuming the journey to his village. Otherwise, she would lose too much blood.

Tearing another strip from the hem of her skirt, he wound it tightly around the wound. Her breathing was raspy, and her eyes still closed as she lay unconscious. He felt she was gravely wounded, and the thought caused him great pain.

Suddenly, Johanna stirred and moaned softly.

Hawkeye sat back on his heels, feeling a great relief that she had come around. With her conscious, it would be easier to determine her injuries.

She moaned again, and her eyelashes fluttered open. He was sitting off to the side of her, but easily recognized the dazed look in her eyes. He remained silent, giving her time to recover her senses.

She lifted a trembling hand, touched the cut on her head, then looked at the warm blood on her fingers.

He started to reassure her, to make light of her injuries, but something about her . . . something about the way her body suddenly went still, and the way her expression became a study in concentration, held him silent.

She closed her fingers together and reached for the wound again. Then, placing her palm over the cut, she closed her eyes.

For a moment he thought she had lost consciousness, then, realized he was in error, for she seemed to be concentrating on something unnamed . . . something unseen . . . something deep within herself.

He looked at the wound again and his eyes widened as wonder and disbelief mingled furiously within him. Incredible as it seemed, the wound had actually closed. Only a shallow scratch remained to show it had ever been there. He might almost have thought he had imagined the wound had it not been for the blood drying on her skin.

How could such a thing be possible?

He had been taught by the Comanches that miracles were possible through the efforts of the Great Spirit who looked over all his people, but his white blood denied such things could happen.

And yet, he had seen it with his own eyes. His gaze fell on a blood-tipped arrow, and only then did he remember his own wound. A wound that was no longer there. Somehow, Johanna had removed the arrow and healed him. Not just once, but twice.

Johanna's lashes fluttered. She opened dazed eyes and found Hawkeye staring at her, his gaze dark and probing.

"There's nothing to fear," Hawkeye said gruffly. "You're safe now."

"The Indians?" she whispered unsteadily.

"They can't hurt anyone now," he said.

There was something about his voice. Something she couldn't quite put her finger on. He seemed to be struggling with some kind of emotion. "Are you all right?" she asked.

"Yes," he said, regarding her coolly. "I am now. What about you?"

She swallowed hard and pushed herself to her elbows, then winced with pain. Her gaze dropped to the bandage on her arm and she grimaced. "Except for the arm, everything seems fine," she said.

"Perhaps you should take care of it," he suggested softly.

Johanna felt stunned. Her gaze flew to his face, met dark eyes that seemed to see through to her very soul, dropped to his smooth, unblemished chest, before lifting to meet his gaze again.

He knew.

Silence hung heavy between them, the tension so thick it could almost be cut with a knife.

"How did you do it?" he asked.

It was a moment before she found her tongue. "D-do what?" she stuttered. "I don't know what you're talking about." Perhaps she could convince him he had imagined his wounds as she had done before. Perhaps . . .

"It won't work this time, Johanna," he declared harshly, seeming almost to guess her thoughts.

"Won't work?" she whispered. "What do you mean?"

"How did you heal my wounds?"

The words, although spoken softly, sounded like a death knell to Johanna. But she refused to give in so easily. "I-I—didn't heal—" She broke off as he continued to gaze steadily at her.

"There is no question about what you did," he said shortly. "Only of how you did it."

She felt trapped, suffocating. "I—I don't know," she said, looking everywhere but at him.

"You don't know?"

Johanna expelled her breath on a sigh. "No," she said at last. "I really don't know."

"Would you care to explain that?"

Clearing her throat of an obstruction, she said, "I can't explain," in low, uneven tones. She twisted her hands nervously together. "Don't ask me more," she begged.

"How can I not?" he asked. "You must know that what you did was impossible. And yet, I saw you do it."

Tears welled into her eyes and spilled over, trickling softly down her cheeks. Now he would be like the others. He would either fear her or he would want to use her.

"You have no need to cry," he said gruffly.

"I'm not crying," she snapped, rubbing her eyes with the back of her hand.

"Perhaps you have something in your eye, then?" His voice was gently teasing.

"Yes."

He tilted her chin up with the tip of one finger. "Like maybe a tear?"

His voice was so gentle that the tears overflowed again. He softly stroked them away with his other hand.

Then, gathering her into his arms, he lowered his head, and kissed her lightly on the lips.

A sob caught in her throat, and without another thought, her arms slid up around his neck, and her fingers wound their way through his dark hair.

He knew! her heart sang. Hawkeye knew her secret and it didn't matter. Another tear slipped down her cheek, and was quickly kissed away.

When he released her, she felt incredibly shy of him. Her innermost secret had been exposed. But he would have none of her shyness. He tilted her head, forcing her to meet his eyes.

"What are you going to do?" she asked nervously.

"Nothing," he said roughly.

"Nothing?" she repeated, trembling slightly. "You know what I am now," she whispered. "Aren't you afraid of me?"

His lips curved in amusement. "Why should I fear you?" he asked.

"People usually do." She studied him curiously "Haven't you ever heard of witches?"

He gave a shout of laughter and her green eyes glinted with anger. "What's so funny?" she asked.

"You are," he teased lightly. "Are you claiming to be a witch?"

"No!" she snapped. "I most certainly am not!"

His lips twitched. "I didn't think you were."

Her anger died away, and she eyed him soberly. "I'm glad," she said. "What happens now?"

"First, you'd better take care of that arm," he said, unwrapping the bandage and exposing the long gash. "It's still bleeding."

She knew he was right, and laid her palm across the wound. For some reason, the healing was becoming easier. A moment later, she looked up at him.

"How do you do that?" he asked, his gaze lingering on the healed flesh of her arm.

"I don't know," she said. "It . . . just happens."

He lifted his eyes to hers. "What are you, Johanna? And where do you come from?"

She looked away. "Ireland is my homeland," she

said, answering his last question first. "As to what I am . . . I'm just a woman, the same as any other."

"No," he said. "Not like any other." he was silent for a moment. Then he spoke again. "You did something to me at Washington town, didn't you? I wasn't mistaken about being so gravely wounded."

"No," she admitted softly. "You weren't mistaken. I was afraid you were going to die."

"Why did you try to hide what you had done?"

"I learned early not to trust people," she said. "We had to leave Ireland because I was different from others. As was my mother. She tried to help a neighbor, and death was her reward. She was caught away from home, accused of being a witch and stoned to death." Tears misted Johanna's eyes. "She was still alive when we found her. I tried to save her, but I was so young. I didn't know how to use my gift."

"And you do now?"

"Not entirely," she said, "but I learn more each time I use it. Just as Michael Durant suspected I would."

"Who is Michael Durant?"

"He's a doctor and head of the Durant Institute. He found out about me when I had a carriage accident outside the Institute. My injuries were severe and one of the other doctors decided they healed too fast. It was brought to Durant's attention. He uncovered my secret and held me prisoner there. He tried to force me to work for him." She clasped her hands tightly together. "My father lost his life trying to set me free."

Hawkeye stroked her silky hair. "How could a man profit from such a thing?"

"He intended to use me to heal the rich and wealthy, anyone who could afford to pay the exorbitant fee he intended to charge. He set up tests to determine how long it took before I was drained of strength."

"Poor little girl," he murmured. "The Creator gave you a wonderful gift and, because of it, you have been badly treated."

She grimaced wryly. "It taught me not to trust anyone," she said. "Michael Durant is only one of a great number of men who would use me."

"You won't have to worry any more," he said. "You'll be safe in my village. You'll be revered by all as a gift from the Great Spirit."

"Hawkeye," she said anxiously, "Are you sure they'll accept me?"

"Of course," he said. "You will be the wife of Hawkeye and the medicine woman for the people."

The medicine woman for the people.

Her eyes flickered with regret. Even Hawkeye planned to use her. But at least it wasn't for profit. She would have to be satisfied with that.

"We had best leave," he said. "Are you strong enough to make the journey?"

"Yes," she said. "I'm anxious to leave this place of death."

"As I am," he said, helping her to her feet. "Wait here while I fetch Diablo. He won't have strayed far away."

Johanna watched him move away and her eyes were filled with love for him. She didn't know what the future held in store, but as long as he was with her, she would find the strength to face whatever came.

Chapter Fifteen

The Big Thicket was comprised of totally virgin forest except for a few small meadows that existed where the soil wasn't right for trees. Southern magnolias grew to enormous size, as did sugar maples, buckeye, beeches, and pines. Forty species of wild orchids bloomed in the Thicket and roughly three hundred species of birds lived there.

It was into this setting that Johanna and Hawkeye rode late one afternoon. They traveled for hours, beneath the branches of the tall trees, through a deep thicket of woods where the sun's rays never reached, where the trees closed around and over them like a green tunnel.

At first, Johanna had marveled at the east Texas forest, exclaiming over the beauty surrounding her, but as time passed and still they traveled, weariness overcame her and she slumped back against Hawkeye's large frame.

"We are nearly there," Hawkeye consoled. "Soon you'll be able to rest."

The news didn't make her feel any better; rather, it made her nervous and her body stiffened within his encircling arm.

It was only a matter of minutes before they left the woods, broke into a clearing, and discovered the sky had darkened ominously.

Hawkeye, after casting a frowning look at the heavy gray clouds, said, "We must hurry, or else we'll be caught in the storm."

He urged the stallion forward.

The wind began to blow as their path took them up a hill that was curiously devoid of growth of any kind. Although the stallion was strong, the velocity of the wind, combined with the weight of his two riders worked against him, slowing down his progress as the hill became steeper.

Casting another look toward the angry, rolling clouds, Hawkeye dismounted, took the reins and began to lead the stallion the rest of the way. The nearer they came to the top, the harder the wind blew until Johanna thought they would surely be blown away.

She closed her eyes as the wind whipped her dark hair this way and that, seeming intent on pulling every hair from her head. Even with her eyes closed she knew when they reached the crest, for the wind grew even fiercer, howling like a thousand banshees as it whipped and tore at her clothing.

Then suddenly there was a cessation of all

movement.

Opening her eyes, she caught her breath with surprise.

They were on the downward slope and the Trinidad River stretched out like a narrow band of silver in a valley far below them. On its west bank was a long line of cottonwood trees, the branches showing white through the leaves. Sheltered among the trees was the Indian encampment—nearly fifty conical skin lodges with smoke-blackened tops.

As Hawkeye mounted behind her, she cast a look at the dark clouds in the sky. "What happened to the wind?" she asked.

"It seldom reaches the valley floor," he said, "It is a good place to stay because the mountains on both sides protect the valley from tornadoes." He smiled tenderly at her. "We have come home, Johanna."

Johanna tried to hide her fear as they began the descent into the valley. She could see the designs painted on the lodges, earth-colored drawings of animals, circles, stars, lines, bands of ocher, yellow, and black.

Thin columns of smoke drifted skyward from countless cookfires around which women dressed in deerskin dresses busied themselves. The Indians seemed unaware of their presence, undisturbed even by the storm raging only a short distance away. Children played unattended through the camp, running, laughing together . . . while copper-skinned warriors lounged near a rolled-up lodge, some repairing weapons while others were busy making new arrows.

As the stallion drew nearer, Johanna's attention was caught by the giant tepee near the center of the enormous camp. The dwelling was much larger than the others and it was her guess that it served as a council lodge.

Suddenly a dog barked, heralding their approach and it seemed for a moment as though all activity stopped as heads turned their way. Even the children stopped their play to stare at them.

Johanna flinched back against Hawkeye's chest. Her instincts told her to turn around and leave this place, to get as far away as she could.

"We have a welcoming committee," Hawkeye said.

Johanna's heart filled with trepidation; her gaze followed his and she saw even more of the savages emerge from the tepees.

As though sensing her fear, Hawkeye's arm tightened around her waist. "Don't be afraid," he said. "You're as safe here as you were in Washington town."

Was she really? she wondered. She could feel the eyes of the Indians upon her, and her throat tightened and she swallowed hard. Hawkeye seemed so certain that she would be welcomed here as his woman. But one glance at the crowd told her he was wrong. They would never accept her as one of them.

Hawkeye pulled Diablo up in front of a large, central tepee. Almost immediately the lodge flap opened and an Indian wearing buckskin breeches and moccasins stepped out of it. The man watched silently as Hawkeye slid off Diablo, then reached for Johanna.

Sensing her fear, Hawkeye smiled encouragingly at her. "This is Big Bear," he said. "Chief of the tribe." He turned to the man and greeted him in the Comanche language.

"Were you able to get the rifles?" Big Bear asked in the same language.

"Yes," Hawkeye told him. "They are well hidden until we return for them."

"That is good," the chief said, then turned his dark gaze on Johanna's bowed head. "You have brought a white captive with you. This was not a good time to do so."

Hawkeye's eyes darkened. "Johanna is no captive," he said. "She is the woman I have chosen for a wife."

Johanna stared at the ground, wishing she could understand the harsh, guttural language the two men were using. She had recognized her name and assumed that Hawkeye was explaining her presence. Even so, she could still feel the hatred in the eyes of the Comanches who surrounded her. She garnered a slight comfort from Hawkeye's nearness as he talked with the chief.

"You would take a paleface for a wife?" Big Bear asked.

"That is my intention," Hawkeye replied shortly.

"You must not do this thing," Big Bear said. "Our people will not accept her. Two moons past Lame Wolf was killed by the white-eyes. All our people share his mother's grief. If she stays, the white girl will be made to pay for the deeds of her people."

"Johanna had nothing to do with it," Hawkeye said. He felt saddened by Lame Wolf's death. The boy had only seen fifteen summers. "Are you certain it was the white-eyes who killed him?"

"Yes," Big Bear said. "We found the tracks of shod horses and the prints of the white man's boots where Lame Wolf lay. The boy was on his vision quest when the white-eyes found him. His body was mutilated and he cannot enter the happy hunting grounds."

"I am sorry this thing has happened," Hawkeye said gravely. "And I understand the feelings of my people. But Johanna is not like the other white-eyes. They have abused her badly and she can no longer live among them."

"What you say may be true. But it would be better to take her away from here. She could not live here in safety."

"Then I will go as well," Hawkeye said quietly. "She is my woman and I will keep her with me. But if we leave, the people will lose a wondrous gift."

Big Wolf turned his attention to Johanna, his gaze traveling the length of the girl as though wondering what she could possibly have that would interest him. "What kind of gift?" he asked slowly.

"The woman is a healer," Hawkeye said. "It is my belief she has been sent to us by the Great Spirit."

Big Wolf's dark eyes narrowed on Johanna, studying her in minute detail. "Come into my tepee," he said. "We will speak more about her. And we will decide."

He stepped back into his tepee.

Hawkeye looked uneasily at Johanna. He could not take her into the chief's tepee without having first been invited to do so. And neither was he willing to leave her alone with the others.

"Wait for me in my tepee," he said softly. "It's the one with the hawk on it." He pointed it out to her.

"Why aren't you coming with me?" she asked in a trembling voice.

He reached out and stroked her soft cheek, hoping to calm her fears. "Do not worry so," he said gently. "The chief has invited me into his dwelling to talk."

"C-can't I come with you?" she asked, her voice wobbling slightly. She felt terrified at being left alone with the Indians. "The—your people didn't seem to like me," she whispered.

"Go into my tepee," he repeated. "You will come to no harm. You have my word on it."

Swallowing around a lump in her throat, Johanna walked the short distance to the tepee Hawkeye had indicated, lifted the lodge flap up and stepped inside. Only then did she turn for one last look at Hawkeye. But it was too late, for he had already entered Big Bear's dwelling.

Johanna's heart dropped with a sickening thud to the pit of her stomach and she stood frozen, her eyes on the spot where Hawkeye had been. She was aware of the crowd staring at her, and each face seemed to regard her with malevolent eyes.

Hurriedly, she dropped the flap and moved farther inside the dwelling. She tried to get her mind off the Comanches who waited outside by concentrating on her surroundings.

She found the tepee surprisingly roomy. It was clean, and the air was freshened by the use of fragrant sage. There was a fire pit in the center of the dwelling that could be used for heat and light as well as cooking when the weather was too cold for cooking outside.

Several skins hung from the lodge poles. While weapons were stored near the entrance.

She had barely sunk down on a folded buffalo robe before her worst fears were suddenly realized. The flap was flung open abruptly and a woman with cropped black hair, her face mottled with rage, entered.

Before Johanna could react, fingers wrapped around her wrist. The woman seemed to have the strength of ten men as she dragged the panic-stricken girl to her feet and pulled her outside to face the angry crowd.

As though encouraging the woman's madness, black clouds boiled in the sky, turning the afternoon nearly as dark as night. The wind howled and lightning ripped through the heavens, while thunder reverberated across the land. The faces of the Indians surrounding her seemed to echo the fierce tempest that threatened and Johanna swallowed hard, trying to still her heart that was suddenly pounding with dread.

Another crack of thunder sounded and it seemed to act as a catalyst, for suddenly, one of the Indian women reached out and grabbed a handful of Johanna's hair, giving it a sharp yank. Tears of pain stung Johanna's eyes but she clamped her lips tightly together, determined to utter no sound.

An old hag in front of Johanna reached out a gnarled hand and pinched her hard on the arm. Johanna tightened her lips and backed away from her. Then hands reached out, pushing and pulling at her. Feeling as though she couldn't breathe, Johanna struck out wildly. The peaceful scene of a few hours ago had exploded into a madhouse.

Suddenly, the Heavens opened up and released their fury. The rain came down in torrents, driven by fiercely gusting winds, and pandemonium broke loose. Johanna found herself lifted off her feet as several of the Indians carried her away from the tepee where Hawkeye lived.

"Hawkeye!" she screamed, but his name was carried away on the wind.

Terrified shrieks escaped her lips, but she had waited too long to cry for help and her cries seemed to amuse the Indians. The ones nearest her grinned widely.

Suddenly a roar of rage stopped the Indians. They fell silent, their tormenting fingers stilled. Johanna found herself dropped to the ground in a crumpled heap.

"What is the meaning of this?" Big Bear asked angrily as Hawkeye hurried to the trembling girl. "This woman belongs to Hawkeye. He left her in his dwelling."

"She is a paleface, a captive," the woman who

had started the trouble replied. "Her kind killed my son." A chorus of angry mutters accompanied the woman's words.

"The woman is not responsible for what the other white eyes did," the chief said. "The woman agreed to come with Hawkeye. He believes she was sent to us by the Great Spirit."

"The Great Spirit would only send a white-eyes to us for a sacrifice," the woman said. "My son is dead. He can not find his way to the happy hunting grounds."

His dark brows lowered in a fierce frown. "Do you claim to know the purpose behind the Great Spirit's will?" he asked, turning hard eyes on the squaw.

Her eyes immediately fell to the ground. "No, my chief," she mumbled.

Big Bear raised both hands. "Listen, my people," he said. "Hawkeye tells me the woman is a healer." Several heads turned to look at Johanna. "She has been sent by the Great Spirit. But there are those who would take her from us if they knew she was here. Not only the white-eyes but other tribes as well. If we are to keep her with us, we must keep silent about her. Hawkeye has told me he will take her for a wife. That is the way everyone will know her. She is to be spoken of in no other fashion."

The crowd shifted uneasily. There were low murmurs of discontent but no one dared speak out against their chief. They had heard his words, but Hawkeye knew many were disbelieving. Only time would prove Johanna's worth.

He led her away to the tepee that bore his mark.

Johanna threw herself into Hawkeye's arms as he closed the tepee flap behind them. "They hate me," she whispered shakily. "I should never have come here."

"Don't say that," he said, lifting her chin and forcing her to meet his eyes. His gaze was hard, troubled, as it rested on her fine features. "Give them time to know you."

"Time?" she asked. "Time won't make a difference." She turned away from him, sinking wearily down onto the sleeping mat that was padded with a bed of moss and pine boughs. He was asking too much of her. She couldn't live here among these savages. How could he even expect it of her?

Dropping to a crouching position beside her, he smoothed her dark curls away from her face. "You belong with me, Johanna. Nothing can change that."

His gaze fell on a bloody scratch on her arm and he swore softly. "They hurt you," he said.

She ignored his words. "Can't we live among my people?" she asked desperately. "They've already accepted you as one of them. And you really are. You don't belong here any more than I do."

He lifted his head to stare at her. "Don't say that, Johanna," he said sternly. "The Comanches are my people. I could never be happy living among the whites." His voice softened as he stoked her arm caressingly. "Be patient, love. Give my people time and they will come to love you as I do."

"You're wrong," she said sadly. "They will never

accept me. Please take me back to Washington."

"Don't ask such a thing of me," he said. "You belong to me. I won't let you go."

Feeling a desperate yearning to be held in his arms, she reached out for him and he gathered her close against him.

"Don't talk of leaving me," he said gruffly. "We'll work things out here. There was a reason my people reacted the way they did. A young boy was found dead. Killed by white men. They thought only to take revenge for his death."

"I didn't kill him!" she sobbed.

"Shushhh," he said gently. "We will sort it all out later." His lips found hers, soothing away the hurt. Then he held her close until she fell asleep.

Johanna moaned softly, in the grip of a nightmare. She was locked away in a small room that was empty except for a bed. She heard voices raised in anger and recognized one of them as her father's.

"Da!" she called, running to the door and pounding on it. "Da! I'm here! Please let me out!"

"Johanna!" The cry was anguished. A scuffling noise sounded nearby and a shot rang out.

Her body shook as she put her ear against the door. "Da?" she whispered. "Da! Are you there?"

There was only silence.

"Da!" she shrieked. "Where are you?"

Something heavy was being dragged, and she knew that her father was dead.

Then Michael Durant was there. Lifting her

hands to his lips, he kissed them softly and smiled at her. "Mustn't hurt those precious hands, dear," he murmured. "They're worth more than gold."

"Where's my father?" she demanded. "What have you done with him?"

"I had to kill him, Johanna." His voice sounded reasonable, and he turned her hands this way and that, searching for the slightest injury to them.

At that moment his face wavered, became indistinct as the scene changed. Now she was in a graveyard, kneeling before her father's grave, it was moving back and forth, as though rising and swelling with the waves in the sea . . . The headstones had become wagons rolling across the prairie.

The Comanches swooped down on them, brandishing tomahawks and spears. An arrow struck Frau Hoffman in the chest and Johanna was lifted and carried aloft by naked savages while the wind shrieked and howled around them.

"Da!" she screamed. "Help me!"

"Wake up, Johanna," her father said. "You're dreaming."

She opened her eyes to find Hawkeye leaning above her.

"Are you all right?" he asked. "You were crying out for someone."

"I had a nightmare," she said, shivering.

Hawkeye wrapped his arms around her, pulled her close against him and lowered his face until his cheek was touching hers. "Tell me about it," he said softly.

She opened her mouth and the words spilled

out. She told him about the nightmare, then about Durant and his experiments. She told him about her escape, and then she told him about her mother's death and her sisters left behind in Ireland, because once she got started, she couldn't seem to stop. And all the time she talked, he gently stroked her back, easing away her tension until she finally fell silent.

"Poor little girl," he murmured, his voice unusually deep and gruff. "You've been through so much. But you're no longer alone. I'll take care of you now."

Johanna found her fears lulled by the soothing tones of his voice. Her body ceased its trembling and she slowly became aware of the sheer maleness of him. Her lips brushed his chest in the fleetest of caresses. Then, opening her mouth, she tasted the sweetness of his flesh with the tip of her tongue.

She was stunned by his response.

His body hardened and he caught his breath sharply. His shaft became hard and seeking as his hand spread over her flat stomach, moving downward until it brushed against the feathery softness between her thighs.

Her body trembled beneath his touch, her thighs parted as his shaft sought the source of her womanly heat.

An intolerable ache began to burn inside her and she felt a sweet anguish, that gave way to fierce craving to feel his spear buried inside the sheath of her body. His lips moved against hers, his tongue snaking out to slide over hers. He cupped the mound of her womanhood, allowing his fingers to settle in the moistness within. Then he began to stroke her gently.

She whimpered and writhed, her body bucking beneath his hand, as he stroked the fires of passion that burned deep inside her body. She was ready when he entered her, and they climbed together, reaching unimaginable heights until they reached the peak and went soaring together among the clouds.

Chapter Sixteen

Johanna woke to the sound of children's laughter. Opening her eyes, she found a young girl with brilliant blue eyes watching her. The girl's golden hair was braided, the ends bound with the same soft deerhide that her dress was made of.

Johanna, aware of her nakedness beneath the blanket, tucked it securely beneath her arms and pushed herself up on her elbows. "Hello," she said softly. "Who are you?"

"They call me Naduah," the girl said, ducking her head shyly.

"Naduah?" Johanna repeated. "What a pretty name."

"It means Keeps-Warm-With-Us," Naduah said.

Johanna wondered how Naduah came to be with the Comanche tribe. Her golden hair and blue eyes told of her parentage. Had she been taken from a settlement?

A movement beyond the girl's shoulder caught Johanna's eyes. In the darkened shadows of the tepee, she saw a dark-haired girl, dressed in the same manner as Naduah, watching her with curious eyes.

Johanna pushed her tousled hair from her face and sat up on the sleeping mat. Her eyes returned to Naduah, "Did you come to wake me?" she asked.

Naduah nodded. "Hawkeye told me to bring you this," she said, handing Johanna a hide-wrapped package.

Upon opening it, Johanna found a doeskin dress, soft, velvety, fringed, worked, and embroidered with porcupine quills. The dress smelled sweetly of wild sage. Along with it were a pair of neatly fitting moccasins and a pair of fringed leggings.

"It's beautiful," Johanna exclaimed. "I've never seen such exquisite work before." She lifted her eyes to Naduah. "Hawkeye wants me to wear this?" she asked.

Naduah's brilliant blue eyes were shining as though she had caught some of Johanna's excitement.

Johanna pulled the dress over her head while the two girls sat watching. "Where is Hawkeye?" she asked, her words muffled by the dress.

"He went hunting," Naduah said.

After Johanna had smoothed the dress over her hips, Naduah handed her a small leather pouch. "I brought a comb and some bear grease for you," she said.

"Bear grease?" Johanna opened the pouch and wrinkled her nose in disgust at the rancid smell which came from the bag. "What's it for?" she asked the girl.

Lifting a small hand to her mouth, Naduah stifled a giggle. "To rub in your hair, of course," she said.

"My hair?" Johanna's eyes went to the girl's golden hair, suddenly realizing the same odor was coming from her braids. "You want me to put this stuff in my hair?"

"Yes," the girl said. "It makes your hair smooth and shiny . . . like mine." She picked up one smooth braid and held it out for Johanna to see. "It keeps the mosquitoes away too," the girl added solemnly.

Johanna's lips twitched. She could certainly understand why. No self-respecting mosquito would want to come near such a vile-smelling mixture. There was no way she was going to put the bear grease in her hair, but she tried to soften her refusal for the girl's benefit. "It was thoughtful of you to bring it to me," she said. "But I think just combing my hair will be enough today."

Naduah handed Johanna a comb carved from a bone. "Do you want me to comb your hair?" she asked shyly.

Sensing it was what the girl wanted, she nodded her head. Naduah bent to her work, tugging the comb through Johanna's unruly curls.

Johanna waited until her hair lay curling about her shoulders before she asked. "Do you know when Hawkeye will return?"

Naduah shook her head. "Do you want me to show you where to fill your water jar?"

Johanna looked uneasily at the tent flap. She felt nervous about leaving the dwelling. "Perhaps I should wait until Hawkeye returns," she said.

Naduah seemed aware of her feelings. "It's all right," she said. "The people will not harm you. Big Bear told them you were sent by the Great Spirit." Her blue eyes widened perceptibly. "No one else has seen him except the medicine man. What does he look like?"

"I don't know," Johanna said. "I haven't seen him either."

Puzzlement flickered across the girl's face and Johanna quickly changed the subject.

"Who is your friend," she asked.

"Cactus Wren," Naduah replied. "They sent her to teach you the ways of the Comanche. But she doesn't speak your language so they sent me as well."

Wondering who *they* were, Johanna watched the girl rise and come forward at the mention of her name. Only then did she realize she had been wrong about the girl's age, for her softly rounded breasts said she had reached her womanhood. Johanna judged her to be around fourteen or fifteen years old.

Her lustrous dark eyes were shy as she spoke softly to the young girl in a language unknown to Johanna. Comanche, she surmised.

"She says we must hurry and show you how to care for your man for we have our own work that

217

must be done."

"I'm ready," Johanna said, although she wasn't really. She didn't want to step foot outside the dwelling, afraid of what waited for her there.

But she needn't have worried. No one paid them any mind as they went to the spring to fetch fresh water. Then the girls showed her how to build a fire outside the dwelling and where to find the food stored inside the tepee. The leather bags, Johanna was told, were called parfleches. They held dried foods, sweet potatoes, dried berries, mesquite beans, dried meat, onions and fruit. They opened one bag and found it contained pemmican, put up for the coming winter. Naduah explained it was a mixture of pulverized dried meat, berries, and wild plums and bear grease. The mixture, which reminded Johanna of mince-meat, was packed in the small parfleches and sealed with melted tallow to make the packages airtight.

"You must learn to do this for Hawkeye," Naduah said. "He will need much food for the winter to come."

There seemed so much to learn, but she was assured the two girls would be willing to help all they could. When Naduah said they must leave, Johanna asked the question that had been bothering her.

"Is Naduah the only name you have?"

"I used to have another one," the girl said. "Before I came here."

"Do you remember it?"

She nodded. "It was Cynthia Ann," she said.

"Was that all of it?"

Naduah's brow wrinkled in thought for a long moment, then, "Parker!" she blurted out. "It was Cynthia Ann Parker."

Cynthia Ann Parker!

The girl who had been taken from Parker's Fort two years ago! Johanna's emerald eyes flared. Hawkeye must know about the girl. Might even have helped capture her. She intended to confront him when he returned. She would make him return the girl to her family.

If she had any family left. Johanna couldn't be certain she did. But she seemed to remember something about an uncle who was searching for the girl.

"Would you like to go home to your family?" she asked gently.

Panic filled Cynthia Ann's eyes. "Go home?" she repeated. "I am home. I live with Takes-Down-The-Lodge." It was as though she refuted any life before her life with the Comanches. As though anything else was too painful to remember.

"Have you been badly treated, Cynthia Ann?"

"My name is Naduah!" the girl said, her blue eyes flashing angrily. "It's the only name I have now. And no one would dare to treat me badly. I belong to Wanderer." The last was spoken almost proudly.

Johanna felt troubled as she watched the two girls leave. The girl whom the Comanches called Naduah must be returned to her white family. She couldn't, in all conscience, leave her to the mercy of the savages.

When Hawkeye returned, she broached the subject. His reaction was totally unexpected. "What is this?" he demanded harshly. "I am barely in my home before I am beset with threats."

Her green eyes widened. "I didn't threaten you," she said. "I just asked you to help her."

"Naduah does not need help," he said, seating himself on the sleeping mat and crossing his legs. "Has she said otherwise."

"No, but —"

"She is Comanche," he said, cutting her off. "She is treated very well here. And she is none of your business, Johanna, so keep out of it." He looked toward the cooking pot. "I am hungry, woman. Serve me my meal."

Her lips tightened indignantly, but she dished up a bowl of stew and handed it to him. "Does my master require anything else?" she asked sweetly.

"I require a little less vinegar from you," he growled. "Now sit down and eat with me."

"I'm not hungry," she muttered.

"Very well." Ignoring her, he began to eat his food.

Johanna felt outraged. Although she had told him she wasn't hungry, she was, in fact, absolutely starved, having eaten nothing since yesterday noon. And even then, it had only been a meal of dried meat.

But she wasn't about to let him know.

As though to prove her false, her stomach took that moment to growl loudly. She looked up in time to see the grin spread across his face and fury surged through her.

220

How dare he find her amusing.

She stood up and started toward the entrance.

"Where are you going?" he demanded.

"I'm going outside for some fresh air," she snapped.

"Not until you have finished serving me."

She looked back over her shoulders. "I have finished," she said shortly.

"But I'm not finished eating."

Her emerald eyes glittered. "If you want more, then get it yourself," she muttered.

"A man does not wait on himself when there is a woman to do it for him."

"Well," she sputtered. "This woman doesn't wait around for any man's pleasure."

She pushed aside the flap and started to step outside, but she never made it. Instead, he was on her in a flash and dragging her back inside the dwelling. She found herself tossed onto the sleeping mat and staring up at him with wide eyes.

Suddenly, unreasonably, her eyes filled with tears and she turned her head away so he wouldn't see.

"Now what is this?" he asked, gripping her chin and forcing her to face him. Lifting a finger, he gently wiped her tears away. "Why are you crying, little one. Surely you don't fear me."

"No," she whispered. "Not you. It's the others."

"The others?" He looked toward the tepee flap as though he would find the answer there. "Did something happen while I was gone?"

She shook her head.

"Then why?"

"They kidnapped Cynthia—" She broke off, then corrected herself. "—Naduah, and murdered her family." Her eyes flew to his. "Were you with them when it happened? Did you—" She couldn't finished the sentence, suddenly didn't want to know.

He pulled her against him and held her close, smoothing her hair with one big hand. "No. I wasn't there," he muttered. "But you must realize, Johanna, there is a war between our people. It is not of our making, and yet, it still exists. And where there is war, people get hurt. It is the way of things."

Johanna didn't want to think about such things, and turned the conversation back to the girl. "Naduah is so young," she said. "Please, Hawkeye. Make them send her home. I know you can do it."

"She is home, love. You must realize that. I wouldn't have sent her to you had I known it would make you unhappy. I thought you would feel better to see how happy Naduah was here. I thought it would help you adjust." His dark eyes probed hers. "Couldn't you see that she was happy?"

"I understand that she thinks she's happy. But how can she possibly be? This life is so foreign to her nature. She's not a savage, Hawkeye. Like me, her blood is white."

Instantly, she knew she'd said the wrong thing, because Hawkeye's body stiffened.

"Is this your way of telling me you can't be happy here?" he asked.

"It wasn't," she muttered against his neck. "But it's true I want to go home."

"You would leave me?"

"I don't want to leave you," she admitted.

"This is my home, Johanna," he said sternly. "And it will be yours as well. After we are married, you will forget all your fears and in time, like Naduah, you will be happy here." He pulled her upright. "Now stop this nonsense and eat with me." He smiled coaxingly at her. "I don't like eating alone."

She allowed herself to be coaxed into eating and afterward, they lay on the mat together and made love. But Johanna's fears lingered on, long after he slept.

Chapter Seventeen

Johanna slept late the next morning. When she finally woke, she was alone in the tepee. She barely had time to wonder where Hawkeye had gone when a scratching at the flap warned her of a visitor. Reaching for her dress, she pulled it over her head and smoothed it down her body before hurrying to raise the lodge flap.

Instantly, a smile widened her lips. "Naduah!" she exclaimed, stepping aside to allow the girl entry. "How nice of you to visit me."

"I came earlier," Naduah said. "But you were still sleeping. Hawkeye wants me to help you prepare for tonight."

"What happens tonight?" Johanna asked.

"Didn't he tell you?" The girl's blue eyes lit with mischief. "Maybe he wants to surprise you," she said.

224

"Surprise me with what?" Johanna asked suspiciously.

"If I told you, it would be no surprise," Naduah replied.

Johanna wondered what Hawkeye had in store for her. "Is the surprise something I'm going to like?" she asked.

"I think so," she said, a smile tugging at her lips.

Although Johanna tried to find out more information, Naduah refused to say more on the subject. She stayed with Johanna throughout the day while a parade of women trooped in and out of the dwelling.

The women brought dresses, shawls, rings, bracelets, leggings, and moccasins with them. They dressed her splendidly, braided her hair and painted red dots on her cheeks. All the while, Johanna could hear the sounds of laughter and bustling activity through the thin buffalo hide walls.

Hawkeye had remained noticeably absent during the day, and had it not been for Naduah's presence, Johanna would have been petrified, feeling they were dressing her for a sacrifice. But the girl kept assuring her that she would like the surprise, so she curbed her fears and used the time to learn more about the girl and her life with the Comanches.

The shadows were lengthening when Naduah left her with an admonishment to remain where she was until Hawkeye came for her. She closed the flap on the tepee as she left, leaving Johanna in near darkness.

Then the drums began to beat.

Thrum, thrum, thrum,-thrum. Thrum, thrum, thrum-thrum.

Her pulse began to race as the drums picked up speed. Something was going to happen and she wasn't certain she was ready for it.

A moment later the lodge flap lifted and Hawkeye entered, dressed splendidly in beaded and fringed buckskin and looking every inch a Comanche warrior.

Taking her hand, he led her to the crowd of people who sat in a circle around a central fire, then motioned for her to sit down beside him.

"What is happening?" she asked, her voice almost hushed.

"It is our wedding night," he answered solemnly. "Our people are gathered to celebrate with us."

Her breath caught, and her green eyes rounded with surprise. "Our wedding night?" she repeated.

He nodded his dark head and said, "Now hush and listen to the drums tell of our love for each other."

Although she felt terribly conspicuous, her eyes smiled into his. A warrior stood up and began to dance around the circle. Almost immediately he was joined by other men who soon lost themselves in the music of the drums.

A wild pig had been killed and roasted over a spit. They were served chunks of meat by the women of the tribe, and never had anything tasted so delicious to Johanna. The festivities lasted well into the night and the hour was late when Hawkeye decided it was time for them to leave the others.

Excitement flowed through Johanna's veins and she stared into his dark eyes, warm with a promise of what was to come.

She was surprised when the stallion was brought to him. After lifting her astride the animal, he mounted behind her and they rode out of the village into the darkness beyond.

They had only gone a short distance when Hawkeye pulled the stallion up. The pale light of the moon beamed down on a dwelling festooned with flowers. Hawkeye pulled Johanna into his arms and carried her inside.

"Where are we?" she asked.

"This is our honeymoon bower," he said huskily. "We will stay here for several days to be alone with each other."

Johanna had no quarrel with that. She lifted her face for his kiss.

Hawkeye undressed her slowly, until Johanna stood before him in all her nakedness.

A flame began to burn in his dark eyes and he stared hungrily at her.

When he started to remove his clothing, she reached out and stopped him. "Let me?" she whispered.

His movement stilled, his expression showing his surprise. She had never offered to help him undress before, had even tried to hide her nakedness from him. It was as though all inhibitions had been lifted from her when he claimed her as his bride.

Slowly, she unfastened his buckskin shirt, her fingers fumbling at first, then becoming steadier as they progressed. Slipping the garment over his head, she pressed her lips softly against his. Without giving him time to respond, she moved lower, scattering butterfly kisses across his chest, down his midriff, to the top of his trousers.

She paused only a moment, casting a glance at him with slumbrous eyes, then unfastened the trousers and slid them down his hips. When her lips touched the flat planes of his stomach, he sucked in a sharp breath, and Johanna felt the reaction in his body instantly. His manhood swelled to enormous proportions, making his buckskins pull taut against his hips.

Her lips twitched, and her eyes twinkled as she struggled with the trousers. She paused, opening her mouth slightly to place a wet kiss against his silky flesh.

He began to swear beneath his breath and his hands worked feverishly with the trousers, pushing them farther down his hips, past his protruding manhood.

Laughing softly, she reached for him again, but he would have none of it. With his trousers down around his ankles, he fell on top of her, carrying her to the pallet and burying his mouth against the silky skin of her neck.

His naked body against hers was doing wild things to her body and as he struggled with his trousers, trying to kick them away from his ankles, his movements lit a flame in her body.

"Don't," she whispered, her voice a mixture of

laughter and desire.

"Don't what?" he said, finally succeeding in ridding himself of the confining trousers and spreading his long body out on top of hers. "Just feel what you did to me," he growled, pressing himself hard against her.

"I feel it," she whispered, sliding her arms around his neck. "Now what are you going to do with it?"

With a low growl, he showed her, prying her legs apart with a knee, then plunging deep into her body.

She sucked in a sharp breath, feeling wave after wave of pleasure sweep over her. When he began to move in the age-old rhythm of love, she moved with him until they reached their fulfillment together and lay shuddering in the aftermath of love.

Johanna woke next morning, her lips stretched into a slow, curving smile, her eyes twinkled with mischief as she stared at the man beside her.

She couldn't remember when she had been so richly, gloriously happy.

She wriggled her toes and beamed happily up at the hide ceiling. So this was what love was all about. This feeling of being one with your mate. She wanted to shout aloud with joy. She had never dreamed such happiness existed . . .

Turning on her side, she caressed his naked form with her eyes. She remembered the moment they had awakened simultaneously and reached for each other. Where had he found the strength to continue so many times?

Her eyes sparkled like emeralds as laughter bubbled up and escaped her lips. He was insatiable. But then, so was she. Her gaze dropped to his bare chest, to the heavy cross hanging around his neck. Where had it come from? she wondered. Her gaze dropped lower and lower, until she saw the way his manhood had hardened, then her eyes flew to his face to find him watching her.

She blushed wildly.

"Do you like what you see?" he asked softly.

She nodded her head.

"Come here," he said, pulling her into his arms and shoving his body against hers.

She couldn't believe he had the strength to make love to her again, but he was so intent on proving it to her, she had no time to remark on it.

Later, after they had eaten, they walked through the forest together. Hawkeye stopped beside a clear stream and carved their names on a cottonwood tree. Surprised, she asked him who had taught him to spell. He told her about the trapper who had lived with them when he was a child.

"He taught me how to read and write and how to cipher numbers. He lived with us for three years or better," Hawkeye said. "It was good he taught me so much about the ways of the white men. It enabled me to go among them without being suspected."

A shadow crossed her face. She tended to forget the differences in their upbringing.

Sensitive to her feelings, he tilted her chin,

forcing her to look at him. "Let us not speak of things that make us sad," he said. "This is a happy time for us. The day will come when we will be unable to shut the world out."

She heard the sadness in his voice and raised herself on tiptoes, pressing her lips firmly against his. "Let's go swimming," she said.

Before he could answer, she whirled away from him, lifted her dress over her head and tossed it across a fallen log. Then she stood before him in all her naked glory.

When he reached for her, she laughed and made a dash for the stream. She paused only long enough for him to shed his clothing, then dove, straight as an arrow into the cool water.

They splashed and played together beneath the sun until they were tired. Then they left the water and he lay her down on the forest floor and made love to her.

Johanna's happiness increased as the days passed swiftly by. To her mind, their time together was near idyllic. She was amazed at the depth of love she felt for this man, Hawkeye, her husband, and she wanted nothing more than to spend the rest of her life by his side.

Hawkeye pampered her outrageously, giving in to her every whim. They swam and played together beneath the warm sun during the daylight hours and at night their bodies melded comfortably together, giving them both the feeling they were fated to be lovers.

He made her a bracelet of turquoise, painstakingly drilling the holes with the tip of his knife and fastening them together with narrow strips of rawhide.

When they weren't making love, they spent long hours talking, learning about each other. He told her all he remembered of the day the Comanches had found him. Of the fire that gutted the small house, the gunshots and his parents' blood on his clothing, told her how frightened he'd been when the Indians found him wandering beside the Brazos River. How they had named him for the river where he was found.

"They called you Brazos?" she interrupted.

He nodded his dark head. "I kept the name until I went on my vision quest," he said. "Then I became known as Hawkeye."

He continued talking, telling her about the hawk he had seen on his vision quest, telling her things that he had never told anyone before, wanting her to know everything about him, for he knew without a doubt that he had fallen in love with her completely, irrevocably.

And he felt she returned that love.

There was nothing to distract them from one another, not even the need to cook. Each morning when they rose there was a fresh basket of food in front of the tepee. When she saw it the first morning, she asked Hawkeye where it came from.

"The women of the village prepared it for us," he said. "It is their way of saying you are welcome here."

She looked doubtful.

"It is true," he said. "In time, they will come to love you as I have from the moment I set eyes on you."

"That long?" she asked, her lips quirking in a grin. "You loved me even when you found me with a sprained ankle?"

His dark eyes were solemn as he nodded. "Even then I loved you, little one."

She raised her face for his kiss and he lowered his head obligingly. After a moment he raised his head and, softly putting his hand to her face, he held her chin between his fingers. "You're beautiful," he said, and his voice was full of tenderness. "I never dreamed I would find anyone like you, so beautiful, so brave."

"Brave?" she questioned. To her mind, she was the world's greatest coward.

"Yes," he said firmly. "Brave. You have more courage than any woman I have ever met. Twice you have left your home to make a new life for yourself in a strange land. And yet, never once have I heard you complain. Even that time in Washington town when you were so frightened you never asked for any help." Suddenly he frowned. "You never told me what happened to frighten you so much."

"I saw one of Durant's men getting off the stage. I thought he had seen me and would tell Durant where I was."

The muscles in his face flexed with emotion. "And you did not trust me to help you?"

"I couldn't trust anyone," she said. "My parents taught me early on that the secret must always be kept." A dark cloud settled in her eyes. "Why did you leave me in Washington town?" she asked. The hurt she had felt was in her voice for him to hear.

He felt as though a knife had twisted in his stomach. Drawing her against him, he caressed her shining tresses. "Not because I wanted to," he said gruffly. "I had no choice except to go."

"Why?"

His dark eyes probed her green ones, wondering how he could make her understand? "I bought some rifles from the two men who ambushed me," he said. "I had to follow the trail before the rifles were out of my reach."

"Did you find the men?"

He nodded. "I found them."

Something about his voice had her inquiring, "What did you do?"

"I killed them."

A cold chill swept over her.

As though sensing her feelings, he tilted her chin. "The rifles were important, Johanna. Many lives were at stake."

"Was it necessary to kill them?"

"Yes." His voice was flat. "It was necessary."

"Did you retrieve the rifles?"

"They are well hidden until I can return for them." He pulled her into his arms. "There are things I must do that you won't like, my love. But they are necessary."

"Why do you need the rifles?" she asked in a small voice.

"Must I explain?"

234

"No," she said, looking away from him. "You don't need to explain." She knew without being told they would be used against the Comanches' enemies. Her people. How could she turn a blind eye to such actions? And yet, how could she stop it?

"Listen to me, Johanna," he said gruffly, tilting her chin and forcing her to meet his eyes. "I know what you're thinking. And if I could, I would have things differently. If I hadn't taken the rifles, they would have been used against my people."

"And now that you have them, they'll be used against mine."

Suddenly, she wished they had never started this conversation. And apparently he felt the same, for he suggested they go for a swim. She quickly agreed and followed him up the path to the pool where they spent most of the daylight hours. Johanna knew she must find a way to accept the situation between them. The Comanches were trying to accept her as one of them and Hawkeye had made it plain he would live nowhere but with the Indians. If she was to find happiness with him, then she must accept his people as her own.

Chapter Eighteen

All too soon the honeymoon was over and they returned to the village. As they made their way through the camp, Johanna spied an old man sitting in front of a tepee with many symbols painted on it. His face was weathered, the wrinkles radiating out from the corners of his eyes. He was the oldest man Johanna had ever seen.

His withered body was covered with many skins, worn like shawls, and a skin pouch was draped around his neck, along with several necklaces made of bone and teeth. She was greatly uncomfortable as they rode past, for his eyes gleamed with something like hatred as he stared at her.

"Who is that?" she asked Hawkeye.

"He's the shaman," He answered. "The medicine chief."

She shivered. "I don't think he likes me," she muttered.

Hawkeye didn't answer for a moment. When he did, his words did not relieve her mind. "He has been our medicine chief for many years," he said. "He may resent you at first. But there is no need to worry," he added hurriedly. "Even he will not go against the words of our chief."

It was that night that he told her he was leaving the next morning. "Leaving?" she whispered. "Do you mean to hunt?"

"No, Johanna," he said. "I'm going after the rifles."

"How long will you be gone?" she whispered.

"A while," he answered evasively. "But you'll be safe here at the village."

She clutched his arm tightly. "I don't want to stay here alone," she said. "Take me back to Washington until you come back."

"I can't do that, Johanna," he said, trying to speak calmly. "By now that sheriff knows I stole you away. My life would be worthless if I returned there."

She shook her head in denial. "No," she protested. "I'll tell Eli that I left on my own. He won't do anything."

"Even if it were safe, I wouldn't take you," he growled. "You belong here with me. My people will keep you safe from harm."

"How can you be certain of that?" she flared. "They don't even like me."

There was pain in his eyes when he looked at her. "I have to go," he said heavily. "Don't make

237

the leaving hard."

"Don't you care that I'm frightened?"

"I care," he muttered, pulling her close against him. "But your fears are needless. You are one of us now. You won't be alone," he coaxed gently. "Naduah and Cactus Wren will keep you company. They will teach you our language."

She stiffened with resentment. He sounded like a parent coaxing a willful child. "I'm not a child," she said coldly. "And I don't like being treated like one."

"Then don't act like one," he said abruptly.

Her lips thinned and she turned away from him, her back stiff with resentment. Her anger stayed with her until they retired for the night. Then, at the thought of him leaving her on the morrow, she wrapped her arms around him and held him close against her.

The next morning, Johanna watched her husband mount the black stallion and ride out of the village. He was accompanied by Sky Walker and six other warriors. Johanna watched them leave with dread for the coming days. She knew nothing of the Comanche language, could communicate with no one in the village except Naduah. And she was just a child.

When Johanna could no longer see Hawkeye, she entered their dwelling, threw herself on the sleeping mat and gave way to her tears.

But she wasn't allowed to grieve long. As Hawkeye had promised, Naduah and Cactus Wren arrived to keep her company. During the days to come, they became regular visitors, teaching her

238

much about the Comanche tribe and their legends. And they began to teach her the language of the Comanche. In the beginning the lessons often dissolved into fits of giggles as Johanna tried to pronounce the unfamiliar words.

Although she got on well with the two girls, her relationship with the other women remained the same. They weren't exactly unfriendly, and yet, they kept their distance, as though they were reserving their judgment about her. One day she expressed her concern to Naduah.

"Don't worry about them," the girl said. "They will do you no harm. I overheard them talking. They are mostly afraid of you because Hawkeye said you came from the Great Spirit."

"I don't want them to fear me," Johanna replied. "Neither do I want their hatred." When Naduah made to protest, Johanna went on. "There's one man who watches me all the time. The one who lives in the tepee with so many symbols painted on it."

"That's Bull Otter, the medicine man," Naduah interrupted. "I think you are right and he doesn't like you very much."

"Do you know why?"

Naduah shrugged her small shoulders. "Perhaps he is jealous. Big Bear tells us you have great healing power. But Bull Otter says it is not so."

Johanna was filled with a deep foreboding. Bull Otter was well respected and could cause her a lot of trouble. She was worrying the problem over in her mind when Naduah said she must be going.

Her worries were not groundless, for later that

day Naduah hurried into the tepee without announcing herself, something that was never done as it was considered impolite.

"The shaman's daughter, Quiet Water, just told me her father has gone to see the chief. He's trying to make trouble for you by telling everyone that you're a fake. He said last night the Great Spirit took him up to the sky and told him you had to be killed."

"What nonsense!" Johanna exclaimed. "Surely Big Bear won't believe it." But even as she said the words, her heart filled with dread. The Indians were savages. They would believe whatever their medicine man told them.

A commotion outside caused Naduah to look out. Her blue eyes opened wider. "They're coming," she whispered. "Chief Big Bear and a whole crowd of people. And Bull Otter is leading them."

Johanna refused to cower in the tepee like a frightened rabbit. Neither would she run. She had done enough running to last a lifetime. Taking a deep breath, she stepped out into the sunshine.

A murmur went through the crowd.

Chief Big Bear held up his hand for silence and he turned to Johanna. "Bull Otter has told us you are a false healer," he said.

Although her command of the Comanche language was small, Johanna understood most of his words. "How does he know?" she asked, speaking slowly because her pronunciation still left a lot to be desired. If the old man wanted a fight, he would darn well get it. Johanna refused to be driven out of the village.

"He says he was lifted up into the heavens last night and conversed with the Great Spirit who told him you spoke with a false tongue. He says the Great Spirit endowed him with magical powers that enable him to see into the future. Then the Great Spirit sent him back to earth to impart this knowledge to the people. Bull Otter prophesies that if the people allow you to live, they will be stricken with the dreaded white man's disease."

Johanna knew the Comanches had been stricken hard with smallpox during the last winter. Obviously, Bull Otter was using their fear of the disease against her. She shouldn't really be surprised, had suspected that one day she would have to prove herself. It seemed that day had arrived.

But how could she prove her claim? Except for the two girls, she had been isolated from the others. If anyone was ill in the village, she knew nothing of it.

Her emerald eyes roamed the crowd until they fell on a boy with a festering sore on his elbow. She pointed a finger at him and his dark eyes widened nervously.

"Bring the boy to me," she said, wishing she had found something better than a sore to offer for proof. "I will heal him."

The boy tried to slip away, but the chief gave the orders for him to be brought forward.

She sank down on her knees beside him and searched for the words to reassure him. "Have no fear," she managed in halting Comanche. She hoped the tone of her voice would keep him from being afraid, if nothing else.

241

Taking his arm, she lay her palm against it. Then she closed her eyes.

A murmur of awe swept through the crowd as she removed her hand and revealed the healed flesh.

The boy looked at her in confusion, then slowly a smile broke out on his face. He reached out and touched her cheek with his finger, then turned and held out his arm for all to see.

Johanna was trembling as she faced the chief. He bowed his head before her, then turned and spoke harshly to Bull Otter. The man glared his hatred at her then turned and walked away.

Later that day, Quiet Water came to tell her the old shaman was to be banished from the tribe for his lies about her.

Sensing the girl's distress, Johanna went to find the chief. He was with the old shaman.

"Please don't make him leave." she said.

"The decision is yours," Big Bear growled.

"I will accept my chief's decision," the old man spoke up. His eyes were without expression as they dwelt on her. "I need no one to plead for me."

"There is much I can learn from Bull Otter," Johanna said. "If he will but teach me."

The old man nodded his head as though bestowing an honor upon her, pulled his skins tighter about his withered body and returned to his dwelling.

Feeling as though a tragedy had been averted, Johanna returned to her tepee.

As the days passed, others of the tribe came to her. Each day at least one of the children turned

242

up with a skinned knee that needed healing, and one day, a young woman brought a badly burned infant to her. Johanna was beginning to feel accepted by the Comanches and more than once heard herself referred to as She-Who-Heals.

She began to take a more active part in the community. The women showed her how to make pemmican for the coming winter, pounding the dried meat into mush and adding dried berries, wild plums or even mesquite beans. She learned how to scrape the flesh from hides and how to rub buffalo brains into them to make them soft.

And as each day passed, Johanna's knowledge of the Comanche language increased.

Hawkeye had been gone a week when Naduah came to her tepee and asked her to go for a swim. She accepted the invitation eagerly. On the way to the river, they stopped by the tepee where Cactus Wren lived and invited her to go with them, an invitation that was eagerly accepted.

While they were splashing in the water three of the young braves came by and stopped to watch.

"Ignore them," Naduah said. "Perhaps they will grow tired of teasing and go away."

Johanna was more than willing to oblige, for the young men made her nervous. Cactus Wren, however, was not so shy. She swam near the men and openly flirted with them. Johanna and Naduah splashed for a while longer, and when the braves appeared ready to join them, Johanna decided she had been in the water long enough.

She was conscious of the way her clothing clung to her body as she splashed through the water toward the bank with Naduah following closely behind her. Then she stopped, realizing there was no way to get around the warriors. They stood in the path to the village.

As though she sensed Johanna's unrest, Naduah went ahead of her. One of the braves, not more than sixteen years of age, jumped in front of her, blocking her path. "Get out of the way," the young girl demanded.

"What will you give me?" he asked, reaching out and tugging at one of her golden braids.

She glared at him. "You'll get nothing from me, Broken Lance."

"Then you won't pass," he said.

"Have you nothing better to do than to bother the women?" came a harsh voice behind them.

They all turned to see Wanderer, a young warrior who had seen eighteen summers, glaring at them. The braves mumbled something Johanna couldn't understand and made a quick getaway. Without a word for them, Wanderer turned and strode away.

Naduah stared after him for a moment, and something about the way she looked had Johanna remembering that Naduah had said she belonged to Wanderer. She puzzled over that as they made their way to the village. When they reached the tepee of Cactus Wren's father, the young woman bid them goodbye in a sulky voice and left them.

Naduah stayed with Johanna for a while and they talked together as Johanna sewed colored beads on a pair of moccasins to be given to Hawkeye on his return.

"Talk to me about the white-eyes, Johanna," the young girl suggested.

White-eyes?

"They are your people, Naduah. Why do you call them white-eyes?"

"Sometimes it's hard to remember who I am," Naduah replied. "Sometimes I think that part of my life was only a dream. As though it didn't really happen."

Johanna felt saddened. But she could understand how the girl felt. She was several years older and she was beginning to feel the same way.

"I can remember Christmas," Naduah said softly. "We would hang our stockings on the mantel and when we woke up there would be fruit and nuts, and sometimes even sweets in them."

"Yes," Johanna said, remembering the holidays with her own family. "Da carved a wooden doll for me one year and Momma dressed it in bright colors and fashioned yellow yarn for its hair. I was only nine that year. And still they told me it was a gift from Santa Claus." Her lips twitched. "As though I would believe such a thing at that age. My cousin, Mary, was so jealous of that doll. She offered to trade me the flute that Da had carved her for it."

"Did you trade with her?"

"No. Never. I wouldn't have taken anything for that doll."

"Do you still have it?"

"No," Johanna said sadly. "I brought it with me when we left Ireland. But when I fled New Orleans, I was able to take nothing with me."

245

"Why?"

"There was no time. Michael Durant had found out about me . . ."

"About how you heal people?" Naduah interrupted.

"Yes."

"He didn't like it?"

"He liked it well enough," Johanna said, her lips tightening grimly. "He liked it so well he wanted to teach me how to control it so that he could use it to increase his own wealth. He planned to use the healing power for those who could afford a high price."

"Sounds like he wasn't very nice," Naduah said matter-of-factly. "It's good that Hawkeye brought you to us."

"Yes," Johanna agreed. "It is good."

And it would be even better when Hawkeye returned, she told herself. Suddenly the future looked very bright for her.

If only Hawkeye would return soon.

Chapter Nineteen

Johanna reached for another plum and sighed heavily. Hawkeye had been gone for more than two weeks now, and she missed him terribly. How much longer would he be gone? She wondered, her eyes searching for more plums.

Realizing she had picked all she could reach, she searched for another bush, and found one only a few feet away. Picking up her basket, she moved toward it. At this rate, it shouldn't take her long to pick enough for a pie.

Her eyes brightened. Perhaps Hawkeye would return tonight and she could show him how much she had already learned from the other women. The thought made her pick faster. When she had picked all the plums she could reach, she looked at her basket. It was only half full. She searched for another bush and saw one a short distance away.

She looked around for the other women, but they were nowhere to be seen. She had wandered away from them in her zeal to pick the easiest fruit, but she had been in these woods several times lately. And although they were thick with trees, she was sure she was in no danger of getting lost. She had been warned to look out for bears, but still, the bush was only a few hundred feet away.

Making up her mind quickly, she headed for the bush laden with plums. A moment later she was happily filling her basket. It was almost filled to capacity when a rustling in the brush caught her attention. She turned, feeling slightly alarmed. As she did, the figure of a man leaped out of the dense forest and grabbed her arm.

Johanna dropped her basket, unaware of the plums that she had so painstakingly picked scattering across the ground. She lashed out with her fist and connected with the man's eye. His surprise caused him to loosen his grip and she was quick to take advantage. She twisted away from him and made a wild dash for the village, unaware that two more warriors had erupted from the bushes and given chase.

She hadn't gone more than a few steps when she was caught by the hair and yanked painfully backward. One warrior clamped a hand around her throat and another one over her mouth. While another warrior unwound a horsehair rope to bind her with.

It wasn't in Johanna's nature to give up without a fight. But her heart beat frantically as she kicked out with her feet, struggling wildly against the warrior's greater strength.

What did they want? she wondered. Were they intent on attacking the village?

She tried to scream, to alert the others, but the hand muffled her voice.

Another warrior had joined the first two. Johanna's eyes widened with fear as she recognized him as one of the Apaches who had abducted her. Hawkeye had been able to rescue her that time, but now there was no one to save her. No one she could rely on except herself.

The Apaches' faces were impassive as they bound her hands and stuffed a dirty rag in her mouth. Her efforts at resistance were useless, and she found herself thrown across a horse and her hands and feet tied beneath the belly of her mount with a horsehair rope.

It was only a matter of minutes before they left the Comanche village behind them, along with whatever hope she had of finding any kind of future happiness with Hawkeye.

Soon Johanna began to feel lightheaded and guessed it was the blood rushing to her head. A red haze formed in front of her eyes and she passed out. When she regained her senses, she found herself seated on a horse in front of one of the warriors, held there by his arm around her waist.

Her hands were still tied and, knowing resistance would only cause her more pain, she remained passive. It wasn't long before she noticed the Apaches were keeping a close watch on their backtrail, turning in the saddle often as though they feared pursuit. Johanna found a small measure of hope from that. Perhaps even now she had been missed and a search party organized. From the position of the sun, she knew it wasn't long before dusk. When they stopped to rest for the night, that would give a rescue party time to catch up to them.

When darkness fell, Johanna's spirits were at a low ebb, because the Apaches showed no sign of stopping to rest. The only concession they made was for the horses they were riding. That was when Johanna learned what the extra mounts were for.

The Apaches merely switched mounts and continued on their way.

Johanna knew then that she had been clinging to the hope that the Comanches would somehow find Hawkeye and tell him what had happened. But that hope was completely gone now. No one could follow a trail at night. Not even Hawkeye.

The Apaches continued to move swiftly in a northwesterly direction, and by morning they had already put better than fifty miles between them and the Comanche village.

When the sun sent a golden blush across the horizon, they stopped for a short rest while they fed and watered the horses. One of the warriors untied Johanna's feet and lifted her from the horse. When he turned her loose, her legs would not hold her and she slumped to the ground.

Pulling the gag from her mouth, he held a skin of water to her lips. She wanted to refuse the drink but knew she would only be spiting herself. She swallowed the tepid water greedily until he pulled it away from her.

Wearily, Johanna closed her eyes and lay back on the ground. Her exposed skin felt prickly and she was certain she had burned from too much sun.

It seemed hardly a moment later when she was dragged to her feet and put on the horse again. She mentally gave thanks because they left the gag off and didn't tie her legs beneath the horse. Even though her hands were still bound she would use the first opportunity she could find to escape from them.

As the morning progressed and the sun rose higher and higher in the sky, Johanna's sunburned skin began to turn a darker shade of red. Even worse, her vision began to blur. Could she go blind from too much sun? she wondered.

They were traveling through the Llano Uplift where granite domes thrust skyward like miniature Scottish highlands. Another time she might have found pleasure in their beauty.

Darkness found them near a creek lined with sycamore trees. The warriors stopped and made camp, kindling a fire of dry wood that was almost smokeless in a hole dug a foot deep. Johanna could see the advantage of such a fire, for it was completely hidden unless you were standing directly over it.

The warriors roasted a rabbit one of them had killed and untied her wrists long enough for her to eat, after taking the precaution of binding her ankles to a nearby tree. As soon as she had eaten and drunk from the waterskin, her wrists were secured again.

Now was the time, she decided. She would wait until the Apaches fell asleep before trying to make her escape. What she hadn't counted on was falling asleep before they did.

She woke abruptly, silently cursing herself for failing to stay awake. At least the Apaches were still asleep. But there was no time to lose.

Johanna began to work at her bonds with her teeth. She would escape . . . or die trying.

"You seem to be in a great hurry, Hawkeye," Sky Walker said, pulling his pony up beside his friend.

Hawkeye turned in the saddle and looked at the other warrior with a grin. "So would you be if someone like Johanna was waiting for you in the village. You should think about that. You're not getting any younger, you know. It's time you took a wife and started having sons."

"There's plenty of others who can do that," Sky Walker replied. "Wives think they own you. They complain constantly. I never lack female companionship, so I will keep my freedom."

What he said was true, Hawkeye knew. Sky Walker was a favorite among the women of the tribe. He was especially adored by Cactus Wren.

"You know the chiefs say it is every warrior's duty to have children," Hawkeye said. "We need boys to grow up and be warriors. Girls to become women to help them. The time will come when we'll need all the people we can get in our war with the Texans."

"We can defeat the white-eyes," Sky Walker said. "The chief has become an old woman. He has forgotten how strong we are. We will fight the palefaces, and we will win."

Hawkeye was not quite so confident. He had lived in both worlds. He knew the numbers of the Comanches were few compared to the white man. And these Texans were a different breed than the Mexicans. They had held out against considerable odds at the Alamo. They were not so easily defeated.

At least the rifles didn't fall into their hands, he thought. But he wasn't sure how long that would be an advantage, or how much good it would do. He had learned long ago that the white men were greedy. They had already begun to kill the buffalo for hides. If they weren't stopped soon, they would wipe out the great beasts that were the mainstay of the Indians' way of life in just a few years. Then what would the Indians live on?

A shout up ahead told him the village had been sighted. He looked back to make sure there was no problem with the two wagons that followed, both heavily loaded with the rifles. The next few days would be filled with learning to operate the new weapons, but he intended to take time out for Johanna. He had been away from her far too long.

Eager to see Johanna, he urged Diablo into a gallop. A crowd had gathered to welcome them, but Hawkeye's only thought was for his wife, Johanna. He looked among the familiar faces surrounding him, but failed to see her. Was it his imagination, or did everyone stare at him with pity?

Suddenly, he felt a cold chill sweep over him, along with a dreadful certainty that something had happened to her during his absence.

He dismounted and turned toward his tepee . . . and found his way blocked by Chief Big Bear.

"Your woman is no longer here," he said. "She has left us."

Hawkeye's eyes glinted, narrowing on the chief. "Why has she gone?" he asked.

"No one knows," Chief Big Bear said. "We thought she was happy here. She was picking plums with the other women when she ran away."

Hawkeye could not believe what he was hearing. He hurried to his tepee, but it was empty. Despair flowed through him, then it was drowned in a terrible rage. She had deceived him. All the time she had pretended to love him, and he had believed her. And she had taken the first opportunity to escape.

He left the dwelling and found Chief Big Bear waiting. "How long has she been gone?" he asked.

"Two suns."

"Did you look for her? Perhaps she had an accident?"

"There was no accident," Big Bear said. "If there had been, we would have found her. But your woman was clever and hid her trail well."

"Hid her trail?"

254

"Yes. She used broomweed to sweep it clean."

Hawkeye knew then, with a certainty, that something was wrong. Johanna didn't know how to hide a trail. "Where was she last seen?" he asked.

"She was picking plums with Cactus Wren and the other women. She wandered away from them. And, as is the way of all women, they were gossiping and did not know she was no longer with them."

"Show me the place," Hawkeye said.

Big Bear did, and although Hawkeye searched the area well, he almost missed the sign as the others had. Behind the plum bush, beneath fallen leaves, he found moccasin prints. He knew the tracks were made by Indians, because the toes were turned inward, whereas a white man's would have been turned out.

His face darkened. Several of the warriors offered to help him search for Johanna and they rode off on a trail that was fast getting too cold to follow.

When it was realized how fast Johanna's captors were traveling, a conference was held and Hawkeye, realizing the village could not be left undefended, sent the others back and went on alone.

Chapter Twenty

The moon, riding high in the ebony sky, seemed to mock Johanna's efforts to free herself. Each second seemed an hour, each minute stretched out an eternity as she worked at her bonds with her teeth. Every sound in the night seemed magnified ten-fold; the thrum-thrum, thrum-thrum, thrum-thrum, of her heart, the hoot of a night owl, and far off in the distance, the lonesome wail of a coyote.

As the latter sounded, she paused in her efforts, her gaze searching out the inert forms of the sleeping men, expecting one of them to wake at any given moment and sound the alert.

They remained motionless, unaware, and after a long moment, Johanna began chewing at the bonds again.

She felt a moment of elation when one of the

strands parted. Flexing her wrists, she tried to gather some slack in the rope which bound her. But despite her efforts, the rope remained tight.

Tears of disappointment welled in her eyes, but they were quickly blinked away. Crying was a sign of weakness and would accomplish nothing.

Although escape seemed hopeless, Johanna refused to give up. It was her guess that she was being taken to the Apache village. Once there, they could take their time for whatever fate they had planned for her.

Forcing herself to a calm she didn't feel, she lifted her bound hands again and tugged at the rope with her teeth. A moment later, a strand gave way.

A soft shuffling noise jerked her head up, and she dropped her hands into her lap just as the warrior who stood guard entered the glade. Johanna lay her head back against the tree and pretended to be asleep. The hairs on the back of her neck prickled and she knew he was watching her, knew too, the moment when he passed on.

His moccasins made only a whisper of sound as he walked by.

Opening her eyes to mere slits, she saw him gliding away into the darkness, headed for the rope corral where the horses had been confined.

Instantly, she began her work on the rope again, feeling elated when another strand parted. It was only a matter of moments when she was able to free her wrists. She moved carefully, afraid the slightest movement would arouse the sleeping warriors as she bent to work on her ankles.

Moments later, she was free.

Johanna left the camp on silent feet, cutting a wide berth around the rope corral where the one lone sentry stood guard.

The forest was thick and heavy with shadows, and Johanna had, of necessity, to travel slowly. The woods were filled with obstructions, fallen logs, bushes, holes that could turn an ankle. Although hindered by the darkness, it was also in her favor. She knew her tracks would be harder for the Apaches to follow at night.

Dawn found her at the edge of a clearing. She had been jogging steadily for the past hour and despite the cool air, perspiration dotted her forehead. Johanna stopped for a moment, watching the sun peep over the horizon, painting the woods with a glorious burst of color.

She could hear the wind sighing through the trees, and somewhere, only a short distance away, the sound of running water. The latter made her aware of her thirst, and she changed directions, letting her ears guide her.

The stream proved to be only a shallow creek, but the water was clear, flowing swiftly over a bed of gravel. Sinking to her knees, she splashed the cooling liquid on her face, then lay on her stomach to drink deeply of the sweet, cool water.

Feeling slightly refreshed, Johanna sat back on her haunches and took stock of her situation. According to the position of the sun, she was headed in a southeasterly direction. That way, she knew, lay the Comanche camp, more than a hundred miles away.

But she wouldn't let herself dwell on the distance that separated her from her friends and Hawkeye. Instead, she would concentrate her efforts on filling her stomach.

She had learned much from the Comanches, knew the forest contained an abundance of food. She should be able to find wild berries and onions and poke salad.

Her eyes narrowed on a large patch of green growing on the other side of the stream. Was that watercress? She was almost certain of it.

She leapt over the narrow stream and bent to examine the greens. Breaking off a stem, she bit into one of the delicate leaves. It was definitely watercress, she decided. She would gather—

A loud crashing through the brush jerked her head around. Something heavy was coming fast. It must be the Apaches. They had found her!

Searching frantically for a place to hide, Johanna's gaze fell upon a rocky cliff ahead and she made a dash for it, hoping to find some form of concealment.

Fear lent wings to her feet as she sprinted toward an opening in the rocks several feet up the cliff. Her breath was labored, coming in short gasps, and she had a pain in her side, but fear spurred her on.

The opening was narrow, but looked big enough to squeeze her small frame through. If she could reach it before the Apaches saw her, then maybe . . .

Reaching the base of the cliff, she scrabbled up the surface, creating a small rock slide in the process, clawing with her fingers at the opening. Relief swept through her as she squeezed her body through the small enclosure just as she heard a deep-throated growl.

Wriggling herself around so she could see, her eyes fell on the black bear rumbling toward her.

She stifled a scream.

Undaunted by the cliff, the bear stood on his hind legs and raked a heavy hand across the opening.

Johanna shrank back against the far wall as the bear bellowed with rage and pressed his snout into the hole, filling the enclosure with his foul-smelling breath. The massive beast, furious at being thwarted, beat the rocks with his hairy paw.

Johanna felt as though the earth was shaking beneath her. She heard the rocks crumbling around her and falling to the ground below, and wondered if her fortress would hold against such an onslaught.

Curling herself into a tight ball, she waited for his next attack. Her teeth chattered as shock set in. It seemed an eternity had passed before the beast stopped beating on the rocks and lumbered away.

Johanna lay still, afraid to move lest she incite the bear to return. When there remained no sound from outside, she moved nearer the opening and looked out. The bear sat at the base of the cliff . . . waiting.

Drawing back in the hole, she laid her head on her knees in despair. Her legs felt numb, cramped from their position. She tried to straighten them out, but there wasn't enough room in the small cave.

Eons seemed to pass as she waited in the cave, her heart fluttering wildly in her chest. Had she escaped torture by the Apaches to be killed by a bear?

Hawkeye! she cried silently. *Where are you?*

Despite her efforts at control, her emerald eyes filled with tears. They spilled over, sliding down her face, leaving tracks through the dirt on her cheeks.

A curious sense of resignation washed over as shock set in and a chill rattled her teeth. Silence crowded in around her, not a peaceful quiet, instead, it was the silence of a tomb.

An eternity of time passed, perhaps minutes, perhaps hours. She had no way of knowing. Finally, exhaustion overcame her. Johanna's eyes closed, jerked open, then closed again and she fell asleep.

When Johanna woke, the inside of her mouth felt like cotton. How long had she been asleep? Her gaze went to the sky. She couldn't see the sun, guessed it was at its zenith. Had the bear grown tired of waiting and left?

She had to find out.

Edging closer to the opening, she looked out . . . and breathed a sigh of relief. The bear was no longer there. The great beast had obviously grown tired of waiting and had left.

Crawling from her refuge, she gingerly lowered herself to the ground. She had only gone a few feet when she heard a tremendous rustling and cracking behind her.

God! The bear was coming after her.

Throwing a quick glance over her shoulder, she realized she was too far away from the dubious safety of the small cave, and ran for the woods as fast as her feet would carry her.

Johanna felt dizzy and lightheaded from her overpowering fear. The bear was gaining on her, his furious snarls rending the air around her.

A young cottonwood tree seemed her only hope of refuge and she made a dash for it, scurrying up the trunk with the bear right behind her.

She realized instantly she had made a mistake, for the tree didn't stop the bear. He beat on the trunk with his massive paws trying to shake her out. Wrapping her arms around the tree, she hung on with all her strength.

The bear, seeming to realize he couldn't shake her loose, began to climb the tree. It bent and swayed beneath him, threatening to break under his weight.

Fear lent Johanna strength as she climbed higher, higher into the tree . . . with the bear right behind her.

"Aaa-ii — ee, aaa-ii-ee."

Johanna almost welcomed the sound that such a short time before had struck terror in her. At the moment, the Apaches seemed to be the lesser of two evils. Two of them had appeared from the brush, loosing their arrows at the bear, distracting his attention from the girl in the tree. With an angry snarl, he left the prey he had treed and turned to the intruders who dared attack him. The warriors let loose another volley of arrows and they buried themselves in the beast's thick hide.

"Aaa-ii-ee, aa-ii-ee," The Apaches cried, waving their tomahawks above their heads and dancing around the great beast.

With a thunderous roar, he dropped to the ground and lumbered toward them. They darted away through the thick woods and Johanna quickly slid down the tree and turned in the other direction. She pulled up short. One of the warriors had doubled back and blocked her way.

Hawkeye knelt beside the campfire. Raking through the ashes, he found a few live coals and his eyes narrowed grimly. He judged it to be only hours since the Apaches had left and they had obviously left in a hurry.

He studied the moccasin tracks left behind, located the smallest ones . . . Johanna's. If he was reading the sign right, she had left ahead of the others.

Had she managed to escape them?

Chapter Twenty-one

Johanna and her captors traveled hard for the next three days, stopping only for a short while at night. She continued to watch for a chance to escape, but the Indians were more wary now and never seemed to take their eyes off her. She wondered where they were taking her. It seemed they had been traveling forever; the pain in her lower body had become almost unbearable, and her muscles ached, doubling her frustration.

Her thoughts turned often to Hawkeye. She wondered if he had returned to the village yet. When he returned, would he be able to follow their trail? She felt almost certain he could . . . and would. She knew the Apaches had taken great pains to cover their trail. But if there were any signs at all, Hawkeye would find them.

And he would follow. She was certain of it. To

think otherwise was too painful to even contemplate, and accomplished nothing except to increase her hopelessness. She forced herself to cling to the stubborn belief that he would find her.

On the fourth day it clouded over and the wind began to blow. Lightning flashed overhead and thunder sounded, reverberating through the heavens.

As the rain came down in blinding sheets, the small band sought shelter beneath a cliff overhang and waited for the storm to end. It was late afternoon before the rain let up and they continued on their way again.

Johanna heard the river before she saw it. The waters were in full flood. Uprooted trees and other debris floated in the muddy water, carried swiftly downstream by the swirling current. She viewed it with satisfaction. *We'll never be able to cross,* she told herself silently. But, apparently undaunted, the Apaches merely turned their mounts upstream, obviously searching for a safer crossing.

Her hopes surged again when they found the way blocked by cliffs that stretched straight up from the river. Surely now, they would have to turn back. Again, her hopes were unfounded. The forward scout found a narrow trail that led up and over the cliff.

They started up the trail, two of the warriors leading the way. Then came Johanna with two warriors bringing up the rear, thereby blocking any hope of escape. She tried to keep her eyes away from the ledge and the swollen river below as her mount picked its way up the narrow path with her clinging tightly to its mane.

Suddenly, the Apache in the rear gave a shout and the two warriors in front pulled up their mounts.

What's going on? she silently wondered.

After a short discussion between the four warriors, one of them turned back, leaving the rest to continue up the trail with Johanna.

Moments later, a shot rang out somewhere behind them, followed by a hacking war cry.

Startled, she twisted in the saddle, her eyes widening as she recognized the black stallion, rearing on his hind legs and pawing at the air with his front hooves as a buckskin-clad man fought to control him.

"Hawkeye!" she screamed, yanking back on the reins as she tried to turn her mount on the narrow trail.

The warrior in front of Johanna acted immediately, grabbing her mount's reins and pulling hard at him, forcing him farther up the trail.

But Johanna wasn't to be stopped so easily. Grabbing her mount's mane with her bound hands, she slid from the saddle and hit the ground running. A loud cry from the trail ahead told her at least one of the warriors had left his mount and was after her.

She paid no attention to the savage who had given chase, intent on the fight that was going on between Hawkeye and the Apache down the trail. Her emerald eyes were wide with apprehension. Hawkeye was so close to the cliff. One small slip and he and the stallion would plunge over the edge. And she felt certain they would never survive the fall.

"No Hawkeye!" she screamed. "They—" She was abruptly cut off when a hand clamped around her mouth and another wrapped around her body, pinning her arms to her sides.

But Hawkeye had heard the cry and reacted instantly. A red haze of battle smoldered in his eyes as he dealt his enemy a killing blow, then sent the stallion charging up the narrow path, intent on reaching Johanna.

The one remaining warrior at the rear turned to meet his charge. Hawkeye, realizing another shot could panic the horses, thereby endangering Johanna, grabbed his warclub and swung it at the Apache warrior.

Johanna fought desperately, but her struggles were useless against the superior strength of both savages. She was flung onto one of the horses and held there while a warrior mounted behind her. Then, as though uncaring of the danger involved, the horse was sent galloping up the narrow trail.

Johanna, fearing for Hawkeye's life, twisted her head around, her eyes searching out the battle raging between the two warriors.

Suddenly, with a wild howl that chilled her blood, the Apache gave a wild leap, colliding with the man clad in buckskin and sending both men plunging over the edge into the canyon far below.

Johanna uttered a despairing cry as Hawkeye disappeared over the edge. Tears streamed, unnoticed, down her face, as she watched the black stallion scrabble for support on the narrow ledge.

No! No! she cried inwardly. *He can't be gone!*

But he was. And with the realization came a terrible despair. Her body slumped in the saddle as the fight went out of her. *What was the use in fighting when her life had just come to an end.*

The warriors found Johanna completely docile as they continued their journey. Anguished and bereft, she was obliged to deal with the pain of her loss at a time when she was least equipped to handle it.

She was vaguely aware of the uneasy glances the warriors threw at her. And just as vaguely, wondered why her state of mind should bother them.

Johanna didn't know how much time had passed when they reached the high plains of what was later to become known as the Texas Panhandle. The prairie stretched out as far as the eye could see before them.

She didn't see the chasm, had no idea it was there until her mount was almost at the rim. Then, she stared down in astonishment at what the wind and water over the centuries had etched into the high plains. It dropped away in multicolored grandeur to a vast valley far below where water flowed and the vegetation was abundant. Her astonishment would have been even greater had she known that it measured, at some points, twelve hundred feet deep and five miles wide, about six hundred thousand acres in all.

And the Apaches had found a way down to it

from its head where the erosion continued, still eating away at the plains.

They made their way down a narrow, rugged draw, to the canyon floor with Johanna clinging tightly to her mount's mane. She didn't breathe easy until she had reached the valley. Then her vision swept the walls of the canyon that rose straight to the plains high above. The rock walls had been stratified eons ago and now were cut through, making layers and layers of red and yellow and orange color.

Johanna could see how the Apaches would be pleased with the canyon, for it provided them with good water, wood, and a safe haven from the brutal winters of the high plains as well as a safe hiding place from their enemies. It was late in the evening when they finally reached the Apache village.

It was built in the shelter of an overhang. Around two score wickiups spread out against the cliff. The dwellings were constructed with brush and sticks held together with mud. She found it a very different sight than the tepees of the Comanches. Johanna was weary in mind as well as body. She wondered what her fate would be. If they had meant to kill her, then why had they brought her so far? Perhaps they wanted time to torture her without fear of interruption. The thought sent a shiver traveling up her spine.

As they made their way through the village, the Apaches, dressed in a mixture of white men's garments and buckskins, stopped their work and followed them. By the time they reached their destination, a sizable crowd had gathered.

A warrior, clad in a cotton shirt, breechclout and fringed leggings, stepped from the wickiup and confronted them. Although there was nothing in his appearance that set him apart from his fellow Apaches, something in his eyes led her to believe he was the chief of the tribe.

Johanna's captor slid from his horse, then reached up and pulled her down beside him, holding her upright when she would have fallen.

The man who confronted her spoke in a guttural language, and her captor drew his knife from its sheath.

Johanna's eyes widened and she drew a sharp breath. Her eyes met those of her captor's.

"Do not be alarmed," said the man Johanna had taken to be the chief. Surprise jerked her eyes around, for he had spoken in perfectly good English. "Chama only means to release you."

"Release me?" Johanna asked.

She didn't see the knife slice down and cut through the rope that bound her wrists. Only felt the pain as circulation returned to her hands. She rubbed her wrists, staring at the man who had ordered her release.

"Who are you?" she asked. "And why was I brought here?"

"I am Chief White Eagle," he said. "And you were brought here because we have need of a medicine woman."

Although his words surprised her, she gave no outward sign. "I am no medicine woman," she muttered.

"Do you deny the power that healed the Comanche warrior, Hawkeye."

Hawkeye!

At the mention of his name, hatred flared in her eyes, and her hands whitened into fists. "I deny nothing," she said, her voice cold with remembrance. "But your warriors killed my husband. Why should I help you?"

His black eyes flicked over the two warriors who had abducted her. He spoke to Chama in the guttural language of the Apache, then stood silent while Chama spoke at length.

Finally, Chief White Eagle turned back to her. "Chama did not know Hawkeye was your husband," he said. "Had he known, they would have tried to take him alive. It is too late now."

"If all you wanted was my help, why didn't you ask for it?" she asked.

"Would you have come willingly?"

She considered his words for a moment, then realized she would not have. She would have been too frightened of them.

He read the answer in her eyes. "You see, we had no choice," he said, his face expressionless. "We would like to make your stay pleasant. We have no wish to hold you prisoner."

Her mind worked frantically. She was far from stupid. They could not trust her to stay. No matter what she said, she would be guarded. But if she could gradually make them think they had won her over, then perhaps they would grow careless and she could escape.

Escape to what? she silently asked herself.

271

Hawkeye is dead. What difference does it make where I am?

Johanna was escorted to a centrally located wickiup by a warrior who motioned her inside, then squatted down by the door.

Johanna sank down on the buffalo hide mat, too weary and heartsick to even contemplate her circumstances. A moment later she fell asleep.

When she woke she saw a young woman bending over a black pot which gave off a mouthwatering aroma. She was wearing a doeskin dress trimmed with glass beads and her dark hair was fashioned in a bun at the nape of her neck. When she saw Johanna was awake, she filled an earthenware bowl from the pot.

"Eat this," she said, holding out a bowl. "It's bound to make you feel better."

Johanna's head jerked up. "You speak English," she exclaimed. "You're not one of them."

"No," the girl muttered. "I ain't one of 'em. An' I ain't never gonna be," she added fiercely. "No matter what they got planned for me."

The girl moved, stepping into the light that streamed through the entrance and Johanna saw that she had been mistaken in the color of the girl's hair. Her hair, instead of black, was a dark red color, shining in the sun with bright copper lights. And the girl's eyes were a deep blue, the color of a cloudless sky.

"How do you come to be here?" Johanna asked.

"The same as you," the girl said. "The Apaches stole me."

"What is your name?" she asked softly.

"The Injuns call me Fire Woman. 'Cause of my red hair," she replied. "But my real name is Mary Elizabeth Abernathy."

"Mine is Johanna McFarley," Johanna said. "And you don't know how glad I am to see you."

"Ain't no reason to be glad," Mary said. "I ain't been able to help myself. Don't see how I can help nobody else."

"How long have you been here?"

"Been nigh on to four years now," Mary replied. "I weren't but eleven years old when they took me."

Four years! "Is your family still alive?" she asked gently.

"Might be all dead," Mary muttered. "Pa was killed right off. Brother Jeb, he was fourteen an' out workin' in the field when the Apaches come ridin' in. He mighta got away. Brother Caleb, he went right after Pa." Her voice became hoarse. "Ma . . ." she swallowed hard. "Ma . . . I ain't rightly sure 'bout her. But I hope she died real soon." A dark shadow crossed her face. "Melissa was alive when they took us. Just turned thirteen." Her eyes looked inward. "Ma made her a new dress out of blue cotton. Dress didn't last as long as she did." She shuddered. "They ripped it apart the first night. Took 'er two days to die."

Oh, God! Johanna thought silently. *How could one frail girl have borne such sorrow and retained her sanity? It made Johanna ashamed of her own weakness.*

"Did they . . ." She hesitated, wondering if she should ask the question. "Did they . . . violate you, Mary?"

Tears welled up in Mary's eyes and were quickly blinked away. "No," she said. "I think they was afeared of killin' me like they done Melissa."

"Have you tried to escape?"

Mary's eyes flickered in remembrance. "So many times I lost track. But they always found me and brung me back. An' each time they beat me 'till I thought I was goin' to die." Her eyes were hard. "But that ain't gonna stop me," she said. "I'd rather be dead then give in to 'em."

"We'll find a way to leave," Johanna said tightly, her features set with determination. "Somehow, we'll get away. Durant thought he could hold me captive. And his prison was more advanced than these savages. If I could outwit him, then I can outwit them."

Chapter Twenty-two

Hawkeye had only a glimpse of Johanna's white face before he plunged over the cliff. Then he was falling . . . falling . . . toward the swollen Canadian River fifty feet below. He felt the shock of the cold river as his body hit the surface, then he sank deep in the water where the light was dim and the pressure caused his ears to hurt.

His lungs burned as he called upon all his will-power—his stubborn determination—to fight against the current, to overcome his growing need for air until he could reach the surface. A dull roar began in his ears and bright flashes sparked behind his eyelids as he fought to reach the surface and the precious air that meant life.

And then he was breaking surface. Only for a moment, but it was long enough for one short gasp of air before he was pulled under again.

He renewed his struggles and again broke surface.

Finding himself facing the rocky cliff, he struggled to reach it, but his strength was waning, his efforts useless against the power of the river. It was all he could to do keep his head above water and he was being forced at an alarmingly swift rate downstream.

The tree was upon him before he saw it. Hope flared strong in his weakening spirit and he called upon his remaining strength, lunging for the safety of the branches. He felt its scaly bark beneath his palm, then it swirled away from him, pulled by the current, and he slipped back into the murky depths of the river.

Hawkeye thrashed the water, despairing, even as the current took the tree farther from his reach. It had been his only chance for safety; he was too weak to struggle any longer.

Johanna. Her face appeared before him. She needed him. He must stay afloat, must help her.

From somewhere, he found the strength to keep his head above water, until miraculously, the tree swung around, caught by a whirlpool. Its branches reached toward him, offering safety, and with a strength born of desperation, he fought the raging river . . . swimming closer . . . closer . . . until his fingers caught and wrapped around the limb. His breath came in short bursts as he pulled himself among the branches, then he gave in to the threatening darkness.

Hawkeye opened his eyes to a clear blue sky. He watched a hawk circle lazily high above him, watched it circle lower, until in one great swoop, it darted toward the ground, out of his range of vision, rising a moment later with a rabbit in its claws.

Slowly becoming aware of a rocking sensation beneath him, Hawkeye pushed himself upright, slipped, and found himself sliding into the icy water of the river.

Water filled his nostrils as he sank into its murky depths. When his feet touched something solid, he kicked his way upward and grabbed the tree. It was then he realized what had happened. The tree's branches had become caught at the edge of a gravel shoal that fingered out into the water and led to an outcrop of granite rocks. It swayed slowly beneath him as the current pulled at it, trying to free it from the shoal.

Hawkeye searched for the cliffs from which he had fallen, but they had disappeared. The landscape was unfamiliar to him, the banks of the river low with flat land spreading out beyond them.

How far had he been carried downstream?

It wasn't long before sunset so he must have been unconscious for several hours. He realized he was lucky to be alive, could have just as easily drowned.

Mentally measuring the distance to the shore, Hawkeye released the tree and swam with aching arms toward the river bank.

It seemed an eternity before his feet touched

bottom; his legs threatened to buckle beneath him as he waded ashore and sank wearily down on the sand. He lay there, breathing heavily, unaware of the passing time, until the sun set and a mantle of darkness cloaked the land.

Then he began to shiver.

Realizing the necessity of drying his wet buckskins or risking pneumonia, he gathered wood for a fire and extracted a flint from the possibles bag that was looped at his waist. Minutes later he knelt before the warmth of a fire. He tried to keep thoughts of Johanna, at the mercy of the Apaches, from his mind, knowing that way led to insanity. He waited only until his buckskins were dry before rising and beginning the long trek upriver.

He would return to the place from which he had fallen and resume his search for Johanna.

He traveled hard that night and when the sun rose over the horizon the next morning, he spied the cliffs ahead.

With his goal in sight, Hawkeye increased his pace, but it was mid-morning before he picked up the Apaches' trail again . . . and along with it were the tracks of his stallion.

Hawkeye studied the tracks on the ground. The stallion seemed too great a distance behind the renegade band to be traveling with them. At that moment, a shrill whistle rent the air and Hawkeye's head jerked up. He had heard the sound enough to know it was Diablo.

And he was somewhere nearby.

A wild surge of hope flared through him, clamoring for recognition, just as the black stallion broke through a thick stand of trees. Dust clouds swirled as he screamed, rearing high into the air. He pawed the ground, sending more dust clouds aloft, then shook his mane and raced toward his master. Hawkeye sent a prayer of thanks winging skyward to the Great Spirit, then sprinted toward the horse.

Nothing could stop him now.

He would find the Apache dogs who had stolen Johanna from him, and he would take revenge against them for what they had done.

Hawkeye was so intent on reaching the animal that he didn't see the warrior rise up from the grass until it was almost too late.

The Apache's knife would have found its mark had not the sun glinted off the tip of the blade. Alerted, Hawkeye flung himself sideways, throwing up his arm to deflect the blade. The tip of the knife sliced into his arm and a warm spurt of blood gushed from the wound.

Hawkeye was at the other man's throat in an instant, squeezing it tightly with one hand while his other held the knife away from his body.

The Apache stared at him with hatred as they fought. He thrust the knife downward, striking Hawkeye's shoulder with a stabbing pain. Then, jerking the knife out, he plunged it into the Comanche warrior's back.

Hawkeye grunted with pain, his blood flowing from the stab wounds, his fingers loosing the pressure on the other man's throat. Using all the strength he possessed, he flung the Apache warrior away from him.

The stallion screamed with rage, pawing the air near the two men. His teeth were bared and his ears laid low on his head as he stared malevolently at the Apache warrior. The man regained his feet and lunged for Hawkeye again, and the stallion struck out with his deadly hooves, delivering a blow on the Apache's chest that sent him stumbling to the ground. Diablo's neck and withers were white with foam as he trampled his master's enemy beneath his hooves.

Blood dripped from Hawkeye's wounds and his legs threatened to buckle beneath his weight. He shook his head, trying to force away the red haze threatening to consume him. When his gaze fell on the stallion, he reached for him, missed, then crumpled to the ground beside the body of his enemy.

Something cold prodded Hawkeye's face and he groaned, pushing feebly against the object which proved to be soft and moist. Opening his eyes, he stared up into the moonlit sky.

A soft whinny turned his head. Diablo was standing beside him, head hanging low, the picture of absolute dejection.

Calling on an inner strength, Hawkeye mounted the animal and held himself upright with great difficulty.

He knew his wounds were bad, knew he had lost a lot of blood, but he knew, also, that he had to keep moving. The need to find Johanna had become his sole purpose in life.

Hawkeye clung to the saddle, losing all sense of time as the sun lifted over the horizon and began its upward journey. He was barely conscious of the stallion's hoofbeats thudding against rock . . . or the hard-baked earth.

Was is dark? He couldn't be certain. Perhaps the darkness only came from his inability to keep his eyes open.

Was he even going in the right direction?

Forcing his eyes open, Hawkeye stared for a moment at the ground swaying beneath him. It began to swirl in a kaleidoscope of colors, his fingers became lax on the saddlehorn, and he slid from the saddle and crumpled to the ground.

Hawkeye woke to the sensation of movement. Opening eyelids that seemed incredibly heavy, he peered through narrowed lids and found himself staring up into a cloudless blue sky. He didn't realize he was bound to a litter slung between two poles until he tried to move . . . and couldn't.

Who had found him?

The wind felt cool against his fevered skin and his throat was dry . . . parched, his body a mass of bruises. He had only just reached that conclusion when the litter struck a rock and agony streaked through Hawkeye.

Mercifully, the black fuzzy haze pressed around him and he succumbed to the enveloping darkness.

Fever raged through Hawkeye's body for days.

He was unaware of the warrior who stayed beside him and tended him, caring for his needs as though he were a small child. Finally, the fever abated and he opened his eyes to find himself in a small cave with Sky Walker leaning over him.

"Water," he whispered hoarsely, licking his dry lips.

Sky Walker rose and picked up a waterskin lying nearby. Returning, he held it to his friend's mouth.

Although the water was tepid, it tasted like ambrosia to Hawkeye as it trickled down his throat. He allowed himself only a few drops, knowing more could make him sick.

"Johanna?" he muttered.

Sky Walker shook his head. "You were near death when I found you, old friend. I dared not leave you to follow them. You would have surely died."

"Rather that than see her tortured by the Apaches," Hawkeye said harshly.

"It is my belief they mean her no harm," Sky Walker said. "They must know of the power that lies within her."

Hope flared alive in Hawkeye's eyes. "Do you have reason for such a belief?"

"Only that she still lives."

"Perhaps only until they reach the safety of their village," Hawkeye said.

He remembered how terrified she had looked when she saw him fall. He would find her, and when he did, the ones who had taken her would feel his wrath.

"I have to get up," Hawkeye muttered, struggling to his elbows. "I must find her." But even as he spoke the words, he knew he was too weak.

"No," Sky Walker said, pushing him back down. "You must allow your wounds to heal first. If she's still alive, she will remain so for another day. And you would be no good to her as you are."

Although Hawkeye knew his friend's words made sense, he hated to think about the delay. Johanna must be terrified, thinking him dead and herself alone and at the mercy of her captors.

As she surely was.

And yet, his weakened state forced him to wait.

Two days later the two men mounted their horses and took up the trail that had long since grown cold. At times they lost it completely, but Hawkeye's determination to find Johanna would not allow room for failure.

He would find her, or he would die trying.

Chapter Twenty-three

Johanna strode beside the litter, uncaring that the sweat trickled down her back. Neither did she care that the sun beat down on her, turning her skin to an even darker shade of brown. None of these things concerned her since she had learned their destination was Bent's Fort, located along the Arkansas River in Colorado territory.

That fact alone wasn't the cause of her elation. But she knew Bent was a white man. And, even though her skin had darkened to a golden brown, and her hair was as dark as the savages among which she lived, she knew her green eyes would give her away to any white man who chanced to see her, and surely, even though William Bent was a well known trader among the Indian tribes, he surely would not allow Mary and herself to remain prisoners of the Apaches.

She had become close to Mary in the last three weeks and knew it was imperative they escape soon. The girl was the property of Three Toes and his wife, Willow. Mary was in no imminent danger from them, but she was on the verge of being sold to Chama.

When the band stopped for the night, Johanna found a chance to speak alone with the girl.

"We'll soon be free," she whispered, her eyes glittering emerald.

Mary Elizabeth looked at her uncomprehendingly.

"We're going to Bent's Fort," Johanna explained. "I've heard he is a just man. He'll never allow the Apaches to leave there with us."

"Don't go countin' on no help from Bent," Mary said, looking at her with something akin to pity. "He married a Cheyenne woman an' makes his livin' tradin' with the Injuns. He ain't gonna do nothin' thet'd turn 'em against him."

"But, surely," Johanna protested. "Surely he wouldn't leave us to their mercy."

"Them 'Paches ain't got no mercy," Mary said harshly. Her hand trembled as it pushed an errant curl back from her face.

"Has something happened?" Johanna asked gently.

The girl nodded her head. "Chama offered Three Toes six horses for me," she blurted. "I think Three Toes is gonna take 'em."

Johanna put a comforting arm around Mary's shoulders. What could she say to comfort the girl? "Perhaps they can be persuaded to wait until we reach the fort," she said.

"What good's thet gonna do?"

"Plenty. If William Bent will help us."

"He ain't gonna do thet. An' anyway, I don't know how to stall Three Toes."

They were unaware of the approaching warrior until he wrapped his fingers around Mary's wrist. She jerked her hand away from him. "Leave me be," she snapped, green flecks glittering in her blue eyes and turning them turquoise.

Fury surged in his dark eyes. Although he hadn't understood her words, he understood her actions well enough. "Your tongue is sharp, Fire Woman," he growled in the Apache language. "Perhaps when you are mine, I will silence it permanently."

Mary stared at him in horror, her face blanching at his words. With a low growl, he turned on his heels and strode away from them.

"What's wrong, Mary?" Johanna asked. "What did he say?"

"I think he's plannin' on cuttin' my tongue out after he buys me," the girl said in a quivering voice.

"Oh, God!" Johanna stared at Mary's terrified face. "Surely he wouldn't do such a thing."

"He wouldn't be the first one to do it. When they brung me here, there was a woman like that. She died two years ago, but I'll never forget the sounds she made. They was awful." She squeezed her trembling hands together. "I gotta get away from here," she said. "I'd rather be dead than like that woman."

286

Johanna lay on the buffalo hide mat, her eyes closed as though she were asleep. But in truth, she was wide awake, waiting only for the Indians to fall asleep, before making good her escape.

She had been disappointed when the Apaches made camp at the river several miles from Bent's Fort. Then, the chief and most of the warriors rode out, leaving a handful of warriors behind to guard the prisoners.

Despite Mary's fears that William Bent would not come to their aid, the two girls were planning to escape and appeal to him for help.

Johanna didn't hear her visitor approach. She remained unaware until she felt the hand on her shoulder.

Turning over on the sleeping mat, she stared up into a pair of blue eyes. Mary placed a silencing finger across her lips and bent close to Johanna's ear. "Come help me with the guard," she said.

Johanna looked at her with a puzzlement that was quickly replaced by horror as she saw the dead guard beside the door. She swallowed hard and helped Mary pull the guard inside the wick-iup. Then the two girls left the village on silent feet.

The water swished around their feet as they waded through the shallows, and Johanna feared discovery at any moment. Soon the water grew deeper and they had to swim for it. Johanna was breathless when they finally reached the other side, but Mary allowed her only a moment's rest before they took up the trail of the warriors.

The girls kept at a brisk pace, intent on reaching their destination before the sun came up and left them exposed.

They sighted the fort, built in a sheltered bend of the Arkansas River, as the first glimmer of light signalled the coming of dawn. To Johanna, it represented a haven of safety.

The two girls moved closer, keeping an alert eye out for the Apaches. Mary saw them first and put a detaining hand on Johanna's arm to stop her.

And then Johanna saw them, sprawled every which way, dead to the world, passed out from the whiskey they had bought and indulged themselves in.

Although Johanna was bone-weary from the long walk, she felt elated by the sight of a horse and carriage standing in front of the fort. The carriage surely meant the presence of other white men, and surely that would insure their safety.

When they left the cover of the last bush, Johanna lifted her chin and walked boldly to the porch. Her heartbeat accelerated as she gripped the doorhandle, pushed the door open and stepped inside the dimly-lit interior, followed closely by Mary.

Johanna stopped abruptly at the sight of the man who stood idly at the bar. He was dressed in shiny black boots, tailored black breeches and the open, white silk shirt that denoted a man of means.

He was past forty, with graying dark hair, a beard, and intelligent eyes. His straight back and squared shoulders spoke of a great pride. His features, to the onlooker, were distinguished. But there was something in the lines and creases of the man's eyes and mouth that suggested cruelty.

Johanna recognized him instantly and cold fear battled with rage. It was Michael Durant; the man she had believed to be in Louisiana.

Although totally conscious of her fear, he seemed as startled as herself. But he recovered quicker. "Hello. Johanna," he said, grinning at her. "This must be my lucky day."

"What are you doing here?" she whispered. Her mind spun with the danger, but her wits had returned. Her whole body screamed out, urging her to run. Nervous, trembling with fear, her green eyes flitted feverishly around the room, searching for a way out.

"I was looking for you," he said, with a dispassionate air of boredom that only he possessed, as though these meager surroundings thoroughly taxed his sensibilities. "Although I didn't really expect to find you here." His eyes traveled over the doeskin-clad form. "And dressed like an Indian too. Will wonders never cease. I heard at Washington-on-the-Brazos that an Indian had abducted you. I came here just on the off chance that Bent might have heard something about you." He looked behind her, at Mary, then beyond her slender form. "Where's the buck who kidnapped you?" he asked. "Am I going to have to deal with him before we leave here?"

"Not him," she said boldly. "But you'll have to deal with the Apaches outside. They abducted me

289

from the Comanche camp."

"My, my," he said. "You are having a run of bad luck, aren't you? It's not likely the Apaches will bother us. We happened to be carrying a good supply of whiskey. A drink they are particularly fond of. But just in case . . ." He let his words drift off as his gaze went to a point beyond Johanna. "Take her quietly, Luke," he said.

Johanna gasped and whirled around. Too late. A hand clamped over her mouth and she was lifted off her feet. She looked wildly at Mary who had made a dash for the door. But even as she watched, another man left the shadows and struck Mary a hard blow on the head with the butt of his pistol. The woman crumpled silently to the floor, a thin trickle of blood flowing from a wound in her temple.

As Johanna watched in horror, footsteps sounded on the front porch. Durant nodded toward the back door and Johanna found herself lifted and carried outside.

"What happened?" a voice boomed from inside the room.

"Don't know," Durant's voice answered. "She just came staggering in the house mumbling about the Apaches and fell down unconscious."

"Poor woman," the unfamiliar voice said. "She probably just . . ."

Johanna heard no more as she was carried around the house and put into the waiting carriage. Although she kicked out with both feet, her captor made no sound as she was gagged and bound and thrown to the floor of the carriage.

Then, to her utter humiliation, her captor sat down on her, knocking her breath from her body. A red haze formed around her and she bordered on unconsciousness.

She was vaguely aware of the carriage swaying as someone entered and sat down. Her world at the moment consisted of the dusty floor of the carriage and the man sitting on her crumpled body.

"I'd appreciate any help you can give me," came Durant's voice from somewhere above her.

"If . . . hear anything . . . let you know." She strained hard to hear the voice outside the carriage. It sounded like the same one that had entered the cabin earlier. "Meanwhile," the voice said, "Don't give up hope. Chances are . . . never see her. Indians don't bring white captives . . ."

"I understand," Durant said. "But keep an eye open anyway."

"Sure will," the voice outside said. "Good luck to you. And don't worry . . . Apaches. Whiskey . . . and gold . . . safe passage . . . see you across . . ."

At that moment, the carriage gave a lurch as it began the long journey down the dusty ribbon of road. "You can get off her now," Durant said.

Luke got off Johanna and sat in the seat across from Durant. She glared her hatred at him, this man who was responsible for her father's death, this man who had ordered her held captive to use for his own means.

Bending over, he removed the gag from her mouth. "It should be safe enough to take this off now," he said. "We're far enough away so no one will hear your screams."

"I wouldn't give you the satisfaction," she grated.

"Satisfaction?" He raised an eyebrow. "My dear Johanna," he purred. "I've never wanted to do you harm. Haven't I always treated you decently?"

"How can you say that?" she asked in an outraged voice. "You had my father killed!"

"A necessary action," he said. "If he'd listened to reason, there would have been no need to act in such a manner."

"There's no excuse for what you did," she said. "No excuse at all."

"Let's agree to disagree," he said. He eyed her crumpled form. "You can't be very comfortable down there, my dear. I think it should be safe enough to untie you now. Even you wouldn't be so foolhardy as to try to escape from a carriage traveling this fast."

Bending over, he began to tug at the bonds on her wrists. "Tsk, tsk," he said. "I'm afraid Luke went a little overboard when he tied you. This rope has cut into your skin." He looked at her with a frown. "That really shouldn't be any problem for you, though, should it? I trust you've been practicing your art."

She refused to answer him. When her hands were free, she rose to the seat opposite him. "Is Mary dead?" she asked coldly.

"The woman who was with you?" he inquired. "I'm afraid she might be. Jed hit her too hard."

Johanna took Jed to be the driver of the carriage. "Another unfortunate accident?" she asked.

"Another?"

"Like my father."

"Oh, yes, I see." His expression darkened. "You must believe me, Johanna, that I never intended for him to be killed."

"I don't believe you."

"It's true. If you'll stop and think about it, you'll see that he could have done me more good alive than dead."

"How?" she asked bluntly.

"I could have used him as leverage," he said honestly. "You'd have stayed with us if we'd just threatened your father with harm. When you found out he was dead, you escaped. Up until that point, you didn't resist."

Not outwardly, she thought. And perhaps he was right. But the mistake had been made and her father was dead. That fact would never change. And Durant was the man responsible for his death. For that, she would never forgive him, and she would never stop resisting him.

Hawkeye's narrowed gaze studied the fort. It represented a safe haven to trappers and traders, as well as the Indians. But at the moment it seemed deserted.

Having long since lost the trail of the Apaches, Hawkeye hoped to find some word about Johanna at the fort. He knew it wasn't likely William Bent had seen her, but he might have heard talk of a woman who healed the sick. As he pulled Diablo up in front of the cabin a man stepped out on the porch. He recognized Bent instantly.

"Hawkeye," Bent said as he dismounted. "Didn't expect to see you here this time of year."

"I've come for help," Hawkeye said. "I'm searching for someone."

"Who's that?" Bent asked, spitting a long stream of tobacco on the ground.

"A white woman named Johanna," Hawkeye said.

"Johanna McFarley?" Bent asked, lifting a surprised eyebrow. "You the one who kidnapped her?"

Hawkeye's eyes narrowed on the man. His face became a hard mask, his eyes without warmth. "How do you know about Johanna?" he asked.

"Man came through here yesterday lookin' for her," Bent said. "Word's out she was stole from Washington town."

"The man's name?"

"Michael Durant," Bent growled. "You really take 'er?" His eyes were hard. "You know I don't hold with stealin' women."

Hawkeye let out a ragged sigh. "I took her, but not against her will." He saw no reason to elaborate. "She's my wife, Bent. The Apaches stole her from me."

"The Apaches?" Bent's eyes narrowed thoughtfully. "In that case, there's a woman here that might know somethin' about her."

Hawkeye's heart skipped a beat. *A woman? Could it be Johanna?* "Who is she?" he asked abruptly.

"Don't know who she is," Bent said. "She's been out of her head since yesterday. She come stumblin' in here ravin' about the Apaches. Durant said she just come in and fainted dead away."

"Durant?" Hawkeye's blood ran cold. "Not Michael Durant?"

Bent nodded. "That's him. He spent the night here, but left right after the woman passed out. I was out hitchin' up fresh horses for him when the woman come in. She was already out when I saw her."

"She hasn't said anything at all?" Hawkeye asked.

"Nope. Not a word."

"I want to see her."

"Sure thing."

Hawkeye followed the man into the cabin, passing through the main room into a smaller one. His gaze went to the young woman who lay on the bed and a sigh of disappointment escaped him.

It wasn't Johanna.

Hawkeye approached the bed, bending to study the face of the girl. She was thin, undernourished, and had probably been badly treated. The Apaches were notorious for their cruelty.

Putting a hand on the girl's shoulder, he gently shook her.

She stirred, then moaned loudly.

"M'am?" he said harshly. "Can you hear me?"

His words elicited another moan from her.

"M'am?" he said. "Do you know a woman called Johanna."

Her eyelids lifted and she stared at him with glazed blue eyes. "Johanna?" she whispered.

"Yes," he said urgently. "You were with the Apaches. Do you know where Johanna is?"

Her eyes flickered, then steadied on him. "She was with me," she whispered. "We got away from the Injuns and come here."

"But you came alone," Bent interrupted. "There was no one with you."

"No," she mumbled. "Johanna . . . was . . . with me."

"Must be ramblin'," Bent said. "Durant told me she was alone."

"Weren't you here when she came in?"

"No. Like I said. I was outside. She was lying there unconscious when I came in."

"Someone . . . hit me," Mary said, and her voice was stronger now.

"Who did?"

"Don't know. Couldn't see 'im. Johanna seemed to know one of 'em, was afeared of him." Her eyelids flickered. "Where is she?"

"That's what we're tryin' to figger out," Bent said.

"Durant took her," Hawkeye muttered, feeling certain of it.

"You think so?"

"Yes," Hawkeye said harshly. "But he won't get away. I'll follow him to hell and back if I have to."

And he would. For the love he bore Johanna would not let him rest until he found her. He loved her with an intensity that shook him, loved her laughter, her caring, the tenderness and understanding she carried in her small frame. And he had been so close to her . . . so close . . .

His mouth set in a rigid line, his eyes becoming cold as a winter storm. He would begin his search all over again, and he would never stop searching until he had found her.

And if anyone got in his way, he would see them dead.

clinging tiny feet on her naked hot skin. During
periods her stretch out into each aching bolster up
his proud arm. A light hue flower spread as she
tried to writhe again. He exalting type as when
all out again, and nearing a deep clamoring
much, when death it gently. Here it ceased
Arnd it announce on his breathing would against
quaking up

Chapter Twenty-four

Light fog clung tenaciously to the passenger
ship as the brawny crew made ready the sails. The
captain gave the order for the gangplank to be
lifted and the mooring lines released from the pier.

The deck was crowded, teeming with passengers, most of them, like Michael Durant, were
anxious to get to New Orleans. Johanna reluctantly stood by his side, held there by fingers
clutching her arm like a steel band.

"Well, my dear," Durant said. "We're on our
way now."

Johanna, her back rigid, remained silent.

"Sulking?" he asked, casting a glance at her.
"When will you realize I did you a favor? After
all, if I hadn't come along, the Apaches would still
be holding you prisoner."

Johanna held her silence.

Irritated by his failure to make her talk, Durant turned his attention to the sails being hoisted up the towering masts. When they were secured at the top, the wind gusted, billowing the sails until they resembled clouds. The order was given to hoist the anchor and the ship began a slow movement as the captain skillfully steered it through the crowded docks.

Durant, as though realizing Johanna was safely imprisoned, even though no bars or locks contained her, left her side and sought more genial company.

Relieved of his presence, Johanna allowed her body to relax somewhat. Her thoughts returned to the day she had first seen Galveston. She had come here expecting to find safety. She had never dreamed she would find love . . . and lose it.

Hawkeye.

Her heart ached. It felt as though it were breaking into tiny pieces.

Why did I have to lose you? she cried inside. Was she destined to always be alone?

Clutching her reticule in her hand, she walked slowly across the crowded deck. She barely noticed the people around her, for her thoughts were on her lost love. She tried to call up every moment they had together in her memory, to comfort herself with the short time he had been hers. She didn't see the small girl who slipped past her to the railing, eager to wave a last goodbye to someone who waited on the crowded docks.

"Becky!" a shrill voice called, penetrating her consciousness. "Where are you, Becky?"

Startled, the child turned . . . and tripped over a coil of rope. She went sprawling to the deck and her foot became caught in a loop that was sliding closer to the edge with each sway of the ship.

"Becky! Where are you?" the voice came again.

Johanna located the voice as belonging to a young woman with brown hair blowing around her face, obviously a harried mother searching for a lost child.

"Mommy!" The shriek came from behind Johanna. "Help me, Mommy!"

Turning, Johanna observed a young girl, not more than four or five years old, with golden hair streaming down her back, sliding dangerously close to the ship's rail.

"Becky!" the voice called again, and the anxiety was there for all to hear. "Becky, answer me!"

"I'm stuck!" the child wailed. "I want my Mommy!"

The ship swayed and the child swayed with it.

Johanna, realizing the danger the child was in, and the fact that the mother would be unable to reach her in time, hurried toward the small girl. As the ship gave another lurch, she made a dive for the child and grabbed her just before she tumbled into the ocean.

Turning, she handed the girl to the panic-stricken mother. As she did, she saw a flash of brown out of the corner of her eyes. Just a flash, but she turned back instantly. It took only a moment to pick the man clad in buckskin out of the many waiting on the dock.

Hawkeye!

Her green eyes widened, her breath seemed stuck in her throat as she stared, mesmerized, at the man she had thought lost to her forever.

Suddenly, cruel fingers gripped her wrist and she was jerked away from the railing and pulled toward the stairwell that led to the cabins.

"Let me go!" she protested, realizing it was Durant who held her imprisoned.

"Stop fighting me," he muttered in a low voice. "Do you want to make a complete fool of yourself? The captain is waiting to show us below."

Johanna had no time for the captain, nor for the young mother who was so effusive in her thanks. Johanna's gaze was riveted to the place where she had seen the man in buckskin.

But, to her consternation, the crowd shifted, and she couldn't see the man. Not one face on the dock was the least bit familiar. If it had been Hawkeye, he was gone.

Had it really been Hawkeye? Or had the man been a product of her imagination? One last effort of her mind to persuade her that he still lived.

Sky Walker grabbed Hawkeye's arm to physically stop his friend from diving in the water in an effort to reach Johanna.

"Careful," he said, keeping his voice low. "We must not attract the attention of these white-eyes."

Hawkeye knew he was right but he silently cursed the fates that would always allow him to reach Johanna too late. Although he'd only had a glimpse of the girl on the ship, he knew in his heart it had been her. And she had recognized him. He was certain of it.

"Perhaps is was meant to be," Sky Walker murmured beside him.

Hawkeye cast an angry look at the other man. "What was meant to be?" he growled.

"Perhaps Johanna belongs among the white-eyes."

Rage flowed through Hawkeye. "She is mine," he said coldly. "She will live wherever I am. And it will not be with the white-eyes."

Sky Walker's look was puzzled. "You will follow the ship?"

"To the end of the earth if need be."

"You take great risk, my brother. The bluecoats call you a traitor. They have put a bounty on your head. If you leave our lands to follow Johanna, you may never return."

"Nevertheless, I will go."

Sky Walker nodded, as though he had expected nothing less. "Then I will go with you."

Hawkeye studied his friend. "You are at even greater risk," he said. "Although there is no bounty on you, you have no understanding of the white man's language."

"Then I will remain silent," Sky Walker said cheerfully.

Hawkeye turned his friend's words over in his mind. "It is too much to ask," he said. "You must return to our people. You are needed there."

"Our people need you and your woman," Sky Walker returned. "Together you will make fine sons. But the great ship sails even as we speak. We must hurry if we are to follow."

Realizing the wisdom of his words, Hawkeye ceased to protest. They made their way down the docks until they reached the office to the shipping lines. While Sky Walker waited outside, Hawkeye entered the shipping office and approached the clerk bent over a newspaper.

"What was the **destina**tion of the ship that just left?" he asked gruffly.

The clerk looked up. "New Orleans," he replied.

"How much for two passengers on the next ship going that way?"

The clerk told him, and watched Hawkeye count out the gold. After issuing two tickets, the clerk said, "Be here before dawn next Monday."

"Monday?" Hawkeye questioned, frowning heavily. "What is today?"

The man grinned at him. "Sounds like you just reached town, stranger. Today is Tuesday. Be another six days afore the next ship leaves."

Hawkeye had already counted the days for himself. "I can't wait that long," he said.

"You wantin' to take a ship, you ain't got no choice," the clerk said. "If'n you wanta change your mind about goin', I don't mind givin' you a refund."

Hawkeye shook his head. Although he chafed at the delay, the ship was still the fastest way to follow. He left the shipping office and joined Sky Walker. The two men left the docks, knowing they could do nothing but wait.

Disregarding the stares of the other passengers, Durant dragged Johanna down a flight of stairs to a stateroom. Once inside, he bolted the door and turned his attention to her. "Who was he?" he asked harshly.

"Who?" she inquired casually.

"You know who I mean," he said. "You thought you recognized someone on the dock. I want to know who it was."

"You're quite mistaken," she said, turning away from him. "I recognized no one."

He smiled, but there was no amusement in his eyes. They remained cold. "I've come to know you very well, my dear." His tone was silky. "You think you've found some way out, someone to help you escape me. But whoever he is, I'll be prepared when he comes."

Alarmed, Johanna hurried to convince him he was wrong. If the man had in fact been Hawkeye, then she wanted no surprises when he came. If he came, she silently reminded herself.

"I was only concerned for the safety of the child," she told him. "And relieved that she had not gone overboard. If you've read something else into that, then you are sadly mistaken." Realizing he remained unconvinced, she raised her eyebrows and smiled at him. "But put a guard on me if you wish. It pleases me to cause you inconvenience."

He took her arm in a hard grip. "This is all so unnecessary," he said, his voice smooth and persuading. "Hasn't this little escapade convinced you there's no place where you can be safe? Except with me at the Institute. I have the power to

304

protect you from the people who would destroy you."

She shook her arm free, detesting his touch. "I'll take my chances with the people," she said, looking at him with contempt.

"Would you?" he countered. "Like your mother did?"

"What do you know about my mother?"

"I wrote to Ireland," he said. "I leave no stone unturned to get what I want. You wouldn't believe what I uncovered there. The mayor of your former city was very helpful." His eyes were hard. "With an ancestry like yours, you should be flattered that I still intend to marry you."

She paid little attention to his remark about her ancestry. Her mind had latched onto his last two words. "Marry me?" she gasped. "What are you talking about?"

"Didn't I tell you?" he asked casually. "I've just this minute decided that is the easiest way to insure you won't escape me again. A woman needs protection and I'll certainly be able to provide it."

"I have no intention of marrying you," she said. "Not now, or ever."

"You will," he said. "Make no mistake, my dear. You will. And I shall prove a devoted husband to you, give you every comfort in life. You'll never want for anything."

"Except my freedom," she said stiffly.

"You'll be free to come and go as you please," he said. "As long as you are accompanied by one of my men. In time, you'll come to realize how lucky you are, and have no wish to leave me."

"You can't force me to marry you," she said sharply. But even as she said the words, she wondered if she was wrong. Michael Durant was a powerful man with powerful friends. And Johanna, having of necessity kept to herself, had none. Her thoughts whirled as she sought desperately for a solution. It seemed there was only one way out. "It would be impossible to marry you," she said stiffly. "Since I already have a husband."

He stiffened with shock. "That's not possible!"

"Yes, it is," she said, more calmly than she felt.

Grabbing her shoulders, he shook her hard. "You lie!" he raged. "Admit it. You lie!"

"It's the truth," she spat defiantly, her eyes blazing hate at him from a face devoid of color.

His face was red with fury as he released her. Then, reaching out, he struck her a hard blow across the face, knocking her to the floor. He stood over her, his hands bunched into fists.

"There was no mention of a marriage in Washington," he said grimly. "If you had married, they would have known about it there."

She stood up shakily, her hand on her stinging cheek and stood defiantly before him. Contempt for him blazed in her green eyes. "They didn't know. I was married after I left there."

Seeming to recognize the truth in her words, he grabbed her shoulders and dug his fingers cruelly into her flesh. "Who is he?" he demanded.

"His name is Hawkeye," she said, lifting her chin proudly.

"Hawkeye?" His laugh grated harshly in her ears. "The savage who stole you? You let that

Indian trash have you?" He released her abruptly. "You're ruined," he said. "No decent man would take the leavings of a savage."

She couldn't keep the triumph from blazing in her eyes. Durant saw it, and a sly smile spread across his face. "There are other ways to get what I want," he muttered. With a hard glare, he left the room and closed the door. A moment later Johanna heard the grate of metal against wood as she was locked in.

Chapter Twenty-five

New Orleans had reached its most picturesque period. In England, it was described as a place of tropical luxury, a strange city in which more than forty thousand people lived. Founded by the French, it had been taken over by the Spanish. Now it was Creole, a blending of both. In an atmosphere of the Old World, in a luxurious community, filled with opera, theater, music, balls, gambling, and bullfights, there lived rich and cultured people, fiery men and passionate women who loved pleasure and lived for excitement that stirred the senses.

Johanna had never been a part of that world. Nor did she have any desire to do so. Life with her father had been peaceful . . . until fate had intervened in the form of a carriage accident outside the gates of the Institute.

She had been taken there to receive medical treatment and had never left again, until her father had been killed and desperation for her father's plight had spurred her escape.

Now she had returned. Once more a prisoner.

Despite the warmth of the midday sun, icy fingers of fear trickled down Johanna's spine as the high brick walls of the Institute came in sight. From her position in the carriage, she could see the drab, two-story brick building with heavily barred windows that lay beyond the walls.

Few people knew of the secrets harbored behind those walls, secrets that could radically change the world if they were to become known.

Therein lay the reason for the high walls, the barred windows. It had only been Cissy's intervention that had allowed her to escape just a few short months ago. Johanna seriously doubted she would be allowed a second chance. Once she was behind those gates, it was very unlikely she would ever come out again.

Michael Durant, seated beside her, seemed to sense her panic. Reaching out, he took her wrist in a hurting grip as though to insure she wouldn't try to run before the gates closed behind them.

Two guards were posted at the gate. One remained in the gatehouse while the other, a stout, fiftyish man with massive shoulders, a stranger to Johanna, stepped out to greet them.

"Have a nice trip, Doctor Durant?" the guard asked. Although his face was expressionless, his eyes flickered to Johanna before returning to Durant.

"Yes," Durant said smugly. "And a very profitable one as well."

The guard unlocked the gate, swung it wide and stepped aside until the carriage rolled through the entrance. Then he closed the gate with a clang of metal and locked it again.

Joshua was waiting at the door. The Negro man barely glanced at Johanna as he began to unload the baggage.

Once inside, Durant turned to her. "You know the way to your room, my dear," he said. "You'll find everything the way you left it. Except for Cissy, of course."

Joshua had just entered the hall with a bag under each arm. He froze at the mention of Cissy's name, but it was only a moment's pause, barely noticeable, then he mounted the stairs and went on his way.

"I'll have the housekeeper assign another maid to you," Durant was saying. "I'm afraid she won't be as useful as Cissy, but I feel certain you'll understand."

He was playing with her, just as a cat would play with a mouse. And like a cat, he was deriving great enjoyment from his cruelty.

Weariness, worsened by her sense of hopelessness, weighed heavily on Johanna's shoulders as she climbed the stairs to her room. Durant was determined to cage her healing power, to learn everything there was to know about it; he was determined to train it, and bend it to his will. How long could she hold out against him? she wondered.

The maid came and prepared her bath, keeping her eyes averted from Johanna as though unwilling to engage in conversation. *By Durant's orders?* Her meal was brought to her on a tray and she felt relieved that she didn't have to eat in Durant's company.

The next day Durant sent for her, intent on resuming the experiments. Although she was forced to go to him, she refused to cooperate.

"Don't be a fool," he said harshly. "You can only delay the experiments by your stubbornness. Eventually you'll have to come around."

"No," she said, holding his eyes with a steady calm. "You can hold me prisoner. But you need my cooperation for the experiments. And I refuse to give you that cooperation."

Realizing the truth in her words, he left the room and slammed the door behind him.

That night he sent word by her maid that her presence was required in the dining room.

"Please convey my apologies to Doctor Durant," she told the maid. "But I don't feel the least bit hungry."

It was only a matter of minutes before he came to her room. "There's no reason to be so foolish," he said. "It will accomplish nothing."

Her emerald eyes glittered. "And neither will you accomplish anything," she said sweetly.

His expression darkened with fury. For a moment she thought he would strike her. Instead, he spun on his heel and left her alone.

Trembling from reaction, Johanna seated herself in a chair beside the window. She felt completely unnerved by the confrontation. She realized she was only delaying the inevitable. She would either have to join him for meals or starve to death.

But the thought of helping the man who had killed her father was completely abhorrent to her.

The next day Johanna kept to her room, but by evening, hunger forced her to join him. He smiled when she joined him at the table and inquired politely about her health. He seemed intent on ignoring the altercation of the preceding night.

She was surprised when he invited her to go riding with him the next day.

Johanna had been intent on her food and the question came as a total surprise. She laid her spoon aside and looked up. "You're inviting me to go riding outside the Institute?" she asked.

"Naturally," he said blandly. "There's not enough room on the grounds to ride."

Although Johanna wanted to refuse, she was also eager to leave the Institute. She craved the fresh air, the wind blowing though her hair, the sense of freedom she would feel, false though it would be, outside the high walls. She found herself agreeing.

"Excellent," he said, his lips curving into a satisfied smile. I expect you'll find the fresh air relaxing."

Johanna did. And the ride became a daily routine that she came to look forward to, especially the times when Durant could not accompany her and she was escorted by one of his men. Then came the day when she discovered the reason for her small pleasure.

The sky was a cloudless blue as she made her way to the stables, expecting the horses to be saddled and waiting. Instead, she was given a message that Durant wished to see her in the laboratory.

Irritably, she made her way there and was ushered into a room where Durant waited with a stranger.

"Here she is," Durant said. "Johanna, I'd like to introduce Charles Parker. Charles, this is the young woman I told you about."

Puzzled, Johanna held out her hand to the stout man and allowed it to be kissed.

"Charles suffers from gout," Durant continued. "Just a little thing. I'd like you to see what you can do for him before you go riding."

So that is the reason he allowed me to ride, Johanna silently fumed. Her eyes met Durant's and held in a long stare. She was being given an ultimatum. Resume the experiments or be deprived of the one pleasure she was allowed.

She spun around in a flurry of skirts and went straight to her room. She expected Durant to follow and he did. He ranted and raged at her, but she remained adamant in her refusal.

The next day she learned from the maid she was to be taken to an opera.

"Tell your master I don't wish to go," Johanna said.

"He ain't gonna like dat," the maid said.

"No," Johanna agreed. "I don't suppose he will." But she didn't really care whether he liked it or not. He could find someone else to take to the opera. It

313

shouldn't be hard. His money and position made him desireable to most of New Orleans female populace. And the opera house was famous for its productions.

Suddenly, Johanna changed her mind. She *would* go to the opera. And she could enjoy herself. To refuse would only deprive herself of some small pleasure. There were few enough to be found, since Durant had refused to allow her to ride again.

"I've changed my mind," she told the maid. "Please convey my acceptance to Doctor Durant. But tell him I'll need something to wear."

The maid bobbed her head. "Yes, missy," she said.

The girl left the room but returned only moments later with a green silk gown and layers of white petticoats over her arm. Johanna allowed herself to be dressed in the finery and her dark hair arranged in large ringlets that fell to her shoulders. After a short glance in the mirror, she descended the stairs to where Durant was waiting.

The large hall was brilliantly lit with hundreds of chandeliers, broadcasting a silvery luminescence over the crowds of people, all in their finest dress, who milled around the Opera House. Not a single corner remained in shadows.

Johanna enjoyed the performance, and wished it could go on forever, knowing she was destined to return to the confines of the Institute when it ended. Perhaps that had been Durant's plan, she told herself. Perhaps his intention was to show her how her life could change if she cooperated with him.

When the curtain fell on act one, they left their box and made their way downstairs amid the crush of people for refreshments.

"There's someone here I want you to meet," Durant said, handing her a glass of sherry.

Johanna looked at him with suspicion. She had suspected he had an ulterior motive in bringing her. Now, it seemed, she was about to find out what it was.

"The Valdez family is one of the oldest, and wealthiest, families in New Orleans," Durant said. "Yvette's ancestors arrived with the French when the city was first founded, and her husband's family came with the Spaniards. They hold a powerful position here and could do the Institute a lot of good."

Johanna wondered what he was getting at, but refused to show the slightest interest in his words. She garnered a slight pleasure just knowing her attitude was a constant irritant to him.

Voices thundered and receded around her, drowning out the voice of the elderly man who approached them.

"Señor Valdez," Durant said, reaching out a hand to shake the other man's. "How nice to see you." He took Johanna's hand in his. "I'd like you to meet my ward, Johanna McFarley."

What was he up to, trying to pass her off as his ward? Johanna curtsied to the man who bowed from the waist. "I'm pleased to make your acquaintance," she murmured politely.

"She's very beautiful, Michael," Señor Valdez said. "You are a very lucky man."

Although Johanna heard the words, she paid no mind to them. She was wondering why Valdez seemed so familiar. Had they met before? She didn't think so, and yet, there was something very familiar about him.

"I understand you have a special gift for healing, my dear," Señor Valdez said.

Johanna's expression chilled and her lips tightened. She should have known that was Michael Durant's game.

"Yes. Michael told me," the other man said, seeming to read her mind. "And with good reason. These last few years my wife has been very ill. The doctors tell me her illness is hopelessly incurable. I would be much obliged if you would see her."

"I'm afraid it would do no good," she said stiffly. "Doctor Durant is mistaken about my abilities."

Señor Valdez seemed not in the least surprised by her denial. "He said you would be reluctant to use your gift," the old man said. "But before you refuse, would you at least consent to see my wife?"

Johanna flicked a glance of dislike at Michael Durant. He had expected a refusal and prepared for it. But had he told Señor Valdez everything? "Are you aware that Doctor Durant is holding me prisoner at the Institute?" she asked.

"Yes. He told me." His dark eyes offered an apology. "But if you won't stay voluntarily, then he has no other choice, except to confine you."

316

"Then you agree with his methods?"

He cleared his throat and shifted uncomfortably. "You must understand, my dear. You have a duty to others. Such a gift was not meant to be ignored. It must be used. My wife, for instance, is desperately ill. Without help she will surely die."

"How much are you paying Durant?" she asked bluntly.

He averted his eyes, looking at a point beyond her shoulder. "A life is worth more than gold," he murmured.

He green eyes darkened. "Yes," she said. "I believe it is. But Michael Durant does not. He has put a price on life. But it is a price few can afford."

Señor Valdez forced his gaze back to hers. "That should not concern you," he said gently. "Your only concern should be to help others."

"I will not use my gift for profit."

"Then you are among the minority," Señor Valdez said. "For is it not the usual practice for a doctor to collect some kind of fee?"

Her eyes flashed emerald green. "I am not a doctor, sir," she said bluntly. "And if I were, then any monies collected for my services would be mine alone. Not *Doctor* Michael Durant's. And what's more, the whole population would be welcome to my services."

"But I understand the healing drains you of your energy," Valdez said mildly. "Surely your strength would not hold out to healing the masses."

"Something could be worked out," she said stubbornly. "At least the choice would be mine, and not Michael Durant's."

"He has your best interests at heart, my dear. Perhaps it would be best if you left such decisions up to him."

"Michael Durant looks after his own interests, first and last," she said. "He always has, and I'm reasonably certain he always will."

"How can you say such a thing," Durant murmured from beside her. "You insist you want to heal the masses, and yet, those same people would condemn you for a witch."

Johanna felt completely frustrated. She had been watching Valdez and knew that Durant had him completely fooled. He believed every word Durant uttered.

Valdez's dark eyes softened as he spoke. "I understand your mother was accused of being a witch and was killed. Michael is only trying to protect you from such a fate."

She studied Señor Valdez, wondering if the sympathy he expressed was real or feigned. "Did Durant tell you he had my father killed?" she asked bluntly.

Her words seemed to shock the older man. He looked at Durant for an explanation.

"An unfortunate accident," Durant inserted smoothly. "McFarley was raving, wild. He had a weapon. I was only trying to defend myself, and the gun went off."

"I'm sorry, Miss McFarley," the older man murmured. "I can see you have suffered greatly. But, please, don't let it influence you against helping my wife. She's not to blame for what has happened and she suffers from intense pain almost all the time." His eyes grew moist as he spoke of his wife.

She wanted to refuse, but for some reason she couldn't. He was right. His wife wasn't to blame for Michael Durant's shortcomings. A soft sigh issued from her lips. "I'll come see her," she said. "That's all I can promise."

He seemed satisfied with her answer and bid them enjoy the rest of the opera. But when they returned to their seats, Johanna found her enjoyment was gone. Durant, however, seemed to have accomplished what he had come for. And, completely satisfied, settled down to enjoy himself.

Chapter Twenty-six

The sun's position announced a two o'clock hour when the maid came to Johanna's room to tell her Durant was waiting to take her to the Valdez home. She slipped out of her dress and donned a blue gown, tied her hair back with a matching ribbon, then descended the stairway to join him.

Johanna sat silently beside Durant as they traveled the river road leading to the Valdez mansion. The air was heavy, moist, the bank lined with tall pines, interspersed with spruce, sweet gum, and fragrant magnolias. Gnarled oaks rose at intervals and slow bayous twisted about them. They had only gone a short distance when the stately mansion came into view, and they went through a pair of high, scrolled iron gates that led from the carriageway to the sun-splashed greenery of the courtyard. Farther on, flagstoned paths wound among raised flowerbeds bordered by brick.

The door was answered by a snowy-haired butler who bid them enter. He showed them into a drawing room filled with rich mahogany furniture and told them to wait.

Durant seated himself in a comfortable chair, but Johanna was restless. She moved about the room, studying the objects d'art that spoke of quiet elegance. Pictures in ornate frames hung from the wall and she studied each of them in turn, recognizing a younger Valdez with a beautiful woman with dark hair and eyes standing beside him. As she moved to the next picture, her eyes widened in recognition.

The man pictured within the ornate frame was the exact image of Hawkeye.

She was drawn to it, almost completely mesmerized as she stared up at the familiar face. Footsteps sounded outside the door, entered the room, then stopped beside her.

"His name is Pierre Valdez," Señor Valdez said.

"Valdez?" She turned puzzled eyes on him.

"Yes," he answered. "My son."

She looked again at the picture, the image of Hawkeye. The man wore expensive dress and around his neck hung a heavy gold cross.

The cross was identical to the one Hawkeye wore.

How could such a thing be possible? She wondered, turning wide green eyes on Valdez. "Where is your son?" she asked.

A world of sadness was in his voice when he

spoke. "He's departed from this earth," he answered. "Killed many years ago. The news of his death nearly killed my wife as well. She has been in bad health for these past twenty-five years. It was her weakness that made her susceptible to disease."

"Which brings us to our purpose here," Durant inserted smoothly. "And that is the Señora's health." He turned to Valdez. "Would you like us to go to her now?"

"Not us, Michael," Johanna said coldly. "I won't need you for what I have to do."

"Nevertheless, I shall go with you," he said.

Johanna sat down on the ivory satin settee, smoothed her gown over her legs, and folded her hands in her lap. "Then you shall see her alone," she told him.

His eyes darkened threateningly. "We've already been over this once before, Johanna," he said harshly. "You will see no one unless I accompany you."

"Then I will not see her."

Michael Durant's eyes glittered angrily. "Would you leave us alone for a moment?" he said to Valdez.

"No," the older man said. "Señorita McFarley is right, Michael. There is no reason for you to accompany her to my wife's room." "Let me be the judge of what is needed here," Durant growled. "I've already told you, we're conducting research. There's no way I can judge the degree of success if I'm not able to see Johanna perform."

Valdez's lips thinned and his dark eyes snapped.

"Perhaps this time you could dispense with the research." Durant opened his mouth to object, but Valdez continued, "Naturally," he said, "I'll make certain the Institute is adequately compensated for the trouble."

Although Durant still looked angry, he appeared slightly mollified. "In that case," he said stiffly, "Perhaps I could waive the research in this instance."

"Naturally," Johanna murmured. "I expected you could be persuaded."

Durant threw her a killing look, but took a seat when she rose to accompany the older gentleman from the room.

They went up a wide curving stairway and turned right at the top of the stairs. Pushing open a door, Valdez motioned her inside.

Bracing herself, Johanna entered the room.

The chamber was large and square, panelled in pine with a marble fireplace built into one wall. A four-poster bed dominated the room. Johanna's gaze fell hesitantly on the woman lying beneath the blue velvet coverlet. There was hardly anything to be seen. She was so thin the coverlet was almost flat. Her skin was incredibly dry and seemed parchment thin, and the color was as pale as the pillowcase beneath her head.

As Johanna drew nearer she felt the sense of familiarity she had felt with Señor Valdez. She didn't think she'd ever met the woman in the white high-necked gown with ruffles at the neck and sleeves, and yet, she couldn't shake the feeling that she had seen her before.

Señor Valdez stepped around Johanna and approached the bed. "Yvette," he spoke softly. "Wake up, my darling."

The woman opened her eyes and smiled up at her husband. Johanna recognized the intelligence burning in Yvette Valdez's deep-set eyes.

"How are you feeling, my dear?" Valdez asked.

"About the same as usual," she answered weakly.

"I've brought someone to see you, Yvette." He stepped aside so Johanna could be seen. "This is Señorita McFarley."

Yvette Valdez's lips stretched into a smile and she held out a trembling hand. Johanna squeezed the frail hand lightly, feeling the bones would surely crush if she applied the least pressure.

"I don't get much company," the old lady whispered in a faint voice. "Especially none as lovely as . . ." A sudden coughing fit interrupted her, shaking her slight frame. She waited until it had passed and she had recovered somewhat, before she added, "Come closer, my dear, so I can see you better."

Johanna did as she was bid.

The two men were right, she told herself. The woman was obviously very ill. Johanna was unwilling to help Durant, but how could she turn away from a woman who badly needed her help? She felt a curious kinship with the woman.

"I'm afraid I can't get up," Yvette told her. "It's been many years since I've been able to get about."

Johanna knelt beside the bed and looked at the woman's pale face. "What seems to be the trouble?" she asked softly.

"Consumption," Yvette Valdez murmured shakily. "It comes from living too long."

Johanna looked questioningly up at Señor Valdez.

"Yvette makes light of her illness," he said. "She is only three score years and has been delicate for many of them. The doctor tells us she has a lung problem that grows progressively worse each day."

"Pshaw!" the old woman said. Her eyes gleamed with love as they held her husband's. "The doctor is an old fool. He doesn't know what he's talking about." She closed her eyes as though suddenly too weary to keep them open. "I'm just a little weary," she murmured. After garnering further strength, she opened her eyes again.

"Do you mind if I put my hands on you," Johanna asked, holding the woman's gaze. "I'll be careful not to hurt you."

"Put your hands on me?" the woman asked. "Whatever for, my dear?" She looked uncertainly at her husband.

"Please, Yvette," he said. "Let her do this little thing. It may be possible she can help you."

The woman's dark eyes grew pensive. "If it makes you happy," she said, "then I don't mind."

"May I have a chair, Señor?" Johanna asked.

"What am I thinking of to allow you to kneel on the floor?" he scolded himself. He picked up a straight-backed chair and brought it to the bedside.

After Johanna was seated, she placed her palms on the woman's chest, positioned them above the lungs, then closed her eyes. Suddenly the woman gave a stifled cry, her eyes opening wider. Johanna

325

could feel the process draining her of energy, but she continued her ministrations until she felt the healing was complete. Only then did she remove her hands and slump back in the chair.

When she opened her eyes again, the woman was sitting up in the bed and staring wide-eyed at her.

"What a miracle is this?" she asked, and Johanna could hear the strength in the woman's voice.

"Yvette," the man cried, falling to his knees beside the bed. "You are better. I can tell you are."

Ignoring him, the woman took Johanna's hand. "Who are you, child, and where do you come from?"

"Ireland is my homeland," Johanna replied. "I came to America a few years ago with my father."

"You live with your father?"

"No. He's dead. I live at the Durant Institute."

The old woman's eyes were sharp and she was very perceptive. "You live there by your own choice?"

"No," Johanna murmured. "Not by choice."

The woman turned to her husband. "Is that man using this child for personal gain?"

Valdez looked uncomfortable. "Yvette," he chided gently. "Don't you realize what has occurred? Miss McFarley has cured you."

"She is the instrument of God," Yvette corrected. "A gift such as hers could come from no other source. But you haven't answered my question. Is Michael Durant using this girl for his own gain?" Her voice was strong, demanding.

"She must be protected," he said. "You can see

326

how drained she is. Michael is only . . ."

"You should be ashamed," she interrupted. "And so should Michael Durant. I want you to make certain he releases her."

"He has threatened to accuse me of being a witch," Johanna told her. "I'm afraid there's nothing your husband can do."

"For shame, for shame." She looked at her husband. "Bring me my robe," she said. "I want to speak to this man."

"But . . . my dear," he protested. "You can't get up. You're much too weak."

"He's right," Johanna said. "And nothing you could say would dissuade Michael Durant from his purpose. No one could. For the moment I must stay where I am."

But only for the moment, she promised herself.

Chapter Twenty-seven

Johanna thought about Yvette's words as she descended the stairwell. If Yvette didn't condemn her, perhaps others would be as tolerant. She realized Yvette's thoughts were colored by her returned health, while others who had not benefited from the healing gift might see things differently. But if she could make Durant think his threats held no power, then perhaps . . .

She had been deep in thought, unaware she had entered the drawing room until Durant spoked.

"How did it go?"

"Very well," she said, her voice cool. "So well, in fact, that I've decided not to return to the Institute with you."

He raised his eyebrows. "Not going? Now what brought this on, I wonder."

"Yvette Valdez," she said. "She knows about me

and doesn't believe me a witch. Denounce me if you will. But I'll take my chances with the public."

He gave a harsh laugh. "I expected this to happen sooner or later," he said. "And I am fully prepared to deal with it."

"Are you?" she asked, and her voice could have put icicles to shame. "How are you going to deal with it? We're in the Valdez home with plenty of witnesses around. Do you think you can silence them all if you force me screaming out of their house?"

"I don't intend to force you. Screaming or otherwise," he said smoothly. "I'm not stupid, Johanna. I came here well-prepared for this contingency."

"How so?" she asked.

"Come to the Institute with me and I'll show you."

She gave a short laugh. "And once inside those gates you'll hold me prisoner again. No, thank you. I don't intend to leave this house with you."

"And where will you go?" he inquired, his voice smooth as silk.

"I'll go home."

"If you mean the house that belonged to your father, then I'm afraid that would be impossible. It's occupied already."

"What do you mean, occupied?" she asked.

"Alas, it has been sold," he said.

"Illegally then," she snapped. "I didn't sign the papers and the house belongs to me, as my father's rightful heir."

"Not so," he said. "Your father was deeply in debt. The house was sold at auction to satisfy those debts."

"That's not true," she gasped. "My father owed no man. He paid cash for everything we bought."

"I'm afraid there were some things about your father that you didn't know."

Resentment and anger stiffened her body, but her voice was clear and calm. "For instance?" she challenged.

"He was a gambling man, my dear."

Her eyes filled with sparks of rage. "You lie!" she hissed.

"Prove it," he said calmly.

"How do you expect me to do that? My father isn't here to deny such a falsehood."

"How true."

"So you've managed to take my home from me," she said slowly. "But even so, I refuse to return to the Institute."

"No? Perhaps you'd better think twice."

Something in his tone warned her she wasn't going to like what he had to say. She waited silently for him to continue.

"There's a certain Irishman living down in the bayou . . ."

Patrick! Her face turned white. Her hands clenched into fists, but she forced herself to be calm. "I don't know what you mean," she said.

"No? Then let me refresh your memory. It's illegal to help runaway slaves. All I have to do is tell the constable of Patrick's activities and he'll be arrested." His eyes were menacing. "You know what happens to anyone caught helping runaway slaves. Don't you?"

She did. They were lucky if they were only hanged.

Michael Durant walked to the door and opened it. "Are you coming, my dear?" he asked. "Or shall I pay a visit to the constable?"

She recognized the threat barely veiled in his words. "I want to see Patrick," she said stiffly. "I want to talk to him . . . make certain he's all right."

"Of course," he said smoothly. "I've already anticipated your wishes. The old man will be waiting for you at the Institute."

She watched him with unfriendly eyes. He was a handsome man in a cold, calculating way. He reminded her of a rattler, coiled, dangerous, ready to strike at anyone who got in his way.

"You knew this was going to happen," she accused.

"I suspected as much," he agreed. "So I prepared for the incident."

"And if I'd given you no trouble? Would you still have threatened Patrick?"

"Of course not," he said. "I don't care about the old man. It's not up to me to find runaway slaves for their owners."

She knew she had no choice except to go to the Institute with him. Even if Patrick was not there, he knew about him and could get to him any time he wanted. She followed him from the house to the waiting carriage.

She remained silent on the trip back, despising the man she was with, despising the haughty, self-assured arrogance he possessed. He had ruined her father's name as well as taken his life. And there was nothing she could do about it.

When they reached the Institute, Patrick was waiting for her in the drawing room, his eyes glazed with worry. "Leave us alone," she told Durant.

He turned on his heel and left the room.

"What's happenin', lassie?" the old man asked her. "Are we in trouble?"

"No, Patrick," she assured him. "Everything's fine. You haven't been threatened in any way, have you?"

"No, lass. Durant's men came and said he wanted to see me. They said it would be in my best interest to come." His expression was worried. "I thought you got away from here, lass. I thought you were safe from him."

"I thought so, too," she muttered.

"Does Durant plan to keep you locked up here?"

"No," she said. "He won't keep me locked up, Patrick. But I must stay. I have no choice."

"Is it because of me?" he questioned. "I wouldn't want you to worry on my account. You don't have to stay here for me. I'll figger somethin' out."

Although Patrick protested, she could see he was worried, and she silently cursed Durant as she patted the old man's hand reassuringly.

"No," she said. "I'll come to no harm here. We'll let Michael Durant have it his way. For now. A little time is all I need, then the two of us will leave New Orleans."

"Leave?" He blinked at her as though the idea of leaving had never entered his head. "Where would we go?" he asked.

Her thoughts turned inward and she smiled at

him. "There's a place in Texas where Durant would never find us. Even if he did, he would never be allowed to harm us."

"I wouldn't be so sure, lass."

"But I am." Her eyes were moist as she thought of Hawkeye. Even if he was gone, there was still the Comanche Indians. They would welcome her back and she would take Patrick with her.

"What are you plannin'?" Patrick asked. "Where is this place."

"Where you'd least expect it, Patrick. An Indian encampment."

"Injuns!" he exclaimed, fear flickering across his face. "I heered about them redskins an' I ain't wantin' nothing to do with 'em. I aim to keep ever bit of the hair on my head."

She gave a soft laugh. "You don't have to worry about being scalped," she said. "The Comanches are friends of mine."

"Friends, are they? How did you come to be friendly with Injuns?"

"My husband was a Comanche warrior," she said.

His mouth dropped open, and he gawked at her. "Your husband?"

"Yes," she said, smiling at his astonishment.

She proceeded to tell the old man what had happened to her since she had last seen him. Her voice softened as she spoke of Hawkeye, and their love.

"Are you certain he's dead?" the old man questioned.

"I saw him go over the cliff," she told him, tears

333

welling up into her eyes. "He couldn't have survived that fall."

The door opened abruptly and Durant stepped into the room. Johanna jerked her head up and stared balefully at him, but he ignored the look.

"It's getting late," he said. "You need your rest. We have a busy day ahead of us tomorrow."

Patrick glared at him. "It ain't right what you're a'doin' to the lass," he said angrily. "Ain't right at all."

"Shut your mouth, old man," Durant said. "You're lucky I don't report you to the authorities. I've a good mind to do it anyway."

The old man's skin turned a pasty gray and fear erupted through Johanna's body. She knew Durant was capable of almost anything.

"You'd better leave Patrick alone," Johanna said. "I intend to visit him every day and he'd better be in his cabin and faring well."

"My dear Johanna," he said smoothly. "I can't be responsible for what happens to this man. Who can say when some untimely accident will . . ."

"He'd better not meet with any kind of accident," she said grimly. "Not if you expect me to continue the experiments."

His lips tightened. "Very well," he said. "I'll put a guard on the old man."

"No guard!" she said sharply. "But I'll be visiting him for tea every day. And he'd better be there and in good health when I arrive."

Putting her hand in the old man's she said, "I'll see you tomorrow at tea time."

"I'll be there," he said, getting heavily to his feet.

She turned to Durant. "Order the carriage around and have him taken home."

"In my carriage?" he was outraged. "There's a mule out back he can ride. It's good enough for the old man."

When she would have protested, Patrick stopped her. "The mule's better, lassie," he said. "I ain't never been in no fancy buggy before an' I reckon I ain't been missin' much."

She bid him good-bye and watched him leave. Only then did she turn to Durant.

"I mean it," she said sharply. "You'd better not hurt him."

Reaching out, he stroked a ringlet of her hair. She jerked her head away from his touch.

His smile was tight, angry. "Perhaps you'd better retire, my dear. Before you go too far."

"Gladly," she said in a cold voice.

Shivering from the encounter, she went to her room and changed into a light cotton dress. Crossing to the window, she stared down into the gardens. How could she be expected to live without Hawkeye? Was he really gone?

Suddenly overcome by emotion, she flung herself on the bed, burying her face in the pillow, muffling her agonized sobs as she let her grief over Hawkeye's death completely overwhelm her for the first time. She didn't want to live without him.

When the flood of warm tears had abated, she rose, washed her face and tried to compose herself. She could never be sure when Durant was going to enter her room, and she didn't want him to know she had been crying. He was hard, cruel, and

335

unpredictable, and she didn't intend to show the slightest weakness to him. He would be quick to take advantage of it.

Sinking down in a rocker, she lovingly fondled the bracelet Hawkeye had made her. The turquoise was smooth and glittered from constant rubbing. It was all she had left of her lost love, except her memories. Again, the tears came, and she wept for all that might have been.

Chapter Twenty-eight

It was evening and the sky had turned the color of thick soot when the merchant ship that carried Hawkeye and Sky Walker docked.

All along the river front, for nearly two miles, moored to the heavy timbers embedded in the batture, lay the shipping. There were blunt-bowed trading ships from Europe, coasting craft from New England, and twenty or more Mississippi river steamboats, the latest development in American navigation. Cargo flats cluttered the great waterway, loaded with cotton, woolen goods, furniture, farming implements, crude machinery, iron billets, liquors, coffee, and spices. Some bound for plantations, others for towns of Louisiana and Mississippi and other ports up the great river.

The whole waterfront was astir. Negroes sang as they toiled, rolling the hogsheads, carrying the bales. Along the levee swarmed the seamen of a dozen nations, and among them the American river men, hard-living, fearless men, who manned the flatboats, men who loved New Orleans, men who scattered their hard-earned dollars in a debauch which lasted but a single night, then who lingered on the levee to drink and fight, to terrorize the negroes, and to get gloriously drunk. Then, penniless, they would strike out again along the overland trail which took them through hundreds of miles of forest and home again.

Hawkeye stood near the railing silently cursing the delay. The ship's captain had told them they would be unable to unload the horses until morning.

"Town's got a curfew," he said. "It's nearly time for the cannon to be fired off." Recognizing Hawkeye's puzzlement, he explained further. "They fire off a cannon at eight o'clock as a signal for all sailors, soldiers, and coloreds to get off the streets. Them who don't, gets took off to the city prison." He looked gloomily out over the crowded city. "Might just as well stay on board," he muttered. "Ain't no taverns left open after that cannon goes off."

Hawkeye watched a steam ferryboat cross the river from the levee beside the French market. On the opposite shore he could see shipbuilding yards.

"How do they enforce such a law?" he asked the captain.

"Got fifty men guardin' the city."

"Fifty?" Hawkeye questioned.

"Yeah," the captain said. "Last census taken

showed more'n forty thousand people here. Them fifty guards patrol in groups of twos and threes. All of 'em carryin' lanterns and guns."

"How do you come to be so familiar with the city?" Hawkeye questioned.

"Got me a family here," the captain answered. "My boy, he wanted to get on one of them patrols." His lips twisted into a grin. "He ain't 'specially all that law abidin'. Just figgered it was a way of gettin' 'round that ord'nance. But they turned 'im down flat. Seems one of the requirements is to be able to speak both French and English."

"Do you have to wait until morning to leave the ship?" Hawkeye inquired.

"I ain't no common sailor," the captain said angrily. And I don't mean to be treated as such. No matter what the city council says. Besides," he said. "I got me plenty of time to get home afore that cannon is fired off. Happens I don't live very far from here."

"Since you're so familiar with the city, do you know anything about the Durant Institute?"

"Could be," the captain replied. "What do you want to know about it?"

"Where could I find it?"

"Just follow the river road north," he said. " 'Bout five miles down the road you'll see a high brick wall. Institute's behind it." He studied them through narrowed eyes. "You expected there?" Without giving Hawkeye a chance to answer, he continued. "If'n you ain't expected, it's more'n likely you won't get inside. Gate's got guards on it."

"Guards?"

"Yeah. It's a research institute. Don't know what kinda research they're doin', but guess it must be valuable to need guardin'. Hear tell they even got a coupla mean dogs runnin' loose inside that fence. In case anyone gets past them guards. This your first time in New Orleans?"

"I was here ten years ago," Hawkeye said. "But I never heard of the Institute."

"Wasn't here then," the captain said. "It was built 'bout eight years ago. If'n you're goin' there to-night, you're gonna need horses. Happens my brother owns the livery down the street. You can always get good mounts there. Rent or buy, which-ever pleases you most."

Hawkeye's gaze swept over a pair of demoiselles with their father on their way to a steamer. A Negro woman passed them, carrying a basket of fresh fruit, her head swathed in a white turban.

New Orleans hadn't changed much in the ten years since he'd last seen it.

Upon noticing the gangplank had been lowered, Hawkeye thanked the captain, and said they'd be back in the morning for their horses, then the two men left the ship and made their way to the livery stable where they rented two likely looking mounts. Moments later they were riding up the the river road that paralleled the Mississippi River for a distance of several hundred miles.

The taverns and houses were jumbled together, the buildings constructed of brick covered with stucco and the roofs covered with slate or tile. Sky Walker was fascinated by the ironwork and walled gardens of the city. As they neared the edge of the city they found the buildings were built farther apart until finally the town was left behind them. On both sides of the water were dense forests where Spanish moss and ivy-draped live oaks and water sycamores and moss grew in abundance on the forest floor.

But the two men wasted little time on the beauty of their surroundings. They were intent on their destination and what lay ahead of them, as they made their way down the river road.

Hawkeye knew it instantly, for the Institute stood out like a sore thumb. A high, brick fence stretched out as far as the eye could see. In front, directly in the path of the incoming road was a guardhouse.

A lone security guard, pistol holster at his side, stepped out and with a forced smile, said, "This's private property, mister. You'll have to turn back."

Hawkeye tried a smile on the man. "We've come to see Miss McFarley," he said.

At his words, the guard's eyes narrowed ever so slightly. "Miss McFarley ain't receivin' company to-day," he growled. "You can leave your name an' I'll tell 'er you was here."

A muscle thudded in Hawkeye's jaw and his fist tightened into a ball. There was no doubt now that Johanna was somewhere beyond the gate. How could he possibly leave without seeing her? He doubted that she would be told of their arrival, but he left the name of Brazos Jones, hoping if she was informed, she would make the connection. When they left, both men were aware one of the guards had left his post and was following them.

Johanna stood before a mirror, putting the finishing touches to her hair. Michael Durant had insisted she join him for dinner. And, although she had wanted to refuse, the knowledge that Patrick would be the one to suffer changed her mind.

Knowing she could delay no longer, she left her room and descended the stairs. She found Durant waiting for her in the parlor.

"How lovely you look, my dear," he said, rising to his feet, and motioning her to a chair.

She held her silence, seating herself on the gold settee. She didn't need compliments from the likes of Michael Durant.

He poured her a glass of sherry, and brought it to her, leaning unnecessarily close. "I thought you'd be interested to know you had company today," he murmured near her ear.

Her head lifted, but she remained silent. She knew he would tell her what he intended as soon as he wanted to, knew also that her continued silence was a constant irritant to him.

"Aren't you the least bit curious?"

"Not really," she said, lowering her eyes to the glass in her hand.

"That, in itself is curious," he told her.

"How so?" she asked. "I have no friends in New Orleans except for Patrick." She lifted her eyes to him. "And since I saw him only this afternoon, I hardly think it was him."

"No," he agreed blandly. "It wasn't him. The man who came was dressed in buckskins."

Her heart beat a rapid tattoo in her breast as she

342

instantly thought of Hawkeye. *It can't be him,* she chided herself.

"I'm afraid I haven't the vaguest idea who it could be," she said, being careful to appear disinterested. "Did he leave a name?"

"As it happens, he did. He gave the unlikely name of Brazos Jones." There was a smile on his face.

Brazos. Hawkeye's words surfaced in her mind. *The Indians named me for the river where they found me.* Her heart began to race in her breast, but she forced herself to stay calm. *Was it possible? Or was she only fooling herself? There could be a hundred men who called themselves Brazos.*

Dressed in buckskin?

She licked lips that had suddenly gone dry. "What did this man look like?" she asked.

He grinned. "So you *are* interested?"

"Isn't that what you intended?"

"I'll admit I was curious. As to what he wanted, he didn't say. He and his companion checked in at a hotel after they left here."

"You had him followed?"

"Of course. Where you're concerned, I leave nothing to chance." He looked up as the butler announced dinner. "It's time for us to dine," he said, extending his arm, an act which she completely ignored. "We can discuss this matter at another time. Right now, I'm ravenous."

She followed him to the dining room, her emotions in turmoil. If Brazos Jones was Hawkeye, he would come again. The meal seemed endless. Johanna wanted to hurry and get back to her room so she could think about what Durant had told her. As if he sensed her desire, he kept up a running stream of conversation and even insisted she have an after-dinner drink with him.

When she was finally able to retire, she went straight to the window and stared out into the night, hoping she would see something, anything, that would give her some clue to the man who called himself Brazos Jones.

Chapter Twenty-nine

Hawkeye watched the guard leave, then let the curtain fall in place. Easing the window up, he swung his buckskin-clad legs over the window sill and dropped to the ground with a soft thud. A moment later he was joined by Sky Walker.

It was easy for the Comanche warrior to elude the town guards and return to the Institute. They left their mounts hidden in the thick forest, and made their way closer under cover of darkness.

As they drew nearer, Hawkeye saw a carriage stopped near the gate.

Michael Durant?

Intent on finding out, Hawkeye dropped to his stomach and worked his way closer until he could hear the low rumble of voices.

The guard's voice came clearly on the still night air. "Will you be out late, Doctor Durant?"

"No," the man in the carriage said. "Only an hour or so. I'm expecting a visitor later on. His name is Crawford. See that he's let through if he comes while I'm gone."

"Sure thing," the guard said. "Bill and Jake will be along soon. I'll see they get the message."

Hawkeye's eyes narrowed on the man who was his enemy. He curbed the urge to attack, knowing the odds were too great. Two guards rode with Durant and another two were posted at the gate. He wanted to get Johanna to safety before exacting his revenge.

Reluctantly, he watched Durant leave.

Returning to Sky Walker, Hawkeye found he'd already killed a rabbit to distract the dogs. Although he was ready to make his move, he remembered the guard's reference to Bill and Jake. Obviously relief guards, and expected soon. He couldn't take a chance on being surprised, would have to wait until the guards changed.

It seemed an eternity before the two armed men rode in and replaced the two guards in the gatehouse. Hawkeye cursed his luck, knowing he should have acted sooner. Durant could ride in at any moment.

The guards, Bill and Jake, left the guardhouse to begin a security check, and Hawkeye knew it was time to act. While Sky Walker kept the Institute under his eyes, Hawkeye mounted his horse and approached the gate.

The guard was jumpy. He held his rifle threateningly, aimed at Hawkeye. "State your business," he said gruffly.

"I've come to see Michael Durant," Hawkeye said.

He took a chance the guard had never met Crawford. "Name's Crawford."

The guard frowned. "Sure thing, Mister Crawford." He lowered the rifle, reached for the gate and fumbled with the lock.

Hawkeye couldn't hide the triumph he felt. It had been so easy, after all. At that moment, the guard looked up, saw the expression on Hawkeye's face and, with an oath, raised the weapon again.

Too late. Hawkeye leapt from his mount and slammed the gate open with a strength few men could match. He caught the guard's head with the iron, and the man crumpled to his knees. Before he could regain his feet, Hawkeye brought the butt end of his pistol against the back of the man's head. The impact knocked the guard hard against the ground.

When the other sentry returned they were waiting for him. Sky Walker's knife was already at his throat before he was even aware of the danger.

The rabbit took care of the dogs and while they snarled and fought over the dead carcass, Hawkeye ran fleetly toward the building. He found the front door locked and swore softly. Hugging the wall, he moved around to the nearest window. He spent precious time testing the strength of the bars before realizing entry could not be obtained from that direction. He moved around farther, found another door . . . locked as well.

Pulling his knife from its sheath, he inserted it in the edge of the door and tried to work the lock loose. He heard a click as the lock gave way, then the door opened inward to reveal the old negro man standing inside.

Hawkeye pushed the old man aside and stepped into the room, hurriedly closing the door behind him.

The two men stared at each other for a long moment.

Finally, the old man broke the silence. "You lookin' for Miss Johanna?"

Hawkeye nodded.

"Then you best come with me," the old man said. "They's so many rooms here, you ain't gonna find her by your ownself. Leastways, not 'fore Massa Durant come back."

Hawkeye wondered if he could trust the old man. "Who are you?" he asked. "And how do I know I can trust you?"

"You gonna have to if'n you want to help dat girl. My name don't matter nohow. Onliest thing what matters is they killed my girl, Cissy." He shook his grizzled head from side to side. "Cissy never hurt nobody. They shouldn't oughtta shot her." He motioned down the hall. "Miss Johanna upstairs," he said. "I show you where."

Johanna rose with a start, bolting up in the feather bed. Moonlight slanted through the window and across the floor, making bright splashes upon the patterned rug. She peered through the shadows, barely able to make out a dark shape lingering near the bed.

Someone was in the room!

She opened her mouth to scream and a hand reached out, covering her mouth, and stifling her

348

voice.

Raking her fingernails down the intruder's arms, she fought desperately to free herself, and was rewarded by a smothered curse.

"Stop it, Johanna," a familiar voice growled.

She went limp as the voice registered on her consciousness. His hand came away from her mouth.

"Hawkeye?" she whispered, her voice quivering. Was she dreaming? Was her need for Hawkeye so desperate that she conjured him up out of thin air?

"Yes," came the husky reply.

Then, unbelievably, his lips covered hers in the darkness, lips that she had known and loved, lips that stirred the familiar ache deep inside of her.

If this is a dream, then please don't let me wake from it, she silently prayed.

Tears welled up, slipped over and slid down her cheeks, mingling with the kiss. She lifted her arms and wrapped them around his neck, twining her fingers through his thick hair and pressing her body hard against his masculine frame. *He doesn't feel like a dream,* a silent voice whispered inside. The tears fell faster and his arms tightened around her, holding her in the security of his embrace.

He pulled his head back and seemed to be staring down at her. "Johanna?" the voice was questioning. "What's wrong? Have you been hurt?"

"Yes," she said shakily. "I've been hurt since the day you rode out of the village and left me behind . . . hurt since the day you went over the cliff and I thought you perished, since . . ."

"Ssshhh," he said, placing a gentle finger on her

349

lips to silence her. "I've been hurt too, love, hurt terribly. I was afraid I had lost you."

"Never," she said fiercely, burying her head against his chest.

"We must leave this place," he said, lifting her face to his and gently brushing loose tendrils of hair back from her face. "I don't know how long we have before Durant returns. When he finds the guards missing he's sure to know something's wrong."

"You killed the guards?"

"I'm not sure," he said. "I didn't stop to check. We can't talk now, love. I'll explain everything when we have more time. Right now we must hurry."

They left her room and eased the door shut behind them, quietly descending the stairs. They had nearly reached the door when old Joshua, the negro butler, stepped into the room and stopped at the sight of them. Johanna hardly dared to breathe as he stared at them for a long moment.

Suddenly, the old man moved toward them and held out his hand. She thought he meant to stop her, but he passed them by and opened the door.

"Hurry, missy," he said gruffly. "Massa Durant, he be back real soon. If you gonna get away, then you gotta go now."

"Thank you, Joshua," she murmured, slipping silently out the door.

They started across the yard, but they had only gone a few steps, when suddenly, without warning, two snarling dogs ran toward them from the shadows of the night. Barking, teeth bared, the dogs cut off their path to the gate. Hawkeye froze, then slowly pulled his pistol from the holster, but Johanna stayed his hand.

"No," she said. "Don't shoot them." Stepping in front of him, she called, "India — Sheba. Come!"

Instantly the two dogs ceased their menacing growls. They bounded to Johanna's feet, lay down on the ground and looked up at her.

Opening the door of the Institute, she said, "Inside."

The dogs obediently went into the building.

As the door closed behind them, Hawkeye grabbed her hand and they made a dash for the front gate and the safety of the forest beyond. They were just sliding through the gate when Durant's carriage came in sight.

He spotted them immediately.

"Stop them!" he yelled. "Don't let her get away."

A shot rang out, whizzing by Hawkeye's ear and striking the gate with a loud ping.

"Run!" he told Johanna, pushing her toward the safety of the forest and reaching for his pistols.

Dodging behind the guardhouse, he sent a volley of shots toward a running shadow and was rewarded by a cry of pain. But the shots had given his position away. He could hear a man cursing, then the whine of bullets sliced the air around him. He felt a sharp burn in his left arm as a bullet struck him.

Hawkeye's weapons spat flame and a guard fell from the coach. A shot coming from the direction of the forest told him that Sky Walker had joined the battle.

Sending another shot winging toward the coach, Hawkeye made a dash for the cover of the forest where Sky Walker and Johanna were waiting, already mounted. He vaulted on the horse in front of Johanna and she wrapped her arms around his waist as he dug his heels into the animal's flanks and sent the horse into the cover of the forest.

After a short distance he pulled up his mount and turned to Johanna. "Do you know somewhere safe we can stay?" he asked.

She shook her head. "That's the reason I left before," she said. "Durant is a powerful man here in New Orleans." Worry marred her brow. "I forgot about Patrick. We must warn him. Michael Durant will look for me there first. And he'll make certain Patrick suffers for my escape."

Patrick? Who was Patrick? Hawkeye felt a stirring of jealousy. Why was she so concerned about this man? He frowned at her, saw the moistness in her eyes as she worried over the man. His lips drew into a thin line. Although he felt dislike for the unknown man, he hated to see her so distressed.

"We can take him with us," he said grudgingly.

"For all the good it will do," she said. "Michael Durant knows every inch of the city. He'll have every exit blocked."

"Don't worry," he said. "When the time comes, I'll take care of him. You no longer have to face him alone, Johanna. Where does this fellow Patrick live?"

She directed him through the thick forest, beneath overhanging vines, through dense branches and over occasional blankets of moss. They came to a narrow stream and followed it for a while, picking their way across rotted logs and fallen trees. Before long they came to a fork in the creek, and veered off to the right. They continued on that path until they came to the bayou where Patrick lived.

His house was in darkness; he was obviously asleep.

Sliding from the back of the horse, Johanna made her way up the steps to the door and knocked softly. She heard a rustling as the old man turned over on a cornshuck mattress. Then, silence.

She knocked again.

Footsteps sounded, the door opened a crack, and a face peered out.

"Who's there?" the old man asked.

"Johanna," she whispered softly.

He opened the door wider. "What's happ'nin', lassie?" He asked anxiously, motioning her inside.

She was closely followed by Hawkeye and Sky Walker. The old man's hands twisted nervously as he gazed at the two men, then returned his attention to her, a question in his eyes.

"Patrick," she said. "This is Hawkeye and his friend, Sky Walker."

The old man considered them both for a moment, then his shrewd gaze fixed on Hawkeye. "You ain't dead?" he asked.

Hawkeye smiled grimly. "Not yet anyway," he replied, feeling a vast relief that the man confronting him was not a rival for Johanna's love. "But if Durant has his way, it won't be long."

Patrick nodded. "He usually gets what he wants."

"No!" Johanna looked at the old man. "We'll find a way out of this somehow," she said. "Hawkeye will take care of us. But Durant's going to come here, searching for us. You must not be here when he does."

"You're right, lass," he said softly. "He'll likely raise all kinds of hell until he finds you. Ain't nobody gonna be able to stop 'im neither."

"It's time someone did," Hawkeye muttered. "He's had his own way much too long." Suddenly, he sighed and slumped down into a chair. "You better fix my arm, Johanna," he muttered.

Johanna's eyes rounded as she noticed his pale face. Her gaze flew to his right arm, then his left, and her face blanched as she saw the bloodstain on his sleeve. "Why didn't you say you were wounded?" she asked.

"Wasn't time," he muttered.

Turning to Sky Walker, she spoke in the Comanche language. "Watch outside for anyone following us."

Sky Walker went silently out the door and faded into the darkness of the night.

"Patrick, get your things together," she ordered.

Then, pulling off Hawkeye's shirt, she laid the wound bare. It didn't look as bad as she had expected, especially considering the amount of blood he had lost. There was an exit wound in the back of the arm which indicated the bullet had gone clean through.

She laid her palms on both wounds. A moment later the wound was closed over and she rose to her feet.

Patrick had wasted no time in grabbing a gunny sack and cramming his few belongings in it. He slung it over his back, then turned back to the buckskin-clad man. "How you figger we're gonna leave this here town?"

"I don't know yet," Hawkeye said. "Johanna seems to think Durant will cover the shipyards to keep us from leaving that way. We'll have to leave through the forest, but we've only got two horses and they won't be able to travel very fast if they're carrying double. Do you know where we can get two more?"

"I'd have to think on it some," Patrick said. "Ain't nobody gonna let us have none if they get the least idea Durant don't want 'em to."

"Perhaps we'll have to steal some." Hawkeye said.

"Ain't gonna be easy, stealin' horses," the old man said. "Ever'body 'round these parts keeps their horses locked up tight come dark."

Hawkeye considered the problem for a moment, then suddenly, he knew the answer. "I think I know a place where we can stay for a while," he said. "It's been ten years since I've been there, but if she's still there . . ." His voice trailed off.

She? Johanna wondered who he was talking about. Who did he know in New Orleans that he thought would help him?

The question was uppermost in her mind as they made their way to a part of town where Johanna had never been. Hawkeye stopped beside a two story stucco building that spoke of quiet elegance. A gaslight burned in front, a luxury that few people had.

Motioning them to quiet, he led them around to a side door and knocked softly.

The door was opened by a woman dressed in a gown that revealed more than it concealed. Johanna

355

knew she had never seen a woman wear less, at least not in public.

There was no question of her beauty; dark hair tumbled around her shoulders, framing a piquant face and showing her white skin to perfection. Her eyes were the color of cornflowers, a deep, penetrating blue.

"Hawkeye?" Her eyes widened in amazement. Then a big smile widened her lips. "It really is you!" she said. "Where the hell've you been all these years?" Reaching out, she took his hand and pulled him inside. She seemed not to have noticed the others with him as she twined her arms around his neck and kissed him heartily.

Hawkeye untwined himself from the woman's embrace. "Is the house full, Mabel?" he asked.

"Naturally," she said. "How could it be otherwise."

"Do you have a place we could stay without being seen?"

She looked at the others for the first time, seemed to take in the tension in their bodies. "In trouble, are you?" she asked. "Come on, and I'll take you upstairs by the back way."

Johanna stepped inside the elaborately decorated house, vaguely aware of the two men following her. Her thoughts were totally absorbed with who the woman was. And how Hawkeye came to know her. And even more important, why had she kissed Hawkeye so intimately.

When the woman turned her attention back to Hawkeye, Johanna tried to still the surge of jealousy that flowed though her. It was not until they passed a

356

room with an open door and Johanna saw a group of women shockingly dressed in wrappers, or disgracefully low-cut gowns, that she realized where she had been brought.

Hawkeye had actually brought her to a house of prostitution!

Her eyes opened wide and she stared at Hawkeye with a sick feeling in her stomach. Why had he come here to this woman? What was his association with her? And what did she mean to him? They had obviously been close, for he seemed to trust her.

But Johanna was not to get an answer to her questions. Instead, she was shown into a room in the attic, bare of anything except a bed, and was told by Hawkeye that he would come for her when it was safe. A moment later, she found herself alone and wondering where the men had been taken.

Chapter Thirty

Johanna lay on the bed in the darkened room, unable to fall asleep. A slight sound at the door brought her head around just as Hawkeye slipped into the room.

A moment later she heard the rustling of his buckskins as he discarded them and joined her in the bed. His long arms reached for her, and she stiffened against his touch.

Leaning up on his elbows, he probed the darkness, studying her intently. "What's wrong?" he asked softly.

"Why are you here?" she muttered, moving farther away from him.

"Because you are," he answered.

"Oh?" She made her voice uncaring. "Was your mistress already booked up for the night?"

He laughed low in his throat. "You're jealous," he

358

accused.

"Not in the least," she said haughtily. "Whatever makes you think such a thing?"

Even through the shadows she could see the grin on his face. "Mabel means nothing to me," he said. "She's just an old friend."

"Yes," she said drily. "Anyone with eyes could see that. Especially the way she threw herself at you and smothered you with kisses." Her voice became accusing. "And I didn't see you trying to resist. In fact, you seemed to be enjoying yourself."

"She does have a way about her," he admitted. "But you have nothing to worry about."

"I'm not worried," she snapped furiously. "She can have you. And welcome to it."

"In that case," he said, sliding off the bed and reaching for his trousers.

"Hawkeye!" she wailed, making a grab for his arm. "Don't you dare leave this room! You're my *husband!*"

"I thought perhaps you had forgotten," he said, slipping back beneath the covers and reaching for her.

"No," she said, sliding into his embrace. "I haven't forgotten one single thing about you."

"Good," he growled, lowering his lips to hers.

She wound her arms around his neck and returned kiss for kiss. Pressing her body close against him, she held him as though she would never let him go. She had waited so long for this. *So long.*

Her nerves stretched tautly like the strings of a finely tuned musical instrument. Time seemed to stretch endlessly, a kaleidoscope of moments.

359

Hawkeye's kiss was forceful, yet marked with a strange tenderness.

He lifted his head slightly and brushed his lips over her face, nipping gently at her earlobes with his teeth.

Opening her mouth slightly, she tasted his warm, salty flesh. He drew in a sharp breath and his lips found hers again and she succumbed to the sensual press of his mouth.

Desire raged, radiating a warm energy into her, and she writhed slowly beneath him, feeling his maleness grow and harden against her.

His lips blazed a slow trail of fire down her neck, causing delightful shivers to tingle across her skin.

Forcing her lips apart, he slid the tip of his tongue into the warm inner moistness of her mouth. His invasion was deep, slow, hot, and tantalizing.

His hands slid over her breasts, leaving a trail of fire wherever they touched and she felt a tightening knot deep inside her body in the vicinity of her loins. Her breasts tingled from his warm caresses and she felt a warm rush pulsating between her thighs.

His hand drew circles over the tautened peaks of her nipples. Moving his hand lower, he caressed her hips, the naked skin of her abdomen, then his hand slipped between her legs and he rubbed softly against the secret places of her womanhood.

She could hardly stand the pleasure he was creating in her body, and yet, she still yearned for more, for a completeness that she was being denied.

Her breath was coming in short gasps as his finger slipped into the moistness of her womanhood.

"Hurry," she pleaded, writhing against his hand.

"Please, hurry."

"Wait," he growled softly. "Slowly, slowly."

But she couldn't wait. She began to tug at his shoulders, to pull at him, wanting him to join with her, to make them as one.

"Please," she begged him. "Please, Hawkeye. I need you so much."

But still he waited, waited until she thought she would surely die from the pleasure he was creating. When he finally moved over her, she was almost mindless with her need for him.

Then he entered her and she sighed with the pleasure of it. When he began to move, she moved with him, urging him on, faster and faster, deeper and deeper. They began to climb toward the peak, higher and higher, climbing on waves of ecstasy until finally they were soaring upon high with the eagles. A last desperate plunge and they leapt upon a kaleidoscope of feeling and hung together for a moment, totally lost in each other as the world whirled around them.

They lay together, saturated, in the spell of their love.

When Hawkeye's breathing finally returned to normal, he stroked the damp hair back from her face and kissed her gently.

"I missed you, my love," he whispered.

"And I you," she replied. "I wanted to die when I thought I had lost you." Her arms tightened around his neck. "You must never leave me again."

"Never again," he said, gently kissing her lips. Never again."

Moments later they fell asleep in each other's

arms.

Mabel opened the door the next morning.

"So this is where you are," she said, pulling open the window shades and letting the sunshine into the room.

Hawkeye groaned and rolled over to gaze at her with bleary eyes. "It's a little early for you to be barging in here," he muttered.

"No," she replied, coming to stand beside the bed with her hands on her hips. "A little late, I'd say. What are you doing in her bed?"

Johanna gasped and pulled the sheet up over her shoulders. But she needn't have bothered for neither of them paid her the slightest attention.

"Didn't I tell you, Mabel?" he asked. "Johanna is my wife."

"Indeed?" Mabel looked at Johanna as though wondering whether he was to be believed or not. Suddenly she gave a long sigh. "Wouldn't you just know it?" she asked dryly. "The only man I ever gave a damn for would have to get himself married."

Johanna's cheeks were flushed with embarrassment and worry that Mabel would give them away just to get rid of her. Mabel apparently guessed her thoughts.

"Don't worry," she said. "I'm not gonna give you away." Her eyes narrowed on Hawkeye. "But you're gonna owe me a favor. I hope you know that."

"Of course," he said mildly. "Just ask any time. Except right now." He looked at her meaningfully. "Right now you'd better get out so I can get dressed."

362

She grinned. "Time was when you wouldn't have asked me to leave for a little thing like that."

"Mabel," he said warningly.

"Okay, okay," she said. "I was just joking."

But Johanna knew she wasn't. There must have been something between the two at one time, and she didn't want to think about what it was.

A knock at the door was quickly answered by Mabel. She took the bundle of clothing from the serving girl who stood at the door before dismissing her. Tossing the bundle on the bed, she said, "Better put these on before you go out in the streets." She turned back to the door. "Breakfast in ten minutes," she added.

After she left, Johanna examined the bundle. It contained a pair of homespun pants, a boy's shirt and an old straw hat. "What on earth does she expect me to do with these?" she muttered.

Hawkeye laughed. "I think you're supposed to wear them," he said.

"But — but it's boys clothing." Her nose wrinkled. "A stable boy's at that. Why does she expect me to wear such things?"

"I told her to find you a disguise," he said, twirling a lock of her dark hair. "Durant is searching for a young lady. Not a stable boy. The disguise is perfect."

"I don't agree," she said. "A serving girl's clothing would have done just as well."

"No," he disagreed. "Any young woman could be suspect. I think Mabel was using her head when she chose these."

She threw him a heated glance, knowing it was

more than likely that Mabel just wanted to make her look as bad as possible, making herself appear more beautiful, in contrast. *As though the woman needed any help,* she silently grumbled.

After breakfasting, Johanna and the three men left the house and made their way through the market place toward the shipyards. Already, it was crowded. Street vendors hawked their wares. Baskets of produce were stacked beside tables of fish waiting to be sold. Fresh baked bread was piled on long tables and pickaninnies were put to shooing flies off the merchandise.

As they neared the shipyards, Johanna recognized two men standing beside the docks with rifles held in the crooks of their arms. Putting out a hand, she stopped Hawkeye.

"Those are Michael Durant's men," she said, nodding at the guards.

"Damn," he swore under his breath. He studied the dock for a moment, his gaze sweeping back and forth, then turned to her. "There are guards posted all over the docks. They're stopping anyone who tries to cross the gangplanks." He studied her disguise for a moment. "Do those two men know you well enough to see through that disguise?"

She nodded her head. "They're around all the time. If they stop us, they'll be sure to know me."

"Then we can't leave this way," he said. "At least not right now." He looked at Sky Walker. "You'd better stay here with them while I get our horses. You won't pass close inspection either. Not with that dark skin of yours."

"They know me, too," Patrick said. "They came to

my house lookin' for the lass when she escaped the first time."

Hawkeye nodded. "That leaves me to get the horses. Best all of you go back to Mabel's and wait for me there."

Although Johanna didn't like the idea, she saw no other way and left with the others.

Hawkeye had no problem locating the horses. He produced his papers to show ownership, and had just turned to leave when he was hailed by Captain Willis.

"See you got your animals," the good captain said.

Hawkeye nodded. "I expected you to be gone," he said.

"You and me both," the captain replied gloomily.

"What's the holdup?"

"They're lookin' for an Irishman."

"What's he done?"

"Not sure." The captain scratched his head. "Some story set about thet a white girl's been kidnapped by 'im. Don't know how true it is, though. Some folks say it's just the man they're lookin' out for. Orders is, though, if anybody's with 'im, to hold them too."

It seemed Durant wasn't certain Patrick was with them. Hawkeye watched a well-dressed man approach the gangplank. He was stopped by Durant's guard. An argument ensued, then the guard raised his weapon and pointed it at the other man who quickly backed away.

"The guards don't seem to be letting anyone

through," Hawkeye said.

"Wouldn't do no good. Mayor says all ships are impounded until further notice."

Damn! Hawkeye silently swore.

"Thet ain't the whole of it," the captain continued. "I heered all roads leaving the city have been blocked. Nobody goes in or out today."

"All because of one Irishman?" Hawkeye questioned. "Can the Mayor really enforce such an ordinance?"

"If'n he's backed by the city council. And he must be 'cause he's deputized a mighty lot of men to see it's enforced. If'n you wanta see a madhouse, then take a drive outa town. Any way out'll be fine. It's all blocked. Ain't no gettin' around them guards. No way at all."

Hawkeye wondered if the captain could be right. Did Durant really have them trapped?

Chapter Thirty-one

"No!" Johanna said, when told of the blockade on the city. "There must be some way out. Something that Michael Durant hasn't covered." She moved restlessly around the attic bedroom in Mabel's establishment, her thoughts in turmoil.

Reaching out, Hawkeye pulled her into the shelter of his arms. "Don't worry so," he muttered against her ear. "We'll work something out. I won't let Durant have you."

She looked up into the face that was so dear to her. Something in his expression caught her attention. It reminded her of someone . . . of . . . her green eyes rounded with surprise.

Yvette Valdez!

She had forgotten Yvette's promise of help if it was ever needed.

It was needed now, needed badly.

Johanna leaned back and clutched Hawkeye's shoulders. "I think I know someone who will help us," she said, her voice betraying her excitement. "I can't believe I had forgotten her." She frowned. "There is one problem, though. She lives at the edge of the city."

"How can she be of help?"

She explained the family's ancestry, telling him what she had learned about them. "According to Michael Durant, the family is one of the most powerful in New Orleans. Durant's wealth is nothing, compared to theirs."

He frowned. "Could they not help you escape from Durant."

"They could have freed me from him," she said. "But he threatened Patrick." Her gaze was troubled when she met his. "There are few in New Orleans who would sympathize with Patrick," she said. "According to their way of thinking, he deserves to be caught and punished for helping runaway slaves."

"They will help him by helping you," Hawkeye said. "Will knowing that affect their decision?"

She sighed heavily and leaned against him. "I honestly don't know," she said. "Perhaps it would be best if they don't find out about him."

After instructing Patrick to stay with Mabel, Johanna, and the two warriors made their way to the stately mansion. Johanna felt uncomfortable in the stable boy's clothing. But it was the only way she could roam the city at will.

Hawkeye lifted the heavy brass knocker and let it fall against the door. Several long moments passed before they heard the sound of approaching footsteps. The door swung inward, and the butler stepped forward. His dark gaze took in the two men clad in buckskin, and the unkempt stable boy who accompanied them. And, although his face was expressionless, his disapproval was a tangible thing.

Johanna stepped forward and gave him her brightest smile. "We wish to see Señora Valdez," she told him.

As she spoke, his eyes widened with recognition. He frowned heavily at her trousers and shirt and his eyebrows raised, ever so lightly. "The señora is still abed," he informed her frostily. "If you will return at a more convenient time . . ."

"Yvette will see me now," Johanna said, lifting her chin, and doing her best to stare down the end of her nose at him; a feat that proved physically impossible, for he was at least a foot taller than herself. "The Señora will not be pleased if she finds she was not immediately informed of my arrival."

Her words accomplished what her manner was unable to. Although his eyes openly disapproved, he obviously dared not take a chance. Grudgingly, after another pointed stare at her trousers, he stepped back to allow them entry. Johanna curbed the impulse to giggle as the butler led them to the parlor and left to inform his mistress of their presence.

She had forgotten the painting on the wall, until she saw Hawkeye staring at it.

He moved closer to the portrait of Pierre Valdez, seeming utterly fascinated by the face in the picture. Hawkeye's dark eyes examined the portrait in minute detail, taking note of the heavy silver cross that hung from around the man's neck.

His hand seemed to move of its own accord to the identical cross around his own neck, and with a heavy frown, he slid it beneath his shirt and out of sight, leaving Johanna to wonder at his actions.

Hawkeye turned his head and met Johanna's eyes. "Who is this man?" he asked.

"His name is Pierre Valdez," she said softly. "He is Yvette's son."

Hawkeye's body was stiff with tension as his gaze returned to the painting again, and Johanna knew he must be as struck by the likeness as she herself had been.

Neither of them were aware of footsteps approaching until a voice spoke from the doorway.

"What has happened, Johanna?"

Spinning around in a flurry of skirts, Johanna saw Yvette, standing beside her husband. Their expressions were similar, varying between bewilderment and anxiety.

"I must apologize for barging in like this," Johanna said contritely. "But I didn't know where else to turn. You told me if I ever . . ."

She broke off, becoming aware that her words were falling on deaf ears. Neither Yvette, nor her husband was paying her the slightest attention. They were both staring at Hawkeye, as though they had seen a ghost.

Valdez regained his composure first. "Who are you?" he rasped, his voice almost accusing.

Although Hawkeye was puzzled, he gave no outward sign. "They call me Hawkeye," he said.

"Hawkeye?" the old man repeated. "Why are you here?"

"He's with me," Johanna said quickly. "He's my husband."

"I had no idea you were married," Valdez said, his eyes narrowing slightly. "Michael Durant gave me to understand you were going to marry him."

"That would be quite impossible, since I already have a husband," Johanna said.

At the mention of Michael Durant, Hawkeye had taken her arm as though he expected the man to appear and snatch her from his grasp.

"Where do you come from?" Yvette whispered, making the others aware of her presence. She clutched her husband's arm as though she were drowning, and the arm was a lifeline to safety.

"Texas," Hawkeye said brusquely, studying her face through narrowed eyes. "You look ill," he added. "Perhaps you had better sit down."

Yvette Valdez's eyes moved to the picture of her son, then returned to the man who faced her. "Please," her voice quivered. "What is your father's name?"

Hawkeye's fingers clenched on Johanna's arm. His answer, when it came, was low. "I don't know. He was killed by renegades when I was too young to remember."

Excitement sparked in Yvette's eyes and she nodded in agreement. "You were only two years old," she said firmly. "Look at the portrait on the wall. It could be you. But the man pictured there is our son. He left Louisiana with his family . . . a wife and son. They traveled to Texas and, shortly after, were killed in a fire." Her frail body trembled. When her voice came again, it was little more than a whisper. "The body of our grandson was never recovered."

Hawkeye looked at the painting again. "There may be a slight resemblance between us," he said roughly. "But that's all it is. I have no relatives among the white community."

"White community? Exactly what does that mean, young man?" Valdez asked.

"The Comanches raised me."

Valdez looked shocked at his words. "You were raised by savages?" he exclaimed. "It's a wonder you lived to tell about it."

Johanna wondered why Hawkeye hadn't mentioned the silver cross. She turned to remind him of it, knowing he must be the Valdez's missing grandson. There could be no other explanation.

"Hawkeye," she said, "You're wearing the same . . ."

"Johanna," he interrupted sharply. "These good people do not care that I wear buckskins." His eyes were hard, warning her. But why? she wondered. Why should he not admit the possibility that he was this elderly couple's grandson?

"I would like to speak to you further, Hawkeye." Señor Valdez looked at his wife, then back at Hawkeye. "If what you say is true," he said slowly, "you may very well be our grandson."

"I think not," Hawkeye said. "My family did not come from New Orleans."

Yvette's eyes were moist with unshed tears; she lowered her lashes to shield her expression. "How can you be so certain?" she whispered. "You said you were too young to remember."

"You want to find your grandson so badly that

you would accept anyone who even vaguely resembles your son," Hawkeye said. "You must accept his death. If he were still alive, he would surely have returned to you. After all," he added, "it has been thirty years since he was lost."

Johanna saw the expression of joy that crossed Yvette's face, the certainty that her grandson was standing before her. Her aged face seemed to glow with her happiness, as her eyes pleaded for acceptance. When Hawkeye turned away from her, her shoulders sagged and the spirit seemed to leave her body. But only for a moment. Firming her trembling lips, and squaring her shoulders, she said, "Perhaps you are right, young man. As you say, it has been thirty years."

Seeming to dismiss him completely, she turned her gaze on Johanna. "You came for help, child. How can we be of service to you."

"You offered to help me," Johanna said. "I refused it before, but I have come to plead for it now. Michael Durant has closed all the exits from the city in order to keep me prisoner."

Valdez frowned heavily. "You must not leave," he protested. "You are needed too badly. I don't hold with Michael's methods for keeping you here, but you are needed."

"If the child wishes to leave, then she must," Yvette said. "We have no right to hold her against her will. Michael Durant is an evil man and we cannot condone his actions. If we did, we would be as guilty as he."

Valdez sighed heavily. "I suppose you are right, my dear," he said. "But New Orleans would benefit much from Johanna's presence. If you must leave, though, I will have Jason bring a carriage around, and I will personally escort you out of the city."

"No need for that," came a voice from the doorway.

Johanna's head jerked around. Michael Durant and three of his gunmen stepped into the room. They were all heavily armed.

"What does this mean, Michael?" Señor Valdez's face was flushed with anger.

"I could ask you the same thing," Durant said. His gaze fell on the girl he was seeking. "Get over here, Johanna," he ordered, his voice menacing.

Johanna flinched against Hawkeye, and he leaned close to her ear. "Wait for the word, then jump to the side," he whispered.

Her body tensed, her eyes flickering to his stern features. What did he intend to do? she wondered.

"You were not invited here, Michael," Valdez said. "You can leave the way you came."

"I'm staying," Durant rasped. "You had better take your wife and leave the room if you don't want to get hurt."

"Do as he says," Hawkeye told Valdez.

Without another word, Valdez took his wife's arm and hurried her from the room.

"I'm waiting, Johanna," Durant said. "Get away from him."

Releasing Johanna's arm, Hawkeye brought his hands to hover just above his holster, and with his thumbs, surreptitiously slipped the thongs from the hammers of his Colts.

Durant grinned widely. "It'll be a pleasure killing

you," he told Hawkeye.

The butler was pressed against the wall, his mouth open in anticipation of the gunfire.

Hawkeye and Sky Walker stood six feet apart, their bodies tense as they watched Durant and his men.

Time seemed to stretch out endlessly as Durant cocked the hammer back on his pistol and pointed it at Hawkeye's chest. "Get out of the way, Johanna," he warned.

"Move!" Hawkeye hissed.

Johanna flung herself sideways as Hawkeye's weapons came out of the holsters in one swift movement. The room exploded in gunfire and black powder fumes. Johanna was aware of the thud of falling bodies around her, but had little time to wonder who they were. The battle lasted no more than ten seconds and when the noise and gunsmoke cleared, six men lay dead or wounded. Durant was still standing. His eyes met Johanna's for a long moment, then they glazed over, his knees slowly buckled beneath him and he crumpled to the floor, dead.

Chapter Thirty-two

In an upstairs room in Mabel's establishment, Johanna leaned back in the bathtub, luxuriating in the hot water. She had never before felt so incredibly happy. Michael Durant was dead and Señor Valdez had told her he would see that she was financially compensated from the Durant estate for the loss of her home.

It seemed too good to be true.

The sound of the door opening had her scrunching down in the tub and turning a startled gaze on the door. Her pulse leapt wildly as Hawkeye entered the room. The lamplight caught the shine of dark hair above wide shoulders and the glint that appeared in his dark eyes as he saw her in the tub.

She smiled impishly at him. "Isn't it wonderful?" her voice fairly bubbled with happiness. She wanted to sing with joy, to shout her happiness from the rooftops.

"What?" he asked, moving toward her and unfastening his shirt.

"Everything," she said gaily. "You. And the fact that you are the Valdezes' grandson." Her lips curled into a satisfied smile. "You are, you know. Even if you weren't the image of their son, the silver cross is still proof that . . ." She let her voice trail away, realizing for the first time that he didn't seem to share her enthusiasm. "What's wrong?" she asked abruptly.

"What are you thinking?" His gaze was dark and probing.

She looked at him with puzzled eyes. "I don't understand," she said.

"Whether or not I am their grandson makes no difference to me." His voice was flat, cold.

Her stomach tightened. "It doesn't? But —"

"They are not my family, Johanna." The words seemed almost forced from him. "The Comanches raised me."

"Well, I know they raised you, but —"

"The Comanches are my people, Johanna."

"All right," she said uneasily. "I know you think of them that way. But, don't you realize that you are the heir to the Valdez fortune. You will inherit —"

"Fortune?" he growled. "Is that what you are thinking? That you will live in that fancy house?"

Johanna sucked in a sharp breath, feeling as though she had been dealt a severe blow. Her expression was hurt as she looked up at him. "No," she whispered, forcing the words between stiff lips. "I suppose it did . . . enter my —" She broke off and

377

stared at him in confusion. "It doesn't really matter, though. About the money, I mean."

He looked down at her for several seconds, a pulse beating wildly in his jaw. "That is good," he ground out. "Because there won't be any."

The words echoed, reverberating in her mind. "What are you saying?" Her eyes were wide and unblinking as she waited for him to answer.

"We will be leaving for Texas tomorrow," he said harshly, his eyes never leaving her face. "Within a week, two at the most, we will be back at the village of my people."

Her face turned white as her mind struggled to accept what she had heard. "You don't mean it," she whispered. "You would throw everything away?"

"Of course I mean it," he grated harshly. "I came here for only one purpose. And that was to find you. I have accomplished that. Now there is no need to stay."

"But — Hawkeye, even if you don't want to take anything from your grandparents, there is still my inheritance. Your grandfather said he would see that I received it."

"You won't need it," his voice was cold, uncompromising.

It was the last that sent her rage surging forth. He could do away with his inheritance if he wanted to, but he had no right to ask her to give up what was rightfully hers. "You can throw your own away," she said, her eyes glittering furiously at him. "But not mine. It belongs to me."

"Then keep it," he growled, clenching his hands as though he were on the verge of violence. "And welcome to it!" he added, spinning on his heels.

"Where are you going?" she asked.

"Home!" he snapped. Striding to the door, he opened it and stepped through, slamming the door behind him.

Johanna stared incredulously at the door, hardly able to believe what had just happened.

Suddenly becoming aware the water was growing cold, she left the tub and wrapped herself in a towel.

Seating herself before the mirror she stared at her reflection. Emerald eyes looked back at her with a stricken expression.

How had it happened? she wondered. One moment she was so happy, looking forward to the future, but it was a future with her husband beside her. What good was a fortune if Hawkeye wasn't around to share it with her? She reached for the hairbrush and tugged it through her unruly curls.

He wasn't being fair. He knew he was Yvette's grandson. And Yvette knew it as well. It would mean so much to her to have him near. He was a beast. A savage! He had no feelings at all. He was incapable of loving anyone. *Especially me!*

Tears welled up, spilled over and ran down her face. *I hate him! I wouldn't have him if he begged me on bended knees!* She sniffed loudly, then swiped at the tears with the back of her had. *What do I need with a savage like him anyway,* she silently railed. *He wouldn't know how to live among civilized human beings.*

Flinging the hairbrush from her, she lay her head down on the dressing table and sobbed.

Go after him, an inner voice said. *Don't let him*

leave like this.

She gulped back a sob. "He didn't mean it," she whispered. "He wouldn't leave me."

He would! argued the silent voice. *Even at this moment he could be leaving.*

Becoming frantic with the need to stop him, she cast aside the towel, grabbed up her pantaloons and slid her legs into them. After tying the ribbon at her waist, she reached for her dress.

Hurry, hurry, her heart cried. *Don't let him leave.*

She found him in the stables leading Diablo from a stall. She was so relieved that she didn't notice the tears spilling from her eyes.

"Don't go," she choked, throwing herself against him, burying her face against his shoulder and letting the tears flow unchecked down her face. "I don't want it," she cried. "None of it. It's no good without you. Please take me with you."

"I wasn't going anywhere," he said quietly, smoothing back her dark hair.

She looked up at him. "You weren't?"

"No." His mouth twisted in self-derision. "I could not leave you, Johanna. I spoke in anger."

"But you have Diablo . . ."

"I was going to rub him down."

Her eyes glittered with tears. "We'll go tomorrow, like you intended," she said. "I'll do anything you ask."

"I would like for you to understand," he said.

"Then tell me," she said. "Why did you deny being Yvette's grandson?"

"She would expect me to remain here," he said. "I could never do that. Their blood runs in my veins,

380

but my heart is with the Comanches. Our people are only beginning a war that will last for many years. Once we return to Texas, it is unlikely we can ever leave and still remain safe. It would be a kindness for them to believe their grandson was lost long ago."

She smiled at him. "No matter how much you deny it, Hawkeye, Yvette knows the truth. I saw it in her eyes. But she has accepted your wishes. She will never mention it again. Yet, I believe, her life will be happier, just knowing that you still live."

"Perhaps you are right," he said, smoothing a dark curl behind her ears. His eyes were dark and brooding as he studied her delicate features. "I want your happiness more than anything, Johanna," he said. "But I ache inside for my people. They will need me in the years to come."

"Then they shall have you," she whispered. "But only if they will take us both." Her heart sang with gladness. Hawkeye hadn't been leaving her after all. Looping her arms around his neck, she pulled his head down until she could reach his lips. "I love you," she whispered, pressing butterfly kisses against his mouth. "I love you more than anything or anyone in this world."

"And I love you," he said. He cupped her face in his hands and bent to kiss her gently, reverently, on the lips. "I love you, Johanna," he whispered huskily. "Life without you would have no meaning." His dark eyes probed hers. "You won't mind giving it all up?"

"Not in the least," she whispered. "You are all I shall ever need. We'll go home together."

Together, her heart sang. *For the rest of our lives.*

YOU WON'T WANT TO READ
JUST ONE—KATHERINE STONE

ROOMMATES   (0-8217-5206-5, $6.99/$7.99)
No one could have prepared Carrie for the monumental
changes she would face when she met her new circle of friends
at Stanford University. Once their lives intertwined and became
woven into the tapestry of the times, they would never be the
same.

TWINS   (0-8217-5207-3, $6.99/$7.99)
Brook and Melanie Chandler were so different, it was hard to
believe they were sisters. One was a dark, serious, ambitious
New York attorney; the other, a golden, glamourous, sophisti-
cated supermodel. But they were more than sisters—they were
twins and more alike than even they knew . . .

THE CARLTON CLUB   (0-8217-5204-9, $6.99/$7.99)
It was the place to see and be seen, the only place to be. And
for those who frequented the playground of the very rich, it
was a way of life. Mark, Kathleen, Leslie and Janet—they
worked together, played together, and loved together, all behind
exclusive gates of the *Carlton Club*.

*Available wherever paperbacks are sold, or order direct from the
Publisher. Send cover price plus 50¢ per copy for mailing and
handling to Penguin USA, P.O. Box 999, c/o Dept. 17109,
Bergenfield, NJ 07621. Residents of New York and Tennessee
must include sales tax. DO NOT SEND CASH.*

ROMANCE FROM JANELLE TAYLOR

ANYTHING FOR LOVE   (0-8217-4992-7, $5.99)

DESTINY MINE   (0-8217-5185-9, $5.99)

CHASE THE WIND   (0-8217-4740-1, $5.99)

MIDNIGHT SECRETS   (0-8217-5280-4, $5.99)

MOONBEAMS AND MAGIC   (0-8217-0184-4, $5.99)

SWEET SAVAGE HEART   (0-8217-5276-6, $5.99)

Available wherever paperbacks are sold, or order direct from the Publisher. Send cover price plus 50¢ per copy for mailing and handling to Penguin USA, P.O. Box 999, c/o Dept. 17109, Bergenfield, NJ 07621. Residents of New York and Tennessee must include sales tax. DO NOT SEND CASH.

ROMANCE FROM JO BEVERLY

DANGEROUS JOY   (0-8217-5129-8, $5.99)

FORBIDDEN   (0-8217-4488-7, $4.99)

THE SHATTERED ROSE   (0-8217-5310-X, $5.99)

TEMPTING FORTUNE   (0-8217-4858-0, $4.99)

Available wherever paperbacks are sold, or order direct from the Publisher. Send cover price plus 50¢ per copy for mailing and handling to Penguin USA, P.O. Box 999, c/o Dept. 17109, Bergenfield, NJ 07621. Residents of New York and Tennessee must include sales tax. DO NOT SEND CASH.